WALL ST.

KISS ME MIDNIGHT SLEEPER DEADLY

BOOK 2

Copyright © 2023 by Raeder Lomax
Cover Design and Typesetting by SpiffingCovers

1st Edition 2023

ISBN: 0-9884911-1-7
Paperback ISBN 13: 978-0-9884911-1-3
Hardback ISBN: 9798218133535
eBook ISBN: 978-0-9884911-3-7

www.hudsonsquarepress.com

KISS ME DEADLY

MIDNIGHT SLEEPER

BOOK 2

DEADLY

"My cousin's love life is like the rent; it's always late."

Shelby Prevette

For David Godlis, *Click*. Billy Pickett, *Click*. S.L. Darcy and E. Smith for those snapshots of yesteryear. Bert Williams, the forgotten but great vaudevillian artist. And Rufus, my old horse, who could slide any bolt, jump any fence, and hunt any field.

1

Midtown Manhattan, January 1926

Agnes, Helena, Godfrey, and Alphonsus, four of the nineteen huge iron bells of Saint Patrick's Cathedral, rang in a rhythmic arc as the mid-morning snow powdered rooftops and streets far and wide. Chimneys smudged the skyline with gray plumes of smoke which turned snowflakes into dirt and six story walk-ups into shades of soft ash that grayed the waking city. City gentlemen, in long winter coats, hurried up and down Fifth Avenue with ladies in sleek wraps as they avoided the sputtering, honking motorcars veering in and out of the slush. A white gloved traffic cop stepped into Fifth Avenue and allowed a 1925 Blue Isotta-Fraschini Sedan to cut across and park directly alongside the cathedral on 50th Street. Gideon Remley, now halfway up the cathedral's tower, said to the Irish groundskeeper, a rumple of flannel and brogue, "How much more do we have to go?"

"Until ya can hear yerself think again, son."

They continued on until they reached the Gothic bell tower with its cragged edges, jagged light, and deafening bells. Gideon quickly crossed over to the west side of the tower and peered through a gap. Down below, across the avenue, he saw milkmen dressed in white, hauling red crates of bootleg whiskey imprinted with the white logo, Milk & Cream, into a six-story walk-up next to Ed Goulson's speakeasy hidden behind an iron gate and fortified by a double door that had to be opened twice before entering. Once inside, the stairway steeply dropped six steps making it dangerous for anyone wanting quick access, especially Prohibition agents. Ed Goulson guided the milkmen through the walk-up's service entrance. He wore a gentleman's overcoat, a Stetson derby, gray spats which chafed at his heels as he angrily pecked his walking cane on each wooden step. When they reached the rooftop, Ed Goulson turned around and, to the surprise of the milkmen, kicked the red crates over and said, "Tell Artemus Cummins I've got a new supplier." The milkmen, their eyes now on the .45 automatic in Ed Goulson's hand, backed away. "And tell the son of a bitch this whole town is sick of his bullying and that none of us is scared of him." The milkmen, slow to take their eyes off the .45, left the red crates where they were and disappeared down the stairwell.

Gideon turned his gaze away from the rooftop below to the bell-ringer beside him who clung onto long ropes attached to each bell. Every time the bell-ringer pulled one, he was sprung up into the air. Gideon then heard him call out the name of each bell that rang out across the city.

The groundskeeper anxiously touched Gideon's shoulder and opened his hand. "There's no time to waste, son. Mass is about to start."

They exchanged a packet of money and a quart of stretched whiskey for a special key which opened the cathedral. Gideon pocketed it and quickly crossed over to the southern side of the tower and set his gaze below, onto a Saks Fifth Avenue department store office window where he saw his girlfriend, Nettie Gimpel, getting lectured by a male executive on how women were weak, fragile, and highly sensitive creatures who needed the calm, analytical, and stern muscled grip of men raised under the glow of candlelight and the grit of kerosene oil to keep the world in order. Gideon felt the anger in her eyes as the groundskeeper pushed him on. He hurried down the bell tower as if all eyes were on him and then walked through the long nave of the stony cathedral which spooked Gideon with all its holy relics and heavily scented candles. He exited the huge side Gothic doorway and was greeted with a flurry of snow that melted on his face as he stepped into the cold Manhattan streets.

The Isotta-Fraschini whisked Gideon away and turned north onto Fifth Avenue. It quickly dodged a double decker green Fifth Avenue bus and headed uptown. Sal Montero, slick, almost handsome, and always impatient, nudged the kid. "You got the key?"

"Yeah, I got it."

"What about Ed Goulson?"

"He entered the walkup like clockwork," Gideon said. "And you can tell Cummins that Goulson doesn't like Milk & Cream whiskey."

"He'll like it if he knows what's good for him," Sal Montero said. "What about the church?"

"Dark and Catholic."

"Any of the priests see you?"

"I think they were too busy seeing other things," Gideon said.

"Good," Sal Montero said, without telling him why.

The Isotta-Fraschini stopped short. A mother grabbed her child. They hurried across the avenue. The sedan moved on.

Gideon said to Sal Montero, "What's so special about that bell tower anyway? I mean you could've seen what happened on any old roof. Goulson wouldn't have known the difference."

"Just do as you're told," Sal Montero said.

"Yeah, well, I'm beginning to think Cummins didn't want to risk any of his people being seen in the church, so he sent me instead. Police question the groundskeeper; I get the blame for whatever happens."

Sal Montero reached into his coat pocket and pulled out the morning edition of *The New York Daily Mirror*. He shoved the newspaper into Gideon's face. "Your rich Greenwich, Connecticut pal Farnham, one who got sick on the 20th Century Limited train from wood alcohol last December, just died."

Gideon stared at the halftones of his fraternity brother who was wrapped inside a big heavy raccoon coat he had bought for 400 dollars.

In one hand he gripped a Columbia University pennant, in the other a Barnard girl, named Jane, who studied anthropology and danced like an aborigine after a few needled drinks at the weekly rub. "You keep on doin' what we tell you," Sal Montero said, "and you'll get good clean booze. Otherwise, there'll be more corpses in your fraternity." He handed Gideon 10 dollars.

"Fifty, Sal. That's what you said."

"Take 10 or nothin'."

"…Why do you wops always lie?"

Sal Montero told his driver, Sugar Winslow, a Harlemite whose talent was doing what he was told, to pull over to the curb on East 64th Street where the grand castled clumps of William Guggenheim, Frank Jay Gould, and Isador Wormser were located across the street from Central Park. Gideon got pushed out of the sedan and fell hard onto the coarse cement pavement. Gun drawn, Sal Montero fired it as snowfall melted on his hand.

2

Midtown West

Robert Benchley edged through the doorway of Zola Nicholas's small, crammed office at *The New Yorker* magazine. "How are you and that Nachman fella getting along?"

Zola kept her eye on the sheet of paper in her typewriter. "Why do you want to know?"

"Because you're not answering his telegrams."

Zola kept on typing. "Bob, if you came in here to talk about some Mississippi lawyer, I'm not interested. I've got a deadline for this rag and it's not waiting for anyone." She hit the return bar and typed the next line.

"Well, it seems," Mr. Benchley said, "your Mississippi lawyer pal from back home sent Harold, our boss—in case you've forgotten who he is—a little wire and some money from Addison Prevette thanking him for not publishing anything about your cousin Shelby's little mishap on the 20th Century Limited last New Year's Eve." Mr. Benchley let the Western Union telegram float from his hand to hers. "You know of anyone by the name of John Smith?"

"There are a million John Smiths," Zola said, pushing away the telegram.

"Not in Clarksdale, Mississippi."

Zola stared at Benchley: his bow tie as neat as his mustache.

He said to her, "Maybe you should start reading those telegrams Nachman's been sending you from home."

"There's no law says I have to."

"No, but I like Nachman. And so do you." Zola stopped typing, "What're you getting at?"

Mr. Benchley pointed to the pile of telegrams on her desk and said, "You don't want me to know all your business." He tossed her a two fingered salute and went down the hall.

Zola searched quickly through the telegrams on her desk. She found Al's and opened the most recent one.

WESTERN UNION TELEGRAM

CLARKSDALE MISSISSPPI = NEW YORK

YOUR FRIEND ED GOULSON WIRED ME ABOUT A LITTLE PROBLEM CONCERNING HOME STOP HE SAYS HE CAN HELP SHELBYS FATHER STOP IF YOU KNOW A JOHN SMITH WIRE ME STOP IT CONCERNS ARTEMUS CUMMINS STOP DO NOT TELL YOUR COUSIN STOP HER FATHER DOES NOT WANT HER TO KNOW ABOUT THIS

NACHMAN

That morning, John Smith walked into the Alcázar hotel in Clarksdale, Mississippi and pulled out several bills from his roll. He gave them to the front desk clerk and said, "This should be good for the week."

The front desk clerk told him, "Can't give you a room if you don't put down your home address."

"Is it the law?"

The front desk clerk said, "If ya want a room, it is."

John Smith put down Hell's Kitchen. He left the hotel, got into a flivver, and headed down the long dirt road past the flat colorless harvested cotton fields where not a soul could be seen for miles.

3

Someone Else's Sweat

It was a long slog through thin ice and snow as Gideon made his way through Central Park. He edged himself into a formation of ancient rocks which eons ago had violently ripped through the earth. He then opened his coat, felt inside his shirt for blood or a puncture, and found nothing, but it was Sal Montero's intent that was the real wound. Honor was a measurement of pride, not reason, and so was shooting someone. Gideon cupped his hands with newly fallen snow and tried to clean the blood off his face and clothing. Then he buttoned up his shirt. Fixed his tie. Put on his dark brown felt fedora and left the safety of the rocks. He followed the bridle path north into the wealth of upper Manhattan, far away from the Lower East Side teeming with immigrants or the Upper West Side crammed with eastern European intellectuals, blue and wet from the Danube, who spent their days in heated arguments started in the old country. Gideon exited Central Park at the East 72nd Street entrance, crossed Fifth Avenue, and entered his apartment building. He took the "A Line" elevator, which was manually operated by an elevator man, up to his family's duplex. The elevator door opened into the foyer. Gideon hurried out and went up the grand stairway to his bedroom where he quickly washed and changed clothing. He then went down the hallway and passed the children's Victrola room where his two younger sisters made him dance the Charleston. He continued on down the stairway of broad banister and royal width. He crossed the living room, billiard room, reading room, and then stopped at his mother's art studio filled with portraits of Germany's war-ravaged misfits: snarly matrons, winking whores, bloated Prussians in plume, and children blown from spoons, where clerics were crammed in gold carts pulled by jackasses beside bankers with whiskers dripping of someone else's sweat as the Freikorps swilled in ratskellers reloading for the next street fight as the strudel class, paunchy and waterlogged from the Great War's trench folly, weaved in and out of the bumper crop of blind and stump-legged young men and imposters hungrily waving tin cups and Iron Crosses for Pfennigs in the ghostly streets of Berlin. Whether this was art or madness, Gideon wasn't sure, but whatever it was, it wouldn't go away.

He went on and turned into the hallway that led to the breakfast room where his father, Ellis Remley, helmed the table. A yawn slipped through Gideon's lips. Ellis Remley looked up from his grapefruit and warned his son, "How many times have I told you to cover your mouth?"

As Gideon covered it, his mother reached over and touched his face. "What happened to you?"

"A taxi jumped the curb, but I'm okay."

Ellis Remley, unmoved by his son's misfortune, removed the spoon from his grapefruit and pointed it at his son, as if to retouch what he had created. "Your problem is that you don't try to make an effort in life other than to please yourself."

"I told you; I had to see a professor early this morning."

Sarah Remley said, "I'm getting the doctor."

"I don't need a doctor," Gideon said. "There was one on the street and he said nothing's broken. Couple of days I'm brand new." Gideon moved his arms and legs to show her how well he worked.

"He'll be fine," said his father, not concerned with his son's misfortune, just his attitude. "I'd like to know what on earth Nettie Gimpel sees in you."

"What others have been missing," Gideon said.

"I haven't missed a thing," his father said. "Nettie called again wanting to know where you were. She said that you were supposed to meet her for coffee this morning before work. She said nothing about a professor."

"I can't meet her every morning."

"You'll have to one day."

"What do you mean I'll have to?"

"I spoke to Nettie's father at the club last night. He said that you've been courting her for a year as of this month. He thinks it's time that you've made the announcement before you graduate."

"I'm on winter break," Gideon said.

"Proving how lazy you are."

His sisters giggled.

Gideon ignored them and said to his father, "I'm on the Dean's list, if you haven't already forgotten."

"You're not on mine. You do nothing all day but read or get lost in the city. I want you to come down to the office and become a man." Every time Ellis Remley said that to Gideon, he thought of his father swinging through the trees like Tarzan.

"I've been through this routine before," Gideon said. "Get someone else to sharpen your pencils."

"Shut up," his father said, half out of his chair, threatening him with that all too familiar voice.

Everyone stopped eating. Gideon, afraid of his father, but not afraid to stand his ground said, "You seem to forget it was Grandmother Edith, *mother's* mother, who gave you the money for your business."

"What she gave me was trust, something I would never give you."

Gideon, tired of his father's abuse, rose from the table. "Who says I want *your* trust?" He removed an unopened missive from his suit jacket: the weekly installment his father sent him which detailed all of his faults in underlined and boldly printed words. Gideon dropped the letter on the table. "Don't you get tired of sending me this crap?"

Ellis answered with his hand. Everyone at the table felt it. Then he said, "Your allowance is suspended until otherwise notified."

Gideon stared at his father who only bought him things he didn't want and then would complain: *Look at all the money I spend on you.*

Ellis Remley shoved the letter into his son's suit jacket pocket. "This time you'll properly respond, or you'll be living in the street."

Gideon eyed the knife on the breakfast table but reached for a Pullman roll instead.

Ellis Remley said, "Put that down."

"Why?"

"If you can't participate at the breakfast table like a decent human being, then you can't eat from it."

Gideon left the table. Then the building.

4

Clarksdale, Mississippi

John Smith pulled his flivver to the side of the dirt road and folded back the engine cover. From there he could keep an eye on the splendid house set deep into the land with magnificent trees and broad open fields. There were no street numbers in this part of the world. You identified a man's property by what grew or died on it.

A 1925 Pierce Arrow Series 80 Sedan 7 came trundling down the dirt road kicking up dust. It pulled up alongside the flivver. Julius Hadley, the Prevette's houseman and driver, cautiously left the sedan and approached John Smith. "Look like you need a hand, mistuh."

John Smith closed the flivver's hood and took in the tall negro who wore a chauffeur's cap, flared britches, and dusty boots. He lied, "Had a little trouble with the motor, but it's okay now," one eye still on the big house. "Does your boss live here?" he said, pointing to the long dirt road that doglegged through an overgrowth of magnolia trees which protected the house from the casual eye, but not the horses grazing in yonder field, the milking cows scattered like jacks, and the chicken coops where multicolored hens squatted, pecked, and squawked in bunches. Country life, with all its complex scenting, suddenly made John Smith want to roll in the hay and pluck the alfalfa. "I asked you a question, boy, does your boss live here?"

Julius said, with a hint of summons, "I don't know what boss you talkin' about, but you the first person I ever seen stuck out here."

"What's that supposed to mean?" John Smith said.

"Been here all my life."

John Smith caught sight of the child in the back seat of the sedan.

"Who's the little girl?" he said with more than a casual interest. Julius stepped into the view of little Martha Prevette, who was busy talking to a toy skirt-puppet on her forefinger.

Julius said to the white man, "Iffen'ya need help with your motorcar, sir, I can call the new sheriff. He'll direct you where to go. Iffen it's somethin' else, he can do that too."

Little Martha rolled down the window. "I want to go home, Julius."

John Smith said, "Who's the man who lives here?"

"Who the man wantin' to know?"

"You didn't answer my question, boy."

"Nossir, but iffen I did, I'd have more answerin' to do." Julius got back into the Pierce Arrow and kept one eye on the rear-view mirror. Little Martha turned around and looked out the back window. "Who's that man?"

Trouble, but Julius wasn't about to tell her.

5

399 Park Avenue, PH A

Virginia Swain left her bedroom and headed to the foyer wearing a burnt orange cape with gold and blue patterns of silk and velvet trimmed with mink at the neck and cuff. She folded the script of the play she was starring in and put it under her arm. The elevator door opened. Shelby stepped out. "Say, isn't that my coat?"

"*No,*" Virginia said. "You're not the only one around here with good taste."

Shelby handed Virginia the *Wall Street Journal's Broad Street Gossip* column. "Why did you let that idiot bond salesman from First National City Bank sell you this junk the other day?" referring to the bond offering of Soling Consolidated Generator that everyone was following.

"Oh, that little thing," Virginia said.

Shelby pointed to the ad copy where the bank boasted its *Financial Solidity and Investment Acumen*, as well as its *Unquestionable Reliability.* Beneath it was an illustration of an overwhelmed customer listening to a banker who spoke with Plymouth Rock antiquity: *Our goal is to help investors choose safe investments. You no longer need to make a prolonged personal study of the complicated structure of security issues and bonds. We do it for you, safely and wisely.* Shelby handed the newspaper to Virginia, who wouldn't take it. "You believe this crap?" Shelby said.

"The bond salesman swore to me it pays a fantastic return."

"Really? Do you even know where the country is that

Soling's fronting?"

"Sure, I do," Virginia lied.

"What do they manufacture down there?"

"Stuff."

"What kinda stuff?"

"Hell do I know?"

"Well, you *should* know," Shelby said. "What are their exports in relation to their imports?

"Who cares?"

"I would. How much debt does its government carry? Or did your banker pal forget to tell you while he was taking your money?"

"Look, smarty pants, all I know the stock's going up and up and I got in before anyone else."

"You certainly did," Shelby said.

"What's the matter with you anyway today?"

Their Irish housemaid, Caitlin, appeared, and said, "Excuse me, Miss Prevette, that young man, Emmet Parsons, just called about meeting you at the Goede Hoop Carriage House on the West Side. Said he might be late, miss. Something about his college uptown."

Virginia said to Shelby, "Is that the boy you met last December riding in Central Park?"

"Yeah, and we're going on our first ride today," Shelby said, taking her russet brown field boots and flared pinque britches from Caitlin. "Now you call that crooked banker and get your money out right now."

Virginia rang for the elevator and said, "I'll get out of the market when I goddamn please."

"You mean when *it* goddamn pleases."

6

The Prevette Plantation

Julius took the mail from the postman as one of the maids hurried down the grand hallway and said, "Mrs. Prevette says for you to take little Martha to school now."

Julius said, "Tell her I'll meet y'all outside soon enough." He then reached for the hallway telephone and got connected to the Alcázar Hotel where Addison Prevette was at the cotton brokers' breakfast. Addison picked up and Julius said to him, "Mail just come in, Marse' Addie. When I get done droppin' off little Martha, you want I should leave it at your office or just keep it here?"

"Just leave it with my secretary. I'll be over there shortly."

"Very good, sir." Julius slipped on his overcoat and hat and headed out the kitchen door. Little Martha, all bundled up, took the hand of her maid and with one big step got into the Pierce Arrow sedan. Julius took her to school and then drove on into town where he pulled alongside the Second Street curb and got out. He climbed the two flights of stairs of the cotton building and continued down the hallway where men were busy sending out cotton contracts. He left the mail on the secretary's desk, but not before noticing someone familiar standing by the water cooler crushing a paper cup in his hand. This time there was no excuse about his flivver having any trouble.

A half hour later, Addison Prevette arrived. His secretary said to him, "This here man says you have an appointment with him, but I can't seem to find it in my book nor his name in any previous correspondence." Addison stared at the stranger, "What's your name?"

"John Smith."

"I know of no John Smith," Addison said, heading to his office.

John Smith approached Addison. He showed him a photograph which didn't need any explanation. The secretary, curious about the pained look on her boss's face, said, "Want me to call the new sheriff?"

"No," Addison said, turning back to the unwelcome visitor. "Come with me." Addison shut the door to his office. "What's this all about?"

John Smith said, "You need to pay up by the end of the week or—" he sat down, made himself comfortable, and took in the simple office where the only extravagance was the expression on Addison Prevette's face.

"Or what?"

"Or this photograph is going to make your life miserable…"

7

The Flapper

The Goede Hoop carriage house, two blocks off Central Park West, was one of many which had served the neighborhood since the late 1880s when horse carriages had reigned supreme. Now the large spoke wheel buggies gathered dust in the loft as family nameplates got duller under cobwebs and hay dust. Since the war, the building had been converted into a riding ring that served the well-to-do.

Gideon stepped out of the pouring rain and entered through the stable's side door. He hollered for Barney, the stable master: an Irishman thick with the lilt of the bog. Gideon headed to the viewing stand, built three feet off the ring, which was always filled with lilies, peonies, and gladioli on competition days. Behind the stand was a waiting room where tack, tagged for repairs, hung on wooden struts which stuck out from the walls. Gideon entered the room and removed his wet shoes and socks. Sitting all alone on a mahogany wooden chair, propped up against the wall, was a bobbed flapper in riding gear. Already deep into her cool blue eyes, Gideon said to her, "Hey, you're not Jobyna Spaulding's sister?"

"*Who...?*"

"The pretty one who likes to hide upstairs in the stalls," Gideon said, putting his wet socks over the radiator as the steam valve hissed.

The flapper stared at Gideon's bruised face. "No, I'm not her sister, and what happened to you?"

He grabbed his numb foot and said, "Slipped on some goddamn ice in the park."

"You were ice skating?" saying ice like *ahs*, betraying her Mississippi drawl, but not much else.

"I wouldn't exactly call it skating," Gideon said, wondering how a Spaulding sister with a Southern accent could be so incredibly good looking since all the other sisters looked so homely.

"I wouldn't do that," the flapper warned.

"Do what?"

"Do that with your socks."

"Why?" Gideon said.

"They'll shrink."

"Well, I can't walk around in them wet," he said, flipping them over, curious about her accent. "You're not from around here, are you?"

"No."

"…Waiting for Barney?"

"Someone else."

"Well, I know all the girls who ride here. Which one is it?"

"A *boy* and he's late."

"…Which boy?"

She hesitated then said, "Emmett Parsons," stretching the 'r' into a smooth flowing drawl.

Gideon let go of his foot. "You don't mean that kid who was in my fraternity?"

"What do you mean *was?*"

"Emmett Parsons got kicked out of school for cheating on his final exams or didngya know?"

"*When* did he get kicked out?"

"First week of January the scholars figured out his little scheme," Gideon said, touching his socks to see if they were any drier. "You're sure about them shrinking?" he said, touching his raw face where it hurt most.

The flapper said to him, "Pick at it and you'll bleed to death."

Gideon removed his hand. "...You Emmett's girl?"

"No."

"...You anybody's girl?"

The flapper stared at the boy, still not used to New York attitude.

"How do you know Emmet?" Gideon said.

"Met him last December."

"Where?"

"In the park, riding."

"How old are you?"

"Why?" the flapper said, as if having been asked to undress.

"You're not Cassie Bender?"

"*Who...?*"

"My younger sister brought her over the other day then locked the bedroom door like I wanted to get in or something."

"Maybe she had good reason."

Gideon wasn't amused. "Why're you meeting Emmett here?"

"Why do you want to know?"

"Well, I'd hate to ruin your day, but Master Parsons doesn't own a horse and he doesn't belong to this carriage house either."

"He doesn't...?"

"No," Gideon said.

"You sure?"

"Emmett's a born liar."

"Then whose horse was he riding when I met him last December?"

"Mine," Gideon said

"*Yours...?*"

"Yeah, I lent him Augustus because he was a fraternity brother. See, you have to do those things otherwise the fraternity gets wind, and you get thrown out."

Barney came down the ramp with Augustus. Gideon shouted through the office door like the building was on fire. "Hey, Barney! You've been letting Emmett Parsons ride Augustus again?"

Barney put Augustus on cross ties. "Ya told Mr. Parsons yerself he could ride anytime he wanted, because it was part of the deal to get ya into that fraternity ya now say ya hate."

Gideon turned back to the flapper, "I suppose you've got a crush on that four-flusher."

"No," she said, looking away.

"Where're you from anyway? You talk funny."

"Mississippi, and I *don't* talk funny."

"They have horses down there?"

"*One.*"

"Well, all I can say is you better know your onions up here, because motorcars and taxis don't give a damn about horses, and you can forget about trolleys; they run you over—*squish.*"

The flapper reached into her polo coat and took out a flask. "You're gonna get infected if you don't clean your face."

"You a nurse?"

"No, I'm not stupid." She walked over to Gideon and said, "Hold still," as she patted down his cheek with some rye whiskey.

He jumped back. "*Hey*…that burns."

"Too bad," she said, holding his chin firmly in her hand. "You're sure you just fell or was it something else?" She capped the flask and grabbed her coat off the chair.

Gideon licked the spill on his finger and followed her. "Hey, where didgya get this rye?"

"I think you've had enough, young man."

"I haven't had any," catching up to her. "There's not a mothership outside the 12-mile limit which has real rye and most of it's that Godawful Scotch." Gideon reached out his hand for another taste.

The flapper handed him the flask, but slowly as if to warn him. Then she pulled it away, "First tell me what a mothership is?"

"I see you're new around here," Gideon said, as if being new was a fault. "How much didgya pay for that rye?"

"I don't think you have a deep enough anchor for this kind of quality."

"Oh, but *you* do?"

She ignored Gideon and said to Barney, who was busy unpacking new blankets, "I noticed an appaloosa for sale on the board inside the tack room. Is he boned for performance?"

"As good a horse as ever stood on iron, miss."

"Then I'll ride him next time I'm here and if I like him, I'll buy him. And if you have a stall for rent or purchase, I'll take that too. But make sure it's away from this boy's horse."

"Hey," Gideon said. "Augustus is for sale and he's a far better horse than that appaloosa."

"Then I'll ride them both and let you know my decision."

"You're not getting on Augustus unless you know your onions."

"Oh, I don't have a clue what I'm doing," she said, heading to the side door which led to the street.

"Where are you going?"

"Gotta blouse, I'm late."

Gideon, barefooted, mounted Augustus and trotted after her.

The flapper stepped aside. "Before you run me over, tell me what the 12-mile limit is all about."

"I'm not too sure if I should, and what's your name anyway?"

"Shelby."

"Shelby what?"

"Shelby Prevette."

"Never heard of you."

"Never heard of *you*. Now what's the 12-mile limit?"

Gideon said at the cantor, "That's where all the motherships are."

"What's a mothership?" she said, having to turn around as he rode by.

"Tell me where I can get more of this rye, and I'll tell you all you wanna know."

"Does it have to with bootlegging?"

"You buy my horse, and we'll talk."

Shelby opened the street door and as she stepped out said, "I think you're all talk......"

8

The Plantation

Julius entered Addison Prevette's library with more than a misgiving look. "That Smith fella's out back, Marse Addie. Can't get rid of him. Says he wants his supper and a good cigar. Miss Mims is right angry and wants to call the new sheriff, but I told her you don't want that, and she says you done lost your mind. Her words, sir, not mine. Now she in the gun room and wants the key to the cabinet."

"Tell Smith I'll meet him out back," Addison said. "You know what to do. Now hurry on." Addison reached for his army issue 1898 Colt New Service revolver. He put it inside his waistband, closed his suit jacket, and headed to the kitchen.

Mims rushed him. "If you don't kill that son of a bitch, I will."

Addison said to his wife, "I'll give you the pleasure after I talk to him." Addison went down the hall, through the kitchen, and on out back where Smith stood shapeless in the night. Addison showed him the photograph. "You got the negative to this?"

John Smith said, "You got the 25,000 dollar down payment?"

"You get me the negative, then we'll talk money."

"Mr. Prevette, maybe I didn't make myself clear in town earlier this morning. That quarter of a million payment is not a one-time sum. You're going to be paying us that amount every year until you kick the bucket. So, you better get your ass on it now or you'll be the town laughing stock." John Smith headed toward the back door and opened it. "Now what's for supper? I'm starving." He stepped into the kitchen and sat down at the baking table. Ruby was by the stove, protecting her pot. Addison said to her, "Dish him out a plate."

Ruby kept her eye on the intruder as she set a plate of food hard on the baking table. John Smith reached for a fork. Addison for his Colt.

John Smith laughed. "You never used a gun in your life, office boy."

Ruby grinned with pride as her boss pressed the Colt's five-inch barrel deep into the intruder's cheek and said, "On second thought, you don't look so hungry." Addison grabbed John Smith by his suit jacket collar and lifted him straight out of his chair and dragged him through the kitchen doorway, out into the yard, and into the Pierce Arrow where Julius was behind the wheel, ready to go. Quarter of an hour later John Smith was thrown out into the empty nighttime streets of downtown Clarksdale with more than a few bruises. It wasn't the first time he had misjudged a man and it should've been the last.

The following morning Addison Prevette walked into the law firm of Nachman & Brocato, just off the Clarksdale Yazoo and Mississippi Valley/Illinois Central Passenger depot. A legal secretary showed him into Al Nachman's office. It was furnished with a flat-top wooden desk, Dictaphone, and three wooden chairs. Addison took a seat and waited for Al who was on the telephone. Another legal secretary came in with a telegram. Al read it and then showed it to Addison, saying, "Your niece, Zola, says Shelby's doing just fine in New York."

Addison said, "You'd think New York loves my daughter more than I do."

Al finished his call and said to Addison, "New York likes smart people. Now, what about this Smith fella you ran into last night?"

"He told me that if I don't pay his gang what it wants, this photograph of me," Addison handed Al the photo," will get published in every newspaper and, if the papers won't publish it, it'll get sent to everyone by mail...I almost killed him last night."

"I heard," Al said. "Seems the new sheriff found him on the street beaten up pretty badly. Smith wanted you arrested. Made a fuss about it. Thought he was in New York."

"He's lucky he can still think that far," Addison said.

Al looked up from the photograph. "You mentioned something about your nephew, Marston Cobb, when you called before."

"Marston was a runner."

"For whom?"

"A criminal gang up in New York, until he got into a fight and killed someone."

"You mean before he came down here," Al said.

"Yeah."

"What happened up in New York?"

"I don't know other than there was some argument," Addison said. "I had to go up there to pay the fix so he'd get acquitted. Then a few months later I was back in Manhattan, at the cotton exchange. I stopped off to see how Marston was getting along, but he wasn't there. When I did find him, he told me that he was now in the nightclub business, because it fitted his temperament better."

"You mean working for the blackmailers behind this photograph."

"How would you know that?" Addison said.

"Ed Goulson."

"How would you know Ed Goulson?"

"He wired me this morning," Al said.

"Yeah, but how do you know him?"

"I could ask the same of you, but your niece Zola introduced us at his club last December in Manhattan. Seems Goulson is all upset about a bootlegger named Artemus Cummins who's been putting the muscle on him and every other big club owner to buy his liquor and no one else's."

"Are you still seeing Zola?" Addison said.

"…It would be hard to do that with her still in New York."

"You know the rumors," Addison said.

"And I know who's been spreading them," Al said, meaning Mrs. Prevette and all the gossip that she had started back in December. "What exactly did your nephew, Marston, have to do to with this picture of you and the girl?"

Addison said, "When Marston had moved down here, after his trouble with the law, he expected an executive job which he was unqualified for, and when I told him that he would have to start as an overseer and learn the cotton business from the ground up he got into a fit, even threatened me. But as he was my nephew, I had to give him leeway. See, I had the foolish notion I could control him since he was under my supervision."

"That's when he got back in touch with that New York gang?"

"Yeah," Addison said. "See, Marston was sick of living down here and wanted to go back to New York, but they didn't want Marston up there because he's a loose cannon; Marston saw blackmail as his entry back into crime. The gang took the bait."

"But you didn't know that."

"Then I didn't," Addison said, reaching for a cigarette. "See, this Smith fella, when he was in my office, asked me how my nephew was."

"He and Marston knew each other?"

"It seems so," Addison said, getting a light from Al.

"He didn't know that Marston's dead?"

"I don't know if it mattered to him."

Al held out the incriminating photograph. "How did you meet the girl in this picture?"

"Some nightclub."

"Which nightclub?" Al said.

"Smalls Paradise."

"Where?"

"Up in Harlem."

"And...?"

"After the floorshow, some of the girls were at the bar and so we had a few drinks, then went up to Goulson's speak."

"And...?"

"Well, you know, one thing led to another. Look, Smith wants a down payment of 25,000 dollars."

"Give it to him," Al said.

"Just like that?"

"When you give him the down payment Smith will leave town and I'll be on his trail. From there I can start making life difficult for these blackmailers because I've got a suspicion."

"What?"

"That this ransom is part of something bigger and to do with Ed Goulson."

"Maybe," Addison said, "but I want those negatives. That's why I'm here."

"Who else was with you that night at Smalls Paradise?"

"Some business associates," Addison said.

"What about the girl in this photograph?"

"Well, she was one of the girls at the bar."

"Where was this photo taken, because it wasn't at Smalls."

"No," Addison said. "Some place in New York, but the negatives are what I'm after, not where the picture was taken. I want those negatives. That's why I'm here."

"What's the girl's name?"

"I don't know—Carmela something. I'm not even sure it's her real name."

"You're not sure?"

"No," said Addison, "and I didn't care at the time. She just told me that she was having a rough go at show business."

"How so?"

"Well, she'd been arrested several times for assaulting Broadway producers. Seems she's got a bad temper."

"There must be a reason why," Al said.

"They say she's colored. She says she's white."

"She's colored," Al said, staring at the photograph. "Quadroon is colored. Have there been other women?"

"None," Addison said.

"What tempted you then?"

"I was with some businessmen. Had a few drinks. Got stupid."

"Did the other men get stupid?"

"...I suppose so," Addison said.

"Were they blackmailed?"

"Not that I know of."

"Why did you choose the colored girl?"

"She's a quadroon, Mr. Nachman. She's not a nigger."

"Down here she is."

"Well, she looked white enough to me," Addison said. "Problem for her was that she didn't look white enough for the Broadway producers. She said that she'd been detained more than once for fighting with them and that the police always wrote white on her arrest sheet. I guess it all depends on who's looking at her."

"Or what you want to see," Al said. "Obviously, you got to know her quite well. How many times did you see her?"

"Only that once," Addison said, "but she had a lot on her mind and spoke to anyone who was around long enough. Other than that, the whole thing was pretty quick."

"You never saw her again?"

"Never," Addison said.

"When Ed Goulson called me this morning, he—"

"I thought you said he wired you."

"He did at first," Al said, "but then he called me and mentioned something about a woman on Broadway who's connected with the blackmailers and that if you wired him 100,000 dollars he could get you the negatives, which is a lot cheaper than what someone else is asking."

"So, you know about the quarter of a million."

"Yes," Al said. "Now, who's this woman on Broadway?"

"Works for some producer, I heard."

"Which one?"

"I wouldn't know," Addison said.

"You have friends who are producers?"

"None," Addison said.

"You're *sure* you don't know anyone who's a producer?"

"I'm in the cotton business, Mr. Nachman, not show business and I'd like to keep it that way."

"Okay," Al said, "but when I get to New York, because I have no doubt that this is where this Smith will be going, I'll get what I need from Ed Goulson about that woman on Broadway and anything else tied to this blackmail—including producers you may or may not know."

"Just get those negatives."

"That's the idea," Al said. "Now about the quarter of a million, when Goulson told me that you didn't want to wire him the 100 grand, I suppose the main reason was that when a friend asks for a fortune it's only natural to be suspicious. But I need to know if you are or were involved with anything or anyone else who can be tied to this blackmailing?"

"Mr. Nachman, what I want is very simple. Get those damn negatives and do whatever you have to, starting right now." Addison pulled out his billfold and wrote out a check for 500 dollars. "This is for your services."

Al glanced at the check and said, "I just hired two more lawyers, Mr. Prevette. We are a growing firm, and it costs money to do investigative work, especially on a New York criminal gang."

"How much more do you need?"

"Mr. Prevette, we're not talking about someone's cow straying into your yard. We're talking New York where money runs thicker than blood, the way race, down here, runs thicker than mud. And if there's trouble down the road, and I'm sure there will be, someone's going to die."

"I'll give you a grand," Addison said.

Al sat back and watched a passing cloud float by the window.

"I'll go as far as fifteen hundred, Mr. Nachman, but that's it."

Al said, "If you want to fork out over a quarter of a million dollars a year for the rest of your life, go ahead. But if you want me to risk my life to save *your* reputation then you've got to understand that I value my life as much as you your reputation, maybe even more. Now, my firm would require 50,000 dollars, which includes expenses, and *not* because anyone here's greedy, but because someone else put himself in a bad situation and it's going to take a lot of money to get out of it. But then if you feel we're asking too much, I'm not offended. There's a private investigator around the corner who charges 20 sheets a week and I'm sure he'll take your case. But remember, you have to pay people to get them to talk."

"Doesn't mean they'll tell the truth."

"No," Al said, "but suppose you want a door opened that's locked, or access to someone or something that's difficult to get. Or what about that person who feels underappreciated? Money will give him or her self-worth and will get us needed information at the same time. And if you still have doubts, then understand that my method is all about changing a person's behavior, getting into his head and messing with it, and that means changing it from aggressor to mark, and at the moment you're the mark." Al went to the door and opened it.

Addison said, "Sit down." He took out his fountain pen, uncapped it, and wrote out a check for 25,000 dollars. He moved it across Al's desk. "You'll get the other half when I get the negatives."

Ten minutes later, Al left his office and headed to the Alcázar Hotel. The front desk clerk, a veteran of backwater hotels and hardwood saloons turned the guest book around. "There a problem, Mr. Nachman?"

Al went down the list of guests. "Has this Smith fella had any visitors?"

"Not on my watch."

"But someone could've gone up without seeing you first."

"Could have, yes."

Al searched each column for John Smith's name and when he found it Hell's Kitchen had been inked in the "City" column. "You get a lot of people from New York this time of year?

"Get 'em from all over, Mr. Nachman. Travelin' salesmen mostly. Why just the other day a fella come in carryin' a miniature Estate Fresh Air Oven gas stove demonstrator. A real beauty. Green enameled pressed steel, porcelain doors and handles. Heard him say because of it he sold six units to be delivered."

"You buy one?"

The clerk dropped a guest's key into the slot board. "No. I eat all my meals here."

Al headed over to the telegraph office and sent a wire to Zola. Forty minutes later it was on her desk. She took it home with her to Hell's Kitchen.

9

Hell's Kitchen

There wasn't much to Zola's 53rd Street rooming house west of Eighth Avenue, but then for $18.50 a month she had a roof over her head. The kitchen was no bigger than a closet. The icebox always leaked. The small fireplace never worked. Her neighbors across the yard made a living yelling all night long and the couple below them played the Victrola late into the morning as they spooned in silhouette behind curtains which blew heart shapes in the wind. But the real nuisance was the telephone located on the first-floor landing. It served the whole walk-up. Mrs. Buchanan, the widowed landlady, permitted you three minutes on the line and no longer. Repeat offenders were kicked out. Long distance calls were forbidden, and unmarried women weren't allowed to bring male visitors into the building any time of day, so the fire escape got a lot of use.

Zola unlocked the door to her apartment. Shelby followed her inside. The dimly lit living room was occupied by a couch that held impressions of people long gone. The curtains were worn, discolored, threadbare and worthy of quarantine. Zola made her way past the colorless walls and into the path of a sprinting cockroach. She checked the liquor stash by the rim of the fireplace just below a framed newspaper clipping of the dead Irish nationalist, Mícheál Ó Coileáin, who had been shot and killed in Ireland for trying to reason with the unreasonable. Shelby stared at the photo. "Some old boyfriend from the war?"

"The last tenant's," Zola said, "but I share the pain," thinking of her late fiancé, Bartel Pschorr, and his zany mad Berlin: a city that sung out of key and danced on one leg. The family mansion in Grunewald built of Schwarzwald brawn. The Fastnacht festivals in Bavaria where people plunged into the streets wearing costumes with enormous heads, weird teeth, and crazed eyes which mocked you as they marched by in ghoulish waves late into the night beyond the white winter landschaft of moldy snow-flesh lumps that brought you back to your senses with ice cold warmth. Zola collapsed into her creaky rocker, her memory heavy with the dampness of Alpine inns, goose feather beds, and beer clinking fräuleins. She moaned as she looked across the room and then said to her cousin, "This is the dump."

"Better than being on the street," Shelby said.

"It would be a whole lot better where you're living."

"You brought me here to whine?"

"You said you wanted to see my place."

"I've seen enough," Shelby said, heading to the door. "I'm running late."

Zola pulled out the Western Union Telegram which Al had just wired from Clarksdale to her office at *The New Yorker*. "I've been debating whether to bring this up."

"Bring *what* up?"

"Do you know anyone by the name of John Smith?"

"No," Shelby said.

"Marston ever bring him up?"

"What didn't that lunatic bring up?"

"Well, somebody—and don't worry, you're not in any trouble—but somebody wants to know." Outside a garbage can toppled, followed by a screech which ripped through the air. "Strays," Zola said. "Why don't you sit down?"

Shelby looked at the dead couch and then stepped into the hallway. "Some other time."

"What do you think of your father?" Zola said.

"What kind of question is that?"

"The last time your parents went to Europe, did they stop in New York?"

"How else were they to get on a ship?"

"That's not what I meant," Zola said.

"Then what did you mean?"

"How often does your father visit New York?"

"Why?"

"I know he comes up here on business."

"That's his business."

"This John Smith might know your father."

"And if he does?"

"I'm just asking."

"Why're you just asking?"

"Look, Shelby, I'm a journalist now and being nosey is part of the job."

"Well, keep your nose out of my affairs unless you've got something to tell me."

"It has to do with Marston."

"Marston is dead, in case you've forgotten."

"Sure, he is," Zola said, "but he left behind two billion other morons."

"Why are you telling me this?" Shelby said, peering down the hallway where a probing cat was intensely scrutinizing a man trying to open his door.

"There's some kinda trouble back home," Zola said

"What kinda trouble?"

"I don't know as of yet."

"Well, when you figure it out, let me know," Shelby said, hurrying past the cat and the man who couldn't get his door to open. On the way out she passed the landlady, Mrs. Buchannan, who said to her, "You must be that whore I heard about pretending to be someone's sister."

"And you must be that Mrs. Buchannan."

10

Speakeasy

Nettie Gimpel hurried out of Saks Fifth Avenue's main entrance into the crush of rush hour. She hollered, "How many times have I told you to meet me where employees leave? I stood by the side entrance for fifteen minutes like a boob."

"Well," Gideon said, "I figured since your family owns the store you could use any door you wanted." He followed Nettie up Fifth Avenue, tugging at her glamorous long white fox collar coat which stood out in the cold winter night. "...I saw you this morning."

Nettie walked even faster. "*Liar.* I called you at home and your butler had no idea where you were."

"I was in the bell tower."

"...*Bell* tower?"

Gideon pointed ahead to St. Patrick's Cathedral.

Nettie could barely make out the spire in the evening sky. "I suppose you're now the Hunchback of St. Patrick's?"

"Nettie...why can't you ever be nice to me?"

"I'm *too* nice. And what business would you have in a bell tower let alone church?"

"Look, they don't pay me in school to learn, so I had to find work to pay for all the fancy speaks you drag me to."

"So, you got a job in a *bell tower?*"

"No."

"Well, you don't need a job. Your family's worth a fortune."

"And every time you ask someone worth a fortune for a piece of it, they see it as misfortune."

"Well, at least my family's not cheap," Nettie said.

"I agree. So why can't a girl spend money on a boy, especially when she's got it?"

"Very simple: he *might* get used to it," Nettie said, still ahead of Gideon. She crossed Fifth Avenue at 52nd street and headed west. Halfway up the street was Tony Soma's, two blocks away from Ed Goulson's club. Nettie walked in and tossed her coat at the hat-check girl behind the Dutch-door then said to Gideon, "You better have money or I'm outta here."

"That's what I want to talk to you about."

Nettie grabbed her coat. Gideon pulled her back inside and showed her a ten-dollar bill. "Something funny's going to happen and soon."

"That sawbuck is going to disappear?"

"No."

The headwaiter brought them to a table.

"Look, Nettie," Gideon said, sitting down first, "maybe you can help me out."

"You're not getting one penny outta me and you're supposed to wait till a girl sits down first."

"I don't want your money," Gideon said.

"Whaddya want, then?" Sure that he was up to something.

"How much do the police pay for tip-offs?"

"*How* much…?" Nettie said, opening her compact and smoothing her lips as she shifted her eyes toward him. "You *killed* someone?"

"*No*, I'm just asking."

"You never just ask anything."

"Well, I'm just asking now."

"Look, Gideon," she said, closing her compact so that it snapped loudly, "cops don't pay you anything. You gotta pay them and it's called a fix. Read the papers. Now, before I order, take out that sawbuck again.

I wanna make sure I wasn't dreaming." Then she saw his face clearly under the glare of the overhead light. "Say—what happened to you?"

"Nothing," he said.

"You look like you fell off a truck?"

"What if I told you someone's going to get killed."

Nettie stood up. "*What're* you up to now?"

"Sit down," he said, pressing down on her shoulder. "And I know who's behind it all."

"Behind *what*?"

"Behind what I just said."

"Does this have to do with those bootleggers you hang out with?"

"Yeah," Gideon said, "but as of this morning, I'm done with them."

"That's what you say," Nettie said, turning toward the flapper entering the speak and making everyone turn. Nettie nudged Gideon with a hard elbow. "I suppose you know that gorgeous girl?"

"Not really."

"So, why're you gawking at her?" Nettie said.

"I met her at our carriage house this morning."

"So, then you *do* know her."

"Take it easy, Nettie. We said a few words. That's all."

"Who is she? I've never seen her before."

"She's from out of town," Gideon said.

"Oh, some showgirl."

"No."

"Well, her clothing is straight from Paris and don't tell me it isn't, because I'm in the trade," Nettie said. "Now who's taking care of her?"

No one was.

Shelby took her seat at the reserved table. Dottie Parker leaned over Robert Benchley and said to her, "Gideon Remley has his eye on you."

Shelby searched the room and found him. "You know that boy?"

"Everyone does," Dottie said. "He and his family are in the society columns all the time and he's got a speedboat faster than any bootlegger's. I'd marry him, right this second, even though I get seasick."

The waiter came over with a bottle wrapped in a serviette. Dottie said, "Mike, I didn't order champagne."

"I know, Miss Parker." He turned to Shelby, "It's from Augustus." Dottie surveyed the room. "Who's he?"

Shelby said, "A horse."

Dottie said, "Then you better rein him in......"

11

Clarksdale, Mississippi

The 10:13 Yellow Dog rolled into the Yazoo & Mississippi Valley/ Illinois Central Passenger Depot with a plume of smoke which drifted off into gray puffs of billowing clouds that shaded the already dark winter sky. A passing shower, having sprinted through town, left a damp wet wind that iced the streets and froze the windows.

The train consist came to a halt. Engine steam masked the locomotive. The fireman stepped down from the engine cab with a long-necked oilcan, reached into the underbelly and greased the moving parts. Pullman porters, up and down the consist, lowered the heavy steel staircases from the vestibule doors and placed stools underneath them for the last step back to earth. Beau LaHood approached his old friend, Pullman porter Jimmy Quitman, who just got off the train. "How's everythin' goin', brother?"

Jimmy Quitman was amused by the amount of steamship trunks he saw down the platform. "How many you got there, Beau?"

Beau grabbed his grip and told the depot boys to bring along the six big trunks stashed with Shelby's Trusted Rye Whiskey.

"Enough to drown the whole line. Any trouble this week?"

"None at all, Beau. Government ain't got nowheres 'nough liquor agents to put on trains down here." Jimmy Quitman then helped his passengers disembark. A moment later he and Beau headed to the baggage car.

"You deadheadin' with me this ride, Beau?"

"Next train, Jimmy. Gotta see a man in town first."

"Okay, wire me when the next shipment's ready."

"Will do," Beau said as he handed Jimmy ten dollars, a small fortune for any working man, black or white. "Any undercover agents travelin' the lines?" Beau said.

"Ain't seen a tipped hat nor flyin' napkin since we left Chicago."

"Good."

"Beau—"

"What Jimmy?"

"...Remember that white boy up north?"

"There's a lot of white boys up north," Beau said.

"One on your train drunk the wood alcohol last December."

"What about him?"

"Boy's dead, Beau. Just heard from a porter on the Illinois Central."

"Wasn't my fault."

"Lotta of us is nervous though."

"I'm not," Beau said. "So, don't y'all worry."

"Well, you hear anythin', you let me know."

"You'll be the first, Jimmy."

They shook hands and bade goodbye.

Beau crossed the tracks and headed to town. He turned the corner of Delta Avenue and walked up the familiar steps that led to the offices of Nachman & Brocato, Esquires. Once inside, a secretary took Beau down the hall to Al Nachman's office. Al reached into his desk and handed Beau a photograph. "Sit down, Beau. This is what I called you about."

Beau studied the image. "Seems somebody got caught doin' somethin' they shouldn't."

"You see the mark on the girl's forearm?"

"What about it?"

"It's a burn wound," Al said, reaching into his desk, bringing out a pint of Shelby's Trusted Rye Whiskey. He set it straight up on the desktop. "The man whose head is inked out just happens to be Addison Prevette, the man with the money behind your little bootleg operation."

Beau looked up from the photo. "You mean Miss Shelby's bootleg operation. I'm just an employee."

"You're more than an employee and you know it," Al said. "You're making good money now, but without Addison Prevette y'all're out of business, so I need you to help me get a certain situation settled."

Beau said, "Seems Addison Prevette got a thing for colored women."

"I'd say he's got a thing for what any man wants. But what I need to know is whether y'all're supplying any Harlem speaks such as Smalls Paradise?"

"I'm about to see to that when I get up there," Beau said.

"When are you deadheading to New York?"

"Today," Beau said. "Been home since New Year's. This'll be my first trip out since that little incident aboard the 20th Century last December."

"When do you report back to work?"

"Not for some time. See, I'm goin' early up to Manhattan to meet Miss Prevette for some business we got. Just don't let Clementine know. She got more chores for me to do than a dog got fleas."

"I won't say a thing," Al said. "But when you get to the city, I want you to visit every Harlem bucket joint and see if you can find the girl in this photograph. Miss Nicholas will give you a hand. Her beat on *The New Yorker* magazine is nightclubs and speakeasies. In the meantime, I want you to keep the photo. It's a copy I made with my new Leica A." The camera was sitting on Al's desk. He handed Beau a 100-dollar bill and said, "Bird dog fee."

Beau put it away and said, "Tell me more what this is all about."

"First, I need to know which train you're riding out on."

"1:13 to Meridian."

"Good," Al said. "There's a pigeon down here by the name of John

Smith fronting for some blackmailers in New York and he's been on Addison Prevette day and night as if it's his privilege. The railroad office will notify me as soon as Smith books a seat back to New York, so I'll be on the train with him. Now, when you get to Manhattan you keep calling the Biltmore Hotel to find out if I've arrived. And don't say anything to Miss Prevette when you see her or anyone else for that matter. You know how a horse can slip the bridle."

"Yessir. You mind my askin' how much money is involved in this blackmailin' scheme?"

"Let's just say it's equal to Prevette's reputation."

"Funny," Beau said as he studied the photograph. "Iffen I slept with a white woman this pretty it would improve my reputation."

"It would also get you killed..."

12

Goede Hoop Carriage House

Gideon walked into Barney's small office and fell into a leather chair that had its own aches. Barney stared at the boy who seemed to live more in his head than anywhere else. "You don't look too happy."

"I'm not," Gideon said.

"Well, maybe she'll change yer mood," Barney said, turning to the riding ring.

Gideon saw Shelby walking the appaloosa on a leadline. She wore a man's camel hair double-breasted polo coat and she took all the man out of it. But it was her deep blue eyes of the morning sky filled with first light which made the rooster in Gideon's heart crow.

Barney left his office and entered the ring.

Shelby said to him, "Please tack him up for me," as she handed Barney her hunter saddle and D-ring snaffle bit. She then took in Gideon who was standing in front of the appaloosa like a hay bag. "What's your problem today, young man?"

"Whaddya mean what's my problem?"

"You look troubled."

"How can I look troubled, if I'm glad to see you?"

Shelby tried to smile but the effort went nowhere. "You're in a bad mood again?"

"I try to leave what bothers me at home," Gideon said, "but that's not always easy to do." He took the leadline from Shelby and said to Barney, "I'll tack him up."

"Don't bother," she said. "I'll do it." She put a pad under the saddle and moved it up to the withers. "I hear this mount gets skittish on approach."

"Who told you that?" Gideon said.

"Some girl upstairs."

"Give him leg and he'll float right over."

Shelby cinched the saddle. "Barney tells me you teach the kids on weekends."

"When I can."

"He said they all love you, especially the girls."

"That's baloney," Gideon said, as he gave Shelby a leg up.

"Well, if it's baloney why did that girl upstairs say you're the best teacher around?"

"That's because girls are okay until they grow up and get big ideas."

"…You mean like me?"

"Who said you're grown up?"

Shelby tried to smile. "Are you always this charming?"

"Usually it wears off by noon," Gideon said, checking the girth then stepping away from the appaloosa. "You're good to go."

Shelby walked the horse on a long rein several times around the ring before giving heel to a working trot. The gelding went easily on the bit, but Shelby kept his neck long for the moment.

Gideon said to her, "How long have you been riding?"

"Oh, I'm just a beginner."

"Then get off this horse. He'll kill you."

"Good Lord, how you can scare a person," Shelby said. "And I'd like to jump some fences today."

"Not if you're a beginner."

"I already told you I had one lesson."

"I don't care if you've had *two*."

"What's wrong with this horse?"

"Nothing, but when a horse spooks or does something unexpected all you have is a split second for a save and it takes a beginner some time to acquire a secure enough seat to hang on, maybe longer if she doesn't have any talent."

"You don't think I have any talent?"

"Let's just say I watched a very sweet old artist lady take a spill the other day and she ended up with broken ribs. She said it was beginner's luck. I told her beginners don't have any luck, just inexperience."

"Were you her teacher?"

"No," Gideon said.

"How's my seat?"

"…Okay."

"Then put up some rails or whatever you call them. I wanna try some jumping today."

"So ya wanna try some jumping…"

"Yeah."

"Go ahead and kill yourself," Gideon said, heading to the wall to get the rails. He set them up like gravestones. Shelby tracked left into the center ring and breezed over the cross rails several times.

She said, "Level them at two feet."

"One lesson, huh?"

"Yeah. Now hurry up and set up those rails."

He did. Shelby cleared them, did a flying change, and tracked right with the inside forehand leading. She said to Gideon, "Set them at three feet."

"Don't you think you're a little ahead of yourself for a beginner?"

"Not if I've had one lesson," she said, clearing the top rail and tracking right. "Put up a four-foot hogsback."

"Sure. What size coffin do you take?" Gideon set it up.

Shelby cantered twice around the ring then sailed over the hogsback and said, "I want a five-foot ascending oxer."

"You can jump that?"

"No, but he can," Shelby said.

Gideon set it up and Shelby flew over the oxer on the one-stride.

"Maybe you had three lessons," Gideon said.

Shelby ignored him as she rode to a trot and then to a walk. "What's this horse's name?"

"Whiskey. Born first day of Prohibition," Barney said, coming out of his office. "You ride him like a dream, miss."

"Beginner's luck," Shelby laughed, bringing Whiskey to a halt as she swung dismounted.

"There's only one rider I know as good as you," Barney said, "and it's this boy over here, but I could be wrong about that now," winking at Shelby as he patted Whiskey on his neck. "Will ya take him, miss?"

"One moment," Shelby said, handing Barney the reigns. She examined Whiskey with a careful eye and said, "He's got a good topline and his underline extends. I can see that he doesn't hold too much weight on the forehand, and I think that the depth of his girth is just about right." She stood far enough behind Whiskey and said, "Nor does he stand wide, and his tracking marks show that he's neither winged out nor winged in and his neckline is also powerful," she said, smoothing her hand over it. She handed Barney the reins. "I'll take him," and then reached for her coat.

Gideon handed it to her. "How was the champagne I sent over last night?"

"Like all the others."

"I only sent one bottle."

"I know……" Shelby said, laughing and hurrying out the door.

"Where're you going?"

"Gotta blouse. I'm late."

"Busy girl."

Yes. The Northeastern Limited was soon arriving at Pennsylvania Station with Beau on it.

13

Alcázar Hotel, Clarksdale

John Smith reached across his bed for an apple which he had taken off the Prevette plantation after having chased a horse, a cow, and some chickens before moving on to the big house and heading upstairs to the wainscoted hallways laid with highly polished hardwood flooring. There, he found Mims Prevette in her bedroom undressing.

The hotel phone rang. John Smith picked it up. A New York operator came through. Then a familiar but distant tinny voice edged itself through the wire. "You there, John?"

"Yeah, and I can't wait to leave this dump."

"How'd everything go?"

"He's scared as hell, Artemus."

"You get the initial payment?"

"This morning," John Smith said, holding up a $25,000 check, not knowing the account was now closed. "Says it'll take a little time for the rest."

"*How* long?"

"Prevette said he didn't know. Then he tried to get wise. So, I had to rough him up a bit. Told him don't confuse a little time for a long time. Then I put him back on his feet. I'm keeping this check, Artemus. You owe it to me."

"We'll talk about that when you get back."

"You owe me the 25 grand, Artemus."

"You got into the house?"

"Yeah."

"You found the little girl's room?"

"I know exactly where it is."

"You took the measurements from the ground to her window?"

"Of course, I did."

"You got them safely in your pocket, not floating around?"

"Yeah, I got 'em, Artemus. But I don't keep the 25 grand, you don't get the measurements, because no one else but me coulda done this."

"I said we'll talk about it when you get back."

"We're talking about it now, Artemus."

The connection dropped.

John Smith tapped the receiver several times. The Alcázar operator came on. She told him it would take at least 40 minutes or more for a new connection. He put the phone down. Lit up. Thought of Mims Prevette in her bedroom. Her fine body radiant in the morning sunlight. Ruby with her broad face and plumb sized eyes as she slashed him down the hallway while the downstairs servants screamed their heads off.

He picked up the telephone. Tapped the receiver. Bought a train ticket to New York. Went to the bathroom. Removed his shirt. Looked into the mirror. The bleeding had stopped.

14

Pennsylvania Station, New York

Two red caps with luggage carts headed toward the Northeastern Limited train that had just pulled into Pennsylvania station. The overhanging glass ceiling infused shafts of gray winter light which soaked up the morning sky and left a gray mist shrouding the platforms below. Shelby, just behind the Red Caps, greeted Beau as he stepped off the train with his grip in hand. His suit was pressed. His felt hat just over his eyes. The smile on his face generous to a fault.

"A pleasure to see you, Beau."

"As it is you, Miss Shelby."

"How was your ride up?"

"Fine, miss. I see you been ridin' some."

"Yes, but it's not like home. There's no land here. You're stuck in a building or a park full of people who think the bridle path is for dogs they can't control. You've got our product?"

Beau pointed to the trunks filled with Trusted Rye Whiskey that the Red Caps were now hauling down the platform.

"Come along then," she said. "I've got Virginia's chauffeur waiting for us in the carport."

The Red Caps followed Beau and Shelby through Penn Station's 150-foot glass and iron ceiling that was a mythology of ancient Rome and England's Crystal Palace. They hurried past the 60-foot Doric columns of pink Milford granite which suggested, in metaphor, traveling was not limited to mere movement. They continued on through the wide sweeping stairway leading to the gritty, honking, temper tantrum of Manhattan, then realized that the carport was the other way. They went back up and found the maze which took them to Virginia's 1925 Hotchkiss AM2 Coupé Chauffeur limousine with the open driver's section. They loaded the trunks then took off.

"When you were back home," Shelby said, now sitting comfortably in the back seat with Beau, "did you hear of a man named John Smith bothering my family?"

"Uh, no, miss."

"Because my mother wired me not to come home until the situation gets resolved."

"Well, Ruby did speak of somethin' when I visited my Uncle Roy at your plantation, but she didn't give no name."

"Is my family safe, Beau? Please tell me."

"I believe so, miss."

"You *believe* so…?"

"Well, miss, I can't be talkin' about somethin' I got no hold of."

"You do remember Marston?"

"Oh, yes, miss, hard to forget him."

"He once came up to me in town and said he was going to make my life miserable by using the Cummins method on me, and when I asked him what it was, he said I'd find out soon enough. Do you know what he was talking about?"

"No, miss, I don't."

"Do you know this man Cummins?"

"Uh, no miss," Beau said. "How'd you hear about him?"

"I just told you, from Marston," Shelby said, noticing a look on Beau's face that said he was concealing something from her.

The limousine turned east on West 34th Street and 7th Avenue and then headed to 399 Park Avenue.

"Well, don't you worry none, miss," Beau said, avoiding her eyes. "I know a colored policeman up in Harlem used to be a Pullman porter, and I'm goin' to see him later about your product."

"You're hiding something from me, Beau."

"No, miss, I ain't hidin' a thing, but I did hear say that Al Nachman gonna be in town in a few days. I'd look him up at the Biltmore Hotel you got any questions about back home."

"I suppose Mr. Nachman told only you, of all people, that he was coming to New York."

"Well, miss, it was accidental. I just happen to be in his office 'cause some white folk been takin' down our new telephone line. See, they don't like us havin' one also. That's when I overheard somethin', but it weren't directed toward me. I could only make out bits and pieces."

"Bits and pieces of what?" Shelby said.

"Somethin' about somethin' I didn't understand."

"Has my father employed Al Nachman, again?"

"That could be the case, miss, but you speak to Mr. Nachman when he come up. He be sure to tell you what's there to know."

"So, he did tell you that he was coming up here," Shelby said.

"No, jus' somethin' I overheard on my way out."

"What did you overhear?"

"Oh, I don't right remember, miss," trying not to look at Shelby.

The limousine pulled up to the entrance of 399 Park Avenue seven blocks north of The New York Central Railroad building which towered over Grand Central Terminal's north side. It held an extended view of the stone façade grand apartment buildings lining Park Avenue for the next 50 blocks. Two doormen, dressed in military style greatcoats, hurried to open the passenger door. Beau tried to get out to help the doormen with Shelby's Beals & Selkirk wardrobe steamer trunks, but a strong grip on his coat sleeve pulled him back into the limousine. Shelby said to him, "You're not going anywhere until you tell me what *really* happened back home......"

15

Hell's Kitchen

Mrs. Buchanan snooped. Held lengthy deliberations on the condition of her diseases. Went on forever about her husband who had dropped dead at the supper table: his face in his soup, his pipe on the floor, his chicken dinner and batonnet carrots untouched—the image always before her eyes. She would befriend you then demand a loyalty that would turn venomous if you didn't open your door when she came a-calling, something Zola never did. Zola was halfway down the street when she braced herself. Mrs. Buchanan was busy checking the coal ash cans for contraband.

"My leaky ice box still hasn't been fixed," Zola dared to complain as she approached the sexagenarian.

Mrs. Buchanan said, "You're the only old maid living in my building. What you need is a husband not an ice box."

"What I need is that paint job you promised."

"*You* do it," Mrs. Buchanan said, slamming the coal ash can cover as she hobbled up the stoop of her building. Her swollen right leg had to be dragged up each step. As she reached the top of the stoop, she turned back and yelled, "I find out you're one of them girls who masturbates, I'll get the vice squad down here and have you arrested like we did that schoolteacher who forgot to pull down the shades." Mrs. Buchanan then slammed the front door behind her.

Zola, wondering if she had pulled down the shades, headed west to Ninth Avenue where the elevated train tracks split the sunlight into exaggerated shadows which lunged out onto the cobblestone streets. She stepped into a sundry store where every item was stacked to the ceiling, all behind a marble countertop that had a wide roll of wrapping paper adjoined to an iron paper cutter. Behind it was a sliding ladder that brought merchant to product. Zola purchased a can of Dutch Boy White Lead Paint. Then she left the shop and continued down Ninth Avenue and went into the used furniture stores where dark, heavy, muscular empire commodes, chiffoniers, and davenports were piled on top of each other against barroom mirrors imported from the pre- Prohibition beer kingdoms of Milwaukee and St. Louis. There were two-for-one deals on spittoons and beer mugs. Orphaned cuckoo clocks tall as lampposts waited to be adopted. Brass headboards and mahogany dressers, once bright and shiny, were now dulled with soot and sold in sets at steep discounts. Cupboards and side tables were chipped, scuffed, and callused by hard shoes and broomsticks. The shopkeepers made you buy the smaller stuff first, before going deeper in to excavate the remains of the 19th century, but Zola had no money nor room for things she didn't want.

She returned home and heard the noises of people deep into their fits that were venting through doors and spilling out into the hollowness of the hallways. She put her hands to her ears and cried for a moment—long enough to catch her breath. Then she realized that she had forgotten to buy a paint brush. Too tired to go back, she pulled a screwdriver and hammer from under the kitchen sink of her apartment and stood before the photograph of the dead Irish nationalist, Mícheál Ó Coileáin, above the fireplace. She was sick of him staring. His early death, now a lyric, was no concern of hers as she chipped away and shimmied the hammer's claw deep into the gap between the nailed frame and wall. Plaster scattered onto the floor and to her surprise she found a gaping hole.

She reached into it. She felt the rub of burlap, the shape of things yet known. She pulled out a tightly wrapped package. Held it in her hands. Wondered why it had been buried behind the wall. She opened it. Realized it was from the war, put it under the light, and was immediately taken back to France of 1918 and the sound of boys dying under starched hospital sheets. They who had sailed over with glory and song waving goodbye, Stars and Stripes in hand, from trains and ships untouched by what was yet to come.

Then she found something that would change her life forever.

16

Walk on One Leg

Harlem, once a 17th century Dutch outpost, had become a destination for immigrants, and—with cotton at a low—African Americans were now moving in by the droves to the already crammed streets of hustlers, game rackets, beauty parlors, literary salons, and jazz clubs. They worked as maids, haulers, sweepers, movers, porters, shoe-shine boys, journalists, and musicians, but it was the new-found freedom that really brought them up. The strange sensation of being able to stand in line with a white person or drink from the same water fountain without getting lynched was like having been crippled all your life and then all of a sudden being able to walk on one leg.

Beau stepped off the elevated (IRT) Interborough Rapid Transit Broadway train at 125th Street and walked north along the extended wooden platform toward the gingerbread station house. Westward, the Hudson River evening ferries glowed like river chandeliers which pitched beams of carbonated light into the sparkling water. Beau entered the station house which came from an era when even the lowliest edifice had a pediment or gargoyle; when hoopskirts and bustles were built like water engines; when puffed sleeves and plumed helmets were worn with unabbreviated ceremony, and the private ceremony was performed with one foot hoisted on a chair with dress lifted to the knee to expose open drawers for the handheld pan.

Beau descended the long ornate steel stairway. He crossed 125th Street and headed uptown into the precinct of police officer Elgin Bumpus, one of sixty black policemen on the payroll of the City of New York Police Department. He commanded his post with a nightstick that had twenty-one notches carved for the men he had knocked out, and nine more notches, on the other side, for handgun knock-outs. Beau approached his old friend and said, "Elgin, I think I'll stay on the railroad."

Officer Elgin Bumpus said, "You ain't never gonna get me on the train again. Last time I stripped a bed is still too near." He slapped the nightstick into the palm of his hand for his twenty-second knock-out and then nodded to a nervous pedestrian heading up the street. They soon passed one of Harlem's most popular nightclubs, Smalls Paradise.

"Elgin, what's this new club just opened up the street I been hearin' of?"

"You mean the Sugar Cane?"

"Yeah. What's the story behind it?"

"Smalls Paradise got too expensive for folks around here. See, it's the only fancy club allowin' black folk as patrons and is owned by one of us, but our folk is gettin' squeezed out by the cost as the downtown folks head up here every night. So, some boys from the neighborhood felt there bein' a need for another mixed club, opened up the Sugar Cane that's now the place to go iffen you in the know, and it looks no different than a juke joint from back home. You got that picture on you?"

"Got it right here," Beau said, reaching into his coat pocket, handing it to him.

They stepped aside as downtown Puritans in black tie and sequin dresses got out of taxis and limousines, and nervously entered Smalls Paradise. For them Harlem was a primitive, uninhibited world notated by swarms of restless negroes raging with jungle madness. The whites quickly herded themselves into the nightclub where purity could safely petition the devil. "I'll introduce you to the owner," Officer Elgin Bumpus said.

Officer Elgin Bumpus pulled out his flashlight and shined it on the photograph.

"Elgin, you ever hear of the Cummin's method?"

"...Why you ask?"

"'Cause I need to find the girl in the photo you lookin' at now. I'm told her first name is Carmela. I believe she's a dancer. She got a burn wound on her left arm."

Officer Elgin Bumpus studied the image. "Why's the white man's head blacked out?"

"It's the girl I'm interested in."

"Yeah, but what's he doin' with a colored girl?"

"Blackmail," Beau said.

"Well, we don't go after anyone, including whores, unless there be a sweep action."

"Y'all're paid off?"

"Paid or not, folks ain't causin' a ruckus, we leave 'em be." Officer Elgin Bumpus centered the light on the image of the woman. "She looks familiar, this girl."

"You know her?"

"Hard to tell with her on the bed like that," Officer Elgin Bumpus said, "but I'll find out soon enough."

"You got any idea where this picture was taken?"

"Could be over on West End Avenue or Riverside Drive. Maybe a fancy brownstone off Central Park. Maybe Park Avenue or Fifth. Or maybe some other town. But I can tell you this kinda set-up ain't of no Harlem railroad flat—how much money's involved?"

"Lower end a' six figures."

"That's a lot either end," Officer Elgin Bumpus said. "This whaddya do: gimme a day or so."

"How 'bout now, while I'm up here?"

"Can't, Beau. Got a tip on a burglary tonight and I plan on bein' there when the fools tiptoe in."

"What about the Cummins method? Ever hear of it?"

"What about it?"

"So, you know of it then," Beau said.

"Oh, yeah."

"Has it got to do with the girl in this picture?"

"Lemme put it this way, Beau. A girl don't do as she's told, she gets burned. Next time, you don't wanna know."

"How many girls been burned by this Cummins?"

"I don't keep count."

"Police know?"

"It's like back home, Beau. Ain't what you know, but who it is you know."

"Is he white, this Cummins?"

"Oh, yeah, and he got his fingers in everythin' that come along." Officer Elgin Bumpus shivered as if they were in him.

"How long he been at this, Elgin?"

"Long time, way before Prohibition, Cummins had a whole mess 'a saloons. Patron walk in and want a little somethin' extra; bartender give him a card. Come Prohibition that all gone. But Cummins done good for hisself, though it cost some blood to get there." They walked on for a while. Then Officer Elgin Bumpus said, "Conductor Truesdale still on the train?"

Beau laughed. "He always askin' me: *When's that Elgin boy gonna quit foolin' around playin' cops and robbers and get back on the train?*"

"Beau, you tell Conductor Liston Truesdale iffen every white man was like him this would be a free country."

"I think he already knows that......"

17

1:13 Yellow Dog

The railroad office issued Al Nachman a ticket for the 1:13 Yellow Dog and all three connections to New York. The section seat that he was assigned to was the same as John Smith's. They left Clarksdale that afternoon. The train was filled with traveling salesmen. All of them were complaining that too many towns weren't plugged in. One salesman moaned it was hard to sell an electric washing machine when the only plug in the house was what you bit off and chewed.

John Smith, sitting across from Al, thought he was a salesman. "What're you selling?"

"Not a thing," Al said. "How about you?"

"Oh, just passing through."

A woman entered the section-car and saw mostly men. She showed her train ticket to the Pullman porter who reminded her that the ladies' special section was two cars ahead.

Al offered John Smith a smoke. "You got family in Clarksdale?"

"No," John Smith said, taking the cigarette and a light. "Just a friend."

"Well, I'm from Clarksdale and I know everyone in town. What's the name of your friend?"

John Smith turned to the boy staring at him as children do when they find a face which interests them. The boy turned away, but not before catching sight of a salesman coming down the aisle wearing a high collar and a black and white checked tie with a diamond studded horse-shoe pin. The salesman held up a box of Préciosa Cuban cigars and told everyone that his wife had just given birth. He also reminded them that he was the only drummer on the line who carried West Electric Water Wavers for women's hair management and at an exceptional price, because of this special day. No one was interested. No one got a cigar.

Al said to John Smith. "I didn't get the name of your friend in Clarksdale."

"I didn't give it."

"He's not in any trouble. Is he?"

"Why would you think he's in trouble?"

"I don't know what to think," Al said, keeping a straight face. "But I'm from Clarksdale and I know everyone there, including your friend. So, what's his name?"

"Well, it's a personal thing," John Smith said, "and a gentleman minds his business, unless he's minding something else."

The drummer with the cigars came back down the aisle. This time he wasn't selling anything. He leaned into Al's section and said to John Smith, "Ain't you the fella I saw back in Clarksdale?"

"Never saw you in my life," John Smith said.

"How could you have?" the drummer laughed. "You was too busy running away from the cleaver in that niggra's hand."

John Smith got out of his seat, but Al stopped him with his hand and said, "Wait till you get off the train......"

18

A Good Angle

Nettie Gimpel put the candlestick telephone closer to her mouth and said in a hush, "Hey, you weren't kidding the other night, were you?" Her eyes were glued to the six-story rooftop across Fifth Avenue from her office.

"What're you talking about?"

"Ed Goulson. You mentioned Ed Goulson the other night."

"Yeah, what about him?"

"He's dead," Nettie said.

Gideon put down his book. "*Who's* dead?"

"Goulson is. On the rooftop."

"*What* rooftop?"

"Across the street, down below."

"Where are you, Nettie?"

"In my office and you better get out of town fast."

Gideon put the candlestick phone closer to his mouth and ear. "Did you see it happen?"

"You bet I did."

"Is there anyone else up there?" he said.

"Up *where?*"

"On the damn rooftop."

"There were a bunch of them with milk crates," Nettie said.

"Were they red?"

"Were what red?"

"The *milk* crates."

"Who cares?"

"*I do.* You said you saw this."

"Yeah, I saw it," Nettie said. "See, I couldn't find my compact mirror, so I used the window reflection to put on my lipstick and then I see Ed Goulson drop like he got whacked in the head as the milkmen flew down the rooftop faster than rats down a city drainpipe."

"Did you see the men leave the building?"

"Who cares if they left? I called you so you could get out of town."

"Where's Goulson now?"

"On the rooftop, dead. I'm looking at him now," Nettie said.

"Did you call the police?"

"I figured I'd call you first since you did it."

"Whaddya mean since I did it? I didn't kill Ed Goulson."

"Isn't that why you were in the bell tower the other day to get a good angle?"

"I was up there, Nettie, but I didn't know *why* I was up there."

"Yeah, well, I've seen you on your speedboat take down a seagull a mile away with your rifle."

"Doesn't mean I killed Ed Goulson."

"You're lying to me as usual."

"Then *how* could I have gotten home so quickly…?"

Nettie thought about that as the snow powdered Ed Goulson's dead body.

19

The Loot

Shelby floated into the breakfast room wearing a Parisian black silk kimono embroidered with camellias falling over a small pagoda with silver threads of imitation sea that gently rolled to shore. Zola, already on her third cup of coffee, said, "Well, ah declare," as she kept her eye on the man who was on his way out.

"That's Lyle Brush, you fool," Shelby said.

"Who…?"

"His father is my Uncle Marbury, an old family friend."

"So, he's not your real uncle," Zola said.

"Look, Lyle is not some lover or anything."

"Ohh, he's just your pretend first cousin."

"Look, Zola. I don't know how to say this—"

"Say what?"

"Talk to Lyle for a few seconds."

"Why?"

"He's a little—" Shelby waved her hand.

"You mean—?

"Yeah, and leave it at that. Now, I'm going back to sleep."

"Hold on," Zola said, pushing Shelby into a chair. "I've got something to tell you."

"Tell me tomorrow."

"*No.* You remember that photo of the dead Irish nationalist over my fireplace?"

"What about it?" Shelby said.

"I took it off the wall and guess what?"

"You sent it to his mother?"

"*No*. Stashed behind it were passports, sticks of dynamite with a timer, and a Webley Scott pistol that English officers carried in France."

"Is this another one of your war stories, because I'm tired of hearing them."

"*No*," Zola said. "I got ahold of that private investigator our magazine uses when we want dope on politicians and businessmen whom we suspect of being more than just a little crooked and I showed him everything—except the loot."

"Loot...?"

"About a 100 grand in American and English notes."

"Where is it?" Shelby said.

"Got it right here," Zola said, pointing to the valise on the floor beside her.

"Does this investigator know about the money?"

"No—just the dynamite and the foreign passports, which really got his interest."

"Why?" Shelby said.

"Seems it's all tied to the 1920 Wall Street bombing of J.P. Morgan that's never been solved. One of the passports belonged to a John Smith."

"You mean the man who—?"

"Yeah," Zola said, "and another passport belongs to my Hell's Kitchen district leader Colm Haydock, and another to someone the private investigator thinks is related to that dead Michael Collins fella who was on the wall over my fireplace. But there was something else that got his attention."

"What?"

"A bundle of documents," Zola said, "and whoever has them controls New York City politics. And if the newspapers ever get a hold of them this town will burn."

"Why?"

"Because of the kickbacks," Zola said. "It's got everything of who gets what and how much all the way up to Albany and as far away as Washington, D.C. So, I need you to help me out. You know the right people."

"Help you out with what?"

Zola said, "I need to convert the English currency into dollars and then set up a bank account without any government snooping."

"You're asking for a lot."

"You want me to go somewhere else?"

"You've got nowhere else to go," Shelby said, now nose to nose with her older cousin. "You've got *all* the money here?"

Zola pointed straight down to the valise beside her. The cook entered. She set down the breakfast plates and then reached for the valise. Zola pushed her hand away.

The cook said, "Just gonna put it in the hall closet while y'all eat."

Zola clutched the valise. "You wanna ruin my appetite?"

The cook hurried back to the kitchen.

Shelby huddled next to her cousin and said, "This is what we'll do…"

20

The Northeastern Limited

Pullman porter Joe Dawson opened the door of the baggage car and said to Al Nachman, "I just hope this Smith ain't as nutty as that Marston Cobb fella was back in December. Me and Beau had us a handful." Joe Dawson then pointed to the corner. "Smith's grip is over there to the side like you wanted back in Bristol Station."

Al had first seen John Smith's grip in the lobby of the Alcázar Hotel before the bellhops put it on the luggage cart for the run to the depot. "Smith hasn't been back here, has he, Joe?"

"Not that I know of. Like most folk he just got his toilet bag with him for the ride up. I better get back to my car now, Mr. Nachman. Gonna be in New York soon and there be some last-minute things to do."

Al put five dollars in Joe's hand: a day's pay for many.

"Thank you, Mr. Nachman. You mind I ask you somethin'?"

"Go ahead, Joe."

"Why'd you wait till the end of the trip to do this? I'd wanna go through his grip soon as possible."

Al said, "Most folks tend to be pretty careful about how they pack. Had Smith come back here to get something, I wouldn't have wanted to have put any suspicions in his head. Now that we're almost in New York, it won't matter."

"Well, you need anyth'n else, you let me know."

"I'll do that, Joe."

Al waited for the baggage car door to close. Then he pulled a paperclip out of his pocket, opened it to ninety degrees, and pinched it so that the upper end narrowed into a little "o" head. He turned the other end into a handle, slipped the head into the padlock, jiggled it, and then pulled out the shackle. He opened the grip and pressed his hands against each item of clothing feeling for anything unusual.

He found a folding camera under some shirts, but the film hadn't been advanced beyond the first frame, because it had been incorrectly threaded. Al then searched the inside snap pocket and touched something he hadn't seen since the war: a British officer's Webley Scott top-break revolver. It used the same size man-stopping cartridge as the 1911 US Army Colt .45, but the Webley dispersed about as wide as a barn—not anything you'd want outside of a trench. Al thought it odd that Smith had never mentioned the war on their ride up—assuming that he'd been in it. Then Al found a hand drawn map of the Prevette plantation with a detailed sketch of the exterior house and all roads leading in and out. The reverse side had a detailed description of the interior including little Martha's second floor bedroom measured from the ground up to her window. Al slipped the map into his pocket along with the Webley's cartridges. He then returned to his section-car seat and sat across from John Smith who was anxiously looking for something.

21

Wall Street

Shelby had spent the previous evening in downtown speaks hidden off Houston Street where *alte zachen* was hollered by ragtag men on horse-drawn clothing carts which clopped up and down Delancey, Eldridge, Ludlow, Rivington, and Hester Streets: the bones of the Lower East Side of Manhattan and home to the immigrants who came off Ellis Island.

She stepped aside to let a burly Italian get to the subway door. He was of the class that lived on Manhattan's lower floors where, in the dead of summer, people squeezed into open windows or slept on fire escapes in their underwear in fits of sweat and endless street noise just as Shelby's Irish maid, Caitlin, had done in Hell's kitchen where people undressed but never changed, doused themselves but rarely washed, and a bath was a ritual that had to be planned days ahead. Caitlin had told Shelby about all the different tribes that lived in Manhattan, and she made the point that the Hebrews and the Dutch were the first real New Yorkers, not the English whom she despised. Shelby then asked Caitlin if she had ever heard of Mícheál Ó Coileáin or as the English pronounced it: Michael Collins. Caitlin cried, "So you know who we are."

"What I want to know is why someone in Hell's Kitchen would put his photograph up on the wall?"

"Ó Coileáin is a hero and a martyr; that's why, miss."

"Do you know many Irish who live in Hell's Kitchen?"

"Well, miss," trying not to laugh, "I've known a few."

"Why do they live in Hell's Kitchen?"

"It's near the docks where they can find work."

"Tell me about the Irish Republican Army."

"Oh, I'm just a working-class girl, miss, not a politician."

"But you do know of people who would put Collins' photo on their wall."

"Well, miss, maybe I do or don't."

"And your district leader, Colm Haydock?"

"I see you know about him as well."

"I've heard when you need something done you go to him."

"Yes, miss. Are you Irish?"

"No."

"If I may ask, then, miss, why are you so interested?"

Shelby didn't say anything about the meeting she had just had with *The New Yorker's* private investigator. Instead, she said, "I'm new to this town and want to learn everything about it. Now what can you tell me about your district leader Colm Haydock?"

"Well, miss, I rarely go to Mr. Haydock now that I've got a swell job working for you. But he's known to help a person out now and then, if ya know what I mean. See, Tammany Hall has its hands in everything and he's a very big part of it and he controls all the liquor on the West Side and any ship that comes to port better leave him some good whiskey or it'll find itself short of provisions on the way out."

"How do you know all this, Caitlin?"

"My brother's a stoker."

"What do you know about the Rebellion of 1916?"

"Oh, miss, I'd be proud to tell ya all about it, for I was there me'self. Where do ya want to start?"

"From the beginning and don't leave out a thing."

The IRT Lexington Avenue downtown subway arrived at Wall Street.

The New York Stock Exchange is a temple façade of ornate Corinthian columns, capital buds, dipping acanthus leaves, and coiled volutes—an odd-looking place for hot picks and wild rumors. Shelby headed to 14 Wall Street, home of the banking firm of Brush Reed. Its young receptionist, whose function was to greet clients before allowing them through the big double doors, was adjusting a copy of *Photoplay* magazine hidden on her lap. Shelby entered the reception area wearing an authentic Mariano Fortuny velvet, silk, and metallic brocade overcoat, a blowout of green, yellow, blue, and red landscape imprints that managed to perfectly weave fantasy into glamor by color shaping chaos into daydreams. The collar, wristlets, and hem were of real mink, unlike the dull wool used in the receptionist's eight buck coat.

"Good morning," Shelby said to the receptionist. "I'm here to see Mr. Brush."

The receptionist said, "And who are you?

"Just tell him Miss Shelby Prevette is here."

"There are several Brushes. Which one would you have in mind?"

"The elder."

"You need an appointment to see Mr. Brush. You just can't walk in."

"I did just walk in. Now you tell him Shelby is here."

The receptionist clicked the intercom switch and spoke into her head receiver as if she were reporting a crime. "Nan, there's a girl out here who would like to see Mr. Brush and she claims she doesn't need an appointment." The receptionist stared at Shelby. "Your name again?"

"I *already* told you."

In no time, Nan, the plump office manager, came into the reception area carrying an empty cigar box of gin—she had been on her way to the speakeasy on the 10th floor where stocks were supposedly traded in a front room filled with tickertape machines. She wore a drop waist navy blue wool dress with white piping, a new Marcel Wave haircut, and a gold watch that everyone knew someone had given her. In her spare time, Nan was an art photographer. Her specialty was photographing late night mischief behind closed doors, without the blackmailing, and then exhibiting it in galleries where mischief was turned into art. She approached Shelby as if she were royalty and said, "I'm so sorry to have made you wait, Miss Prevette. Mr. Brush will see you immediately."

Shelby said to Nan, "Didn't we meet at Kitty Morton's Tea Room the other night? You were the one taking photographs. I'm pretty sure you were."

"Yes, I was," Nan said, opening the inner sanctum door, "and you were sitting with that vaudevillian fella, Obie, laughing your head off."

"And just what do you do with the pictures you take?" Shelby said.

"I exhibit them. I'm an artist as well as an office manager."

"Then I must see your art," Shelby said.

"Miss Morton has a share in a Greenwich Village gallery that I'll be exhibiting in next month. I'll forward you an invitation."

"Good. I can't wait," Shelby said. "And I want to buy that photo that you took of me and Obie, as well as the negative of it."

"Sorry, Miss Prevette, but you can't own the negative. I'm sure you can understand why."

"For some money, I think you could understand why I could," Shelby said as she turned to the receptionist, who was now standing up. "Your *Photoplay* is on the floor……"

Marbury Brush's office was a large, magnificent chamber with broad windows which opened to a rolling view of Wall Street's skyscrapers. Shelby walked in and immediately felt power on display as Marbury Brush rose from his desk, took her hand, and placed it on his lips. "Please sit down," he said, pulling up a chair for her, his enormous desk making anyone beside it tiny in perspective. "I just spoke to your father."

"You mean about me learning the investment banking business?"

"That among other things," Marbury Brush said, sitting back in his big custom chair which allowed him to swivel and lean, so that nothing was beyond reach, "and we both agreed that that kind of work is unsuitable for a girl."

"I disagree," Shelby said, finding it odd that there was nothing on his desk other than three candlestick telephones: one for the office, one for the stock exchange, and the third for outside calls. A Columbia Gramophone Dictaphone Model 10 Type A, the same one that her father had in his office, sat on a platform beside the desk along with a duckbill mouthpiece which hung on a long chord. She wasn't offered a cigarette, as it was unladylike to smoke, so she took one of her own and said, "I have capital to invest, I need to learn how to short the market, and I need you to explain to me how a pool works. Your son, Lyle, did his best this morning, but I had a feeling he was holding back."

"Well, it's very simple, child. But it's not anything you need to know. What you don't want to be short of is diapers."

"Teach me the banking business and we'll see who comes up short," Shelby said. "Now, how does a pool work?"

Marbury Brush turned to his three phones and imagined that any one of them was ringing. "Very simple."

"How simple?"

"As I said, I just spoke to your father and—"

"How simple?"

Marbury Brush couldn't get out of the way of her intense eyes.

"How simple, Uncle Marbury?"

"Well, as simple as the price of a stock going up along with its corresponding value."

"And…?"

"At a decided moment investors disinvest." Marbury Brush found his pipe.

"You mean they disinvest before it drops *or* so that it will drop? I'm a little confused."

He struck a match. "That does seem to be the preferred approach."

"The dropping or the disinvesting?"

He puffed along. "Did you get our invitation?"

"Yes."

"Everyone wants to see you up at the country club this weekend for the winter ball. There are some boys from very good families that'll be on the lookout for you."

Shelby took two packets of bills from her bag and dropped them on his desk. "What are the conversion rates going for pounds today?"

Marbury Brush removed the pipe from his mouth and sighted the money. "I didn't know you were in England."

"I wasn't. How much are pounds trading for?"

"Where did you get English pounds then?"

Shelby said, "What's at issue is what can be done with them."

"That's always the issue. May I…?"

"Go ahead," Shelby said, pushing the money toward him.

He licked his thumb, took the notes, and flicked through them until they were all pushed into the back of his hand. Shelby was impressed. She had seen payout men at the racetracks do the same thing and not any faster.

"How do I get all this converted into dollars?"

"Why do you ask?"

"Because I've got a lot more where this came from."

Their eyes met. "*How* much more?"

"A *lot* more," Shelby said.

"I can set up a bank account for you and have the funds shifted into it as a loan of an equal amount."

"Why?"

"Because you don't pay taxes on a loan, and it will be all legitimate. You let my people take care of it, child. They do this all the time."

"Really…?" Shelby said. "Now about this shorting business, I want to get into the next pool. In fact, I believe there's one already active."

"And just which one would that be?" Marbury Brush said, striking a match.

"Soling Consolidated General."

He let the burning match hang in his finger. "I suppose Lyle told you about it this morning?"

"No. In fact he told me very little, but I've been reading about it in the *Wall Street Journal*."

"What do you mean reading about it?"

Shelby said, "There are two columns, *Broad Street Gossip* and *Abreast of the Market*, which have been overtly pushing Soling Consolidated General and I would say for obvious reasons—they've been paid to push it."

"And how would you know that?"

"I did a little research of my own," Shelby said, "and it seems the assets of said debtor are dubious and the country's economy not strong enough to act as future collateral should Soling belly up. It may be an American company, but if you read the fine print it's fronted by a holding company which has no real history other than a lot of twisted lawyer's talk—but then what do I know, Uncle Marbury? I'm just a girl," she said, her eyes dead on him.

"…No doubt a smart one," he said, tossing the charred match into the ashtray.

"You still think a woman has no place in investment banking?"

"The point is that it's not for girls, not about having any place."

"You mean you'd hire a boy with half my wit?"

"No…but you wouldn't be accepted into the clubs. You know the expression: 'It's a man's world'? You just can't have a girl sitting around while men are discussing business. It would be highly inappropriate."

"Unless I'm mistaken, Uncle Marbury, we're discussing business right now, and it seems anything but inappropriate."

"Yes…but this is different, and anyway it's not the way things are done. You'll be married soon enough, and you'll be very busy with social tasks along with raising children."

"I'm not getting married so fast."

Marbury Brush stared at the girl whose eyes held onto him the way ice clings to a branch in the dead of winter. "We'll talk about this later," he said, restacking the notes. "But as far as I'm concerned, this whole flapper business has gone too far. Young girls are getting the wrong impression today and sadly, when they grow up, reality will hit them where it hurts."

"Where it *hurts?*"

"Yes."

"What do you mean where it hurts?"

Marbury Brush said, "The location is a metaphor."

"Well, what I'm talking about is for real," Shelby said, getting up. "I can have the rest of the money here in an hour."

He opened the door for her. "Get it……"

Twenty-five minutes later, Shelby walked into her library where Zola was busy writing her column for *The New Yorker*. Caitlin hurried in and said, "Your uncle Marbury is on the phone, miss. I told him you just walked in."

Shelby took the call and then returned. "How much money did you find?"

Zola looked up from her notebook. "Well, I come up with a different number every time I count it, but it's always around 100,000, give or take. It's the pound conversion that I'm not exactly sure of."

"Maybe it's your math."

"Shut up."

"Don't worry," Shelby said. "I'll count it when I take it downtown."

"You mean when *we* take it downtown."

"No, when *I* take it downtown."

"So, you can steal all my money?"

"Zola, in case you didn't know, there'll be a 20% fee to do the currency transaction because of certain complications—unless you want to use pound sterling in Manhattan."

"*Twenty* grand?"

"That's how it's done in the big leagues."

"You mean 20% for you," Zola said.

"If you think you can have English pounds converted into dollars and also open an account all by yourself with stolen money then go ahead and do it."

"*Stolen* money...?"

"Yes, *stolen* money," Shelby said. "That's what that phone call was all about. The serial numbers were just checked. Enjoy living in that hole of yours in Hell's Kitchen."

"You mean the money's useless?"

"No, but you sometimes are," Shelby said, reaching for the valise. Zola wouldn't let go of it. Then crazy Mrs. Buchanan came to mind. The neighbors who made noise all night. The communal telephone on the first floor that reeked of bad breath. The leaky icebox. The dim cataract light bulb that infected her living room. The couch that always smelled of someone else. Zola let go of the valise.

22

Deeper Than Love

Without saying a word, Pullman porter Joe Dawson let the white passenger know that he could get very nasty if push came to shove and that he wasn't the one who was going to feel the pain. John Smith let go of him and in a more restrained voice said, "You find anything in this car that's mine?"

"As I said, sir, I wouldn't know what's yours."

"It's a diagram of my new house."

"Could be you lost it in the transfer. Happens all the time."

"No, no, I had it on me," John Smith said, checking his coat pockets again.

"Well, it can just happen that a man's mind gets out of sorts when he travelin'. Packin' and unpackin' he forgettin' where he put somethin'. But us gonna be in New York soon, so I'll tell the cleanin' gang to look out for it when we get there. Got your name on it?"

"No."

"Your company name?"

"No," John Smith said, compulsively checking his pockets again. "I need to find that diagram or you're not getting a tip."

Pullman Porter Joe Dawson said, "You leave me your address and iffen this diagram be found, I'll get it over to you. And you can keep the tip."

John Smith waved Joe Dawson on and lit a cigarette, not bothered that he wasn't in the smoking car. The train entered the tunnel to Manhattan from Weehawken, New Jersey and went dark for a moment. Then the interior lights went on. Al looked up from the wire which Zola had sent to Bristol Station, Virginia, and said to him "You lose something?"

John Smith, sitting across from Al, didn't reply.

"Happens all the time when I'm traveling," Al said.

John Smith just stared into the blackened window.

"Must be really important. What did you lose?"

"…A diagram."

"Of what?"

"Of my new house."

"It'll turn up," Al assured him. "Those things always do."

"You said that before."

"No, the porter said that." The train rumbled along in the tunnel. "You mentioned that you were born in Ireland."

John Smith picked up a magazine, one he had already read.

"Ever hear of the Irish nationalist Michael Collins?" Al said.

John Smith became very still.

Al said, "I believe Collins was killed a few years back."

"Are you Irish?"

"No."

"So then how do you know about Collins?"

"A girl I know in Hell's Kitchen had a photo of Collins in her rooming house," Al said. "I thought maybe you could set me straight on what he was all about, since I'm not Irish."

"I thought you were going to New York to sell bonds with your brother on Wall Street."

"I am," Al said.

"So, then what's with the girl from Hell's Kitchen?"

"She's from back home."

"What's she doing in New York?"

"Got tired of the farm," Al said.

"She Irish?"

"Scots-Irish."

"Not the same thing."

"No, it isn't," Al said, "But she's a country girl and knows something about guns, so when she found the Webley Scott revolver in her room, she thought maybe it had to do with that picture of Collins."

John Smith sat up. "How did she make that connection?"

"I had mentioned to her that Empire officers used that weapon in the trenches on the Western Front."

"Where in Hell's Kitchen does this girl live?"

"I forget offhand."

"How did she get a hold a Webley Scott?"

"I told you. She found it," Al said. "Someone probably brought it over after the war then forgot about it. You know how it is."

"Where in the apartment did she find it?"

"Oh, I wouldn't know *that*," Al said.

"You said she found it in her apartment."

"I did."

"You didn't ask her where she found it?"

"Why would I ask?"

John Smith didn't reply.

"I'll ask her where when I see her," Al said. "It's not the only thing she found."

John Smith leaned over. "What else did she find?"

"From what I read in one of her letters, I could tell she was pretty much excited."

"Excited about what?"

"A whole lot of things that had to do with traveling," Al said.

"I'd like to meet this girl."

"Would you?"

"I'm a gun collector."

"You never said anything about that before," Al said.

"It's a hobby, not a profession."

"What kind of guns do you collect?"

"All kinds," John Smith said. "See, I'd like to buy that gun. Give me her telephone number and I'll offer her a fair price."

"She's never home," Al said, "but if you leave me your number, I'll have her call you."

"*I'm* never home."

"Then you won't get the gun," Al said.

"Tell her I'll give her 100 dollars for the gun, way more than it's worth."

"What's so special about it?"

"It was an English piece of junk," John Smith said. "But historically important."

"How so?"

"It was a weapon used in the war. So, it's a piece of history."

"You're a historian?" Al said.

"Sure, I am. You don't know your history, you don't know who you are."

"…Who are you, John?"

"What do you mean *who* am I?"

"That salesman, back in Mississippi, said you were chased by a colored woman with a cleaver."

"He mistook me for someone else. I told him that."

"He thought otherwise."

"He thought incorrectly, so get it out of your head."

"Hard to get a knife out of your head," Al said with a smile.

"Then it'll be harder for you and me to keep on talking."

Al offered him a cigarette. "Were you in the war?"

"Why?" taking the smoke.

"You said you're an American."

"I'm also Irish," taking the light from Al.

"Is that why your accent comes and goes?"

"I wouldn't know," John Smith said. "I don't hear myself."

"Generally, a man speaks one way or the other."

"What do you mean, one way or the other?"

"I mean you go in and out of Irish," Al said.

"You're only American."

"What do you mean, I'm only American?"

"You wouldn't understand," John Smith said.

"I hope you're not insulting me by saying that I'm only American."

"Only if you want to take it that way."

"Is it something from long ago?" Al said.

"Could be."

"How long?"

"When I lived in Ireland."

"What happened?"

"As I said, it was a long time ago."

"Not so long to have forgotten it," Al said.

John Smith shrugged as if it weren't worth the time—but it was.

"Someone you loved?"

"Deeper than that," John Smith said.

"How do you get deeper than love?"

John Smith said, trying to end the discussion, "When you look into a girl's eyes, and you can't turn away, then you're looking between this world and the next."

"You mean your wife?"

"No."

"Someone else's?"

"No."

"This girl leave you?"

"…Not in the normal sense."

"What sense then?"

John Smith looked into the blackened window and measured the reflection of his face against his life. So far it had been a waste. He said, "I used to see this girl on her doorstep every day."

"Did you know her?"

"Not in the sense of knowing a girl," John Smith said, "but all I had to do was look into her eyes. Most girls don't have eyes."

"She did?"

"Yeah. Then—"

"What?" Al said.

"I spoke to her and when I did—I heard another accent besides Irish."

"She wasn't Irish?"

"No."

"What was she then?"

"I didn't know what she was," John Smith said. "But when I tried to find out, a hurt look came over her and she ran away. I knocked on her door for days on end."

"Did she open it?"

"Never."

"You still think of her?"

"Always."

"…I guess you see yourself in her," Al said.

"I don't see myself in anybody," John Smith said, turning to the window as the Northeastern Limited pulled into Pennsylvania Station. The light from the glass and iron canopy ceiling saturated the multiple platforms and stairways as the puddling iron of the Eifel Tower, deep into Pennsylvania Station's structure, gave off an otherworldly glow that would one day be demolished and replaced by a soda machine.

The consist rolled to a stop. The luggage was hauled off the baggage car and brought to the claims desk. Al and John Smith received their grips and bade each other goodbye. Al took the second taxi and followed him up Riverside Drive, the Upper West Side of Manhattan, right along the frigid Hudson River that separated two realities.

23

Riverside Drive

The public parks along Manhattan's Riverside Drive were empty except for some swings twisting in the wind. Only the drifting sound of tugboat horns and maritime bells suggested that there was any blood left in the frigid city. John Smith entered a townhouse on 105th Street fronted with tall, fluted columns and sweeping steps. An eight-foot glass panel, shielded by an intricate Beaux Arts ironwork screen, framed the doorway. The chandelier in the foyer, of some grand old reign, gave off enough light to reach Fort Lee across the Hudson River. But it was by the second-floor lighting, flat and dingy, where a tall man's shadow battled the walls and discolored the room. He moved with long angular strides and clenched a black cigarette holder in his teeth and wore a monocle over his left eye: marks to those who feared him. His pale face, of time lost, filled the street window.

Al got out of the cab and set the f/stop of his Leica A to 3.5 and focused the lens. *Click.* Then another shadow took up the wall. *Click.* A heated argument ensued until both shadows merged. *Click.* The lights went out. Al waited. The black metal Ohmer taxi meter ticked away. Seconds, then minutes went by and then a blue Isotta-Fraschini Tipo 8A 4 Door Sedan with bright round headlights and a strapped-on trunk at the rear came down the street. *Click.* Al put the lens on the man in the backseat who wore the monocle. *Click.* Rain bounced off the sedan's wide sloping fenders as it headed south before turning east. *Click.* Al then quickly crossed the street and rang the doorbell of the townhouse.

No one answered. He went around below to the service entrance and stepped down into the kitchen where a middle-aged white cook, wearing a long gray dress and a spotless white apron, was reading a copy of *Laughter Magazine* spread out on the baking table. The cook looked up, not surprised someone whom she didn't know had appeared.

"I have an appointment with Mr. John Smith," Al said. "I rang the front door, but no one answered."

"The front door is not my business," the cook said.

"You work here?"

"Every day now for a month."

"You're the cook?"

The cook looked up at Al, wondering why he was there.

"Are you making supper tonight?"

"Only when they ring," she said.

"Who are *they?*"

"I wouldn't know. I never see 'em. They just ring when they want something," pointing to the dumbwaiter where the requested food was sent up.

"When did they last ring for food?" Al said.

"I don't think they ever have."

"And you just sit here."

"I get paid to sit here,"

"You get paid to cook."

"Are you hungry?"

"No. Do you know John Smith?"

"Smith you say?"

"Yeah, Smith. John Smith."

"There are no Smiths here, mister."

"How do you know there aren't?"

"I would know."

"You're sure about that?"

"Absolutely," the cook said.

"I thought you said you've never met anyone here?"

"That's why I'm sure."

"What about the lady of the house? Doesn't she come down to give you instructions?"

"You'd have to ask her," the cook said.

"I'm asking you."

"Look, I just answered the ad in the paper, mister. They wanted an expert cook. I'm an expert cook." She opened the icebox and showed Al the eggs, the chops, the thick slab of bacon, the block of cheese, the flounder draped over an oval platter, the bottle of whole milk, fruit preserves, pickles, butter, sour cream, and a bowl of shiny apples with their leafy stems still attached.

"When was the last time you ever cooked anything?"

"I never once cooked a thing."

"Don't you find that a little strange?"

"Look, mister. You might as well ask that flounder, in the ice box, who caught him, because I don't know and neither does that fish."

Al left the kitchen. He went upstairs. He entered the street side room on the second floor where the tall man with the black cigarette holder and monocle had paced. Al found John Smith face down on the parquet floor. He looked like roadkill: the kind that thinks a sprint is all it takes to bypass the human world. Al put on his gloves and reached inside the dead man's coat. He found a small black booklet which had Addison Prevette's Clarksdale address where at that very moment Addison was reading the final notice of where to leave the quarter of a million, and it wasn't from John Smith.

24

Dragon Clouds

Ship bells from New York harbor rang through the narrow streets of skyscrapers which stood end to end in downtown Manhattan—daylight got through by appointment only. Marbury Brush, sitting behind his huge desk, counted the last bill of the pile and said, "We've gone through this three times, and it always comes to 387,500 dollars—a lot more than what you thought you had."

"Someone can't count," Shelby said, looking up from the stack of cash and into the dragon cloud drifting by the window. She felt the weight of some unspoken omen as the big office went dark for a moment. "What do you know about the 12-mile limit?"

"What anyone knows—why?"

"I'm curious."

"It's nothing that should concern you."

"Then it should," Shelby said.

"Most 19-year-old girls can only think of boys and necking in the rumble seat."

"What's the 12-mile limit?"

"Now that we've counted the money—"

"What's the 12-mile limit?"

"Shelby, you're a young woman of good breeding."

"I already know that."

"Then you shouldn't bother with things that have nothing to do with you."

"What's the 12-mile limit?"

"It's merely some designation of the international water line. Now, how do you want all this money invested?"

"As we discussed before," Shelby said.

"All of it in the Soling Consolidated General pool?"

"Every penny."

"Good. Now, you said that you needed something else."

"I need to set up a bank account for a Miss Zola Nicholas in the amount of 80,000 dollars—but only to be deposited after the short. All profits earned over that will go into my account."

"All...?"

"Yes," Shelby said. "Unless something has changed."

"Nothing's changed. If it were my money, I'd do the same."

"Have you been out there?"

"Out where, child?"

"The 12-mile limit."

"Only when we sail in summer ocean," Uncle Marbury said as he got up from his desk. "Now, come along. I'll have everything set up."

"You still haven't answered my question."

"All it means," Uncle Marbury said, "is that any ship lying outside the limit is in international waters."

"And that liquor may be sold out there?"

"I suppose a lot of things may be sold out there."

Shelby, still seated, said, "I hear there's a nightclub with a casino on a certain ship which caters to rich men and their pleasures. I assume that it's outside the 12-mile limit."

"I wouldn't know anything about it."

"But you've heard of it," Shelby said.

"Heard of what?"

"That ship or yacht."

"Why should it concern you?"

"I'm new to New York."

"It's not a place for a proper young lady of means."

"Why isn't it?"

"It isn't and that should be enough."

"Is it engaged in immoral activities?" Shelby said.

"I have no idea."

"So, then, how do you know it's not a place for a proper young lady of means?"

"Shelby…what you should be thinking of is the winter ball this weekend at the club and all the potential husbands who'll be there, not some silly ship out at sea."

"I shall *think* what I want."

Marbury Brush said, "I don't like that tone of voice,"

"I shall think what I want, and no one will stop me."

"If you keep up this attitude," he said, "I won't invest your money. Remember, I'm under no obligation."

"If women have the right to vote then they have the right to speak their mind, and *that* is an obligation *not* an offense."

"Yes, but you're not a woman, yet."

"I will be one soon enough," she said, getting up and going to the door.

"Listen to me, Shelby," he said, following her. "There's a lot of trouble a high-minded flapper like you can get into in this town. Your father isn't here, and he told me to give you guidance, and God help me should anything happen to you, because I promised your father nothing would."

"Yes, but your promise to him is nothing without my consent and *that* you do not have and shall not have," she said.

"Young lady—you're lucky that your father and I are old and dear friends."

"And since he's *more* than my friend, my wishes shall be respected, or any loss of respect shall be his. Now, what about Tammany Hall?"

"What about it?" Marbury Brush said, reaching for the door, wanting to get out.

"How easily are its politicians bribed?"

"Too easily. Why?"

Shelby thought of Hell's Kitchen and its district leader Colm Haydock and stepped out the door.

"You didn't answer my question," Marbury Brush said.

But he had answered hers.

25

The District Leader

Rabbi Edmund O'Dorcey lugged a burlap case of bootleg whiskey up a wooden staircase so narrow that it got out of breath before he did. The fourth floor opened to a gaslit gallery where the clacking and racking of billiard balls ticked the air as flies chased whatever light came in through the unwashed windows. The whole walk-up shook to an IRT Uptown Ninth Avenue train rumbling over the elevated tracks. Just feet away, the rooftop pediment façade—dated 1875— sheltered a yellow-rumped warbler. Right below it and through the window, Colm Haydock, the Tammany Hall district leader of burnt orange hair and freckled skin—a giant at six feet six inches—stepped out of his backroom office and shoved a roll of bills into Rabbi O'Dorcey's pocket. He said to the newly ordained cleric, "Maybe ya oughta change yer name to Bernstein while yer at it?"

Rabbi O'Dorcey said, "The government's permit to acquire hooch for religious rites don't require ya to change yer name—but I just might change me friends," and then left the building.

Haydock's assistant, Mugs O'Beer, stepped aside and made a slight bow to the young lady who had just walked in. "Please to meet ya, miss," as if love had struck her first.

Shelby turned away from the worn emerald, "Where can I find the district leader?" she said, suppressing her drawl as best as she could.

"This is not the day for favors, miss. But, bein' I'm a gentleman, I could help ya out, dependin' on what yer little need is," Mugs O'Beer said, letting the dazzle in his eye play her up."

Colm Haydock said, "Don't mind him, miss."

Shelby turned to the giant coming her way with eyes that counted everything twice. "Does he always wear his hat inside and when a lady is present?"

"Mugs ain't as educated as you, miss, nor is he as beautiful."

Colm Haydock folded Mugs O'Beer back into his deck and escorted Shelby to the backroom office. "Is there anything I can do for ya today, miss?"

"My name is Etta Jape," Shelby lied.

Colm Haydock took the unopened case of Glen Trool which Rabbi O'Dorcey had just delivered and set it on the floor beside his desk.

"Would you like a drink, Miss Jape?"

"I only drink milk."

"It's better for ya. Please sit down. Now, what can I do for ya, miss?"

"Have you ever heard of Mícheál Ó Coileáin?"

The district leader stared at the incredibly beautiful girl, half his height, who had risked walking into a men's establishment all alone; and like Mugs O'Beer, he wanted her, but he was wise enough to know that there were consequences for getting stupid. "There's a lot of men with that name, Miss Jape. We could spend all day and the next lookin' for the one ya want and still be nowhere."

"I'm talking about the Irish nationalist shot dead at Béal na Bláth."

Colm Haydock's expression changed from interested to wary. "Are ya Irish, miss?"

"Irish American," Shelby lied, hearing Caitlin's voice in her own. "Do you remember what happened in 1920?"

"A lot of things happened in 1920, miss. Where would ya be wantin' to be startin'? January 1st or Christmas week?"

"Let's start with the bombing of J.P. Morgan on Wall Street."

"...And why there?"

"Because Mícheál Ó Coileáin worked for the Guaranty Trust Company of New York in 1915, which is owned by J. P. Morgan who financed the British war effort and kept England afloat throughout the war."

The district leader walked over to the barely opened window and shut it. He sat down, again, and reached for a cigarette. "Why would someone of your likes be concerned with Mícheál Ó Coileáin?"

"Because, Mr. Haydock, you, Mícheál Ó Coileáin, John Smith, and 1920, are all connected."

Colm Haydock looked down the hall to see if anyone one else had come with Shelby. He didn't believe a girl this refined would come here on her own, even though she spoke with the confidence and determination of someone who had seen things and was no longer under the spell of adolescent impressions. The district leader said to her, "Everyone knows that it was the Italians and Russians behind the bombing, and, anyway, Attorney General Palmer has already put an end to this anarchist business. So, with all due respect to your youth, miss, you've got it all wrong."

"You can think what you want, Mr. Haydock. But the government hasn't closed the case and it would be more than glad to know that I'm in possession of passports, one that is yours, as well as those of the others involved in the Wall Street bombing—which the police are still investigating. I also have the detonators, that you're an expert at deploying and the same kind that were used in the blast, as well as a list of the graft in this town that would be more explosive than any of your bombs."

"…And just how do you come up with such fantasy, Miss Jape?"

"Some say a free Ireland is fantasy. You might as well ask them how they came up with that."

"A man doesn't lose his passport easily," Colm Haydock said.

"Ah, but you were born here, so you have two."

"And how would you know that, Miss Jape?"

"The way I know that your mother came here penniless and when she got tired of scrubbing floors, she found prostitution more lucrative. Then she became pregnant with you and was soon arrested. She gave birth to you in the Tombs prison, downtown. Upon release, she returned to Ireland to leave her shame here."

Shelby opened her clutch bag and took out the mugshot of the district leader's mother taken in 1891 that Zola's private investigator had dug up for her, among other things. "You wouldn't want any copies of this to get around. Would you, Mr. Haydock?" Shelby put the mugshot back into her bag. "And this is a copy of the original should you try to take it away from me," which had been on his mind. "After having lived in Ireland nearly all your life, in the summer of 1914 you returned to this country with a man named Casement to raise funds for the great Irish cause after the protestant Ulster Volunteers had landed over 20,000 rifles in Northern Ireland from a freighter without the British ever batting an eye. The nerve of England to think that we Irish would ever let anything like that go unheeded. But, then, that is the conceit of those in power to disregard those they subject."

"Were you there yourself, Miss Jape?" The district leader's denial now gone.

"Does it matter?"

"A man you're married to?"

"Oh, Mr. Haydock, how you underestimate us women. Just as they did Countess Markievicz, who gave up art for Ireland's cause."

"You knew the Countess?"

"She's like a mother to me and sister to us all who love Ireland and hate the British for plundering our sacred soil to enrich themselves and impoverish the likes of you and me. England will pay in time. But that's not for now. I have a message for you to give Artemus Cummins. Tell him to send the negatives he has of a certain Clarksdale gentleman to this post office box address by the end of the week, or he shall be dead come Sunday; if not, Mr. Haydock, every newspaper in town will publish what I have on Tammany Hall's Tombs' bastard and the payoff list."

"And I suppose you plan on killing Cummins yourself, Miss Jape?"

"Oh, no, Mr. Haydock. It wouldn't be ladylike. You're the one who's going to do it."

Shelby got up and left a small, scented lavender envelope on the district leader's desk to be read at his pleasure, and then left.

Mugs O'Beer followed Shelby down Ninth Avenue and then up the heavy iron stairway of the 50th Street IRT elevated train station. He did little not to be seen. He made flashes of the eye. Showed his teeth and winked when Shelby turned his way, but her cream-colored gigolo hat marked her as she went through the doors of each train car as it rattled above the cobblestone streets. Shelby got off at Times Square and hurried down into the subway tunnels where every twist and turn was crowded with thousands of strap-hangers coming in and out of the countless stairways and platforms and merging into a stream of commuters which quickened onto the crosstown shuttle platform where the train was arriving and opening its doors. The strap-hangers herded themselves inside. The departure bell rang. The doors shut. The shuttle lurched forward. Mugs O'Beer pressed his angry face up against the train's double windows. Shelby was still on the platform, but with her hat off.

26

The New Yorker

Zola fed a blank piece of paper into a 1915 glass key Underwood #5 typewriter that *The New Yorker* magazine had bought at a fire sale. She typed out the beginning of her column: *I'm not going to bother you this week with the usual club openings in and around Broadway nor anywhere else for that matter. The bad ones close faster than the Prohis can get to them, and then there is the theater's inability to produce anything better than that side dish: Abie's Irish Rose. The Big White Way, besides being lachrymose and hoisted by its own retard is nothing but a stopover before the real show begins: spooning, which is playing, free of charge, in all the nightclubs and as far downtown as Greenwich Village. Why just last night, at a table next to mine, the waiter tried to serve dessert to a spooning flapper who complained: I haven't finished with this dish yet!*

Zola stopped typing and looked up. "...The hell happened to you?"

Shelby, exhausted, stepped in and said, "I was chased by a pervert."

"When?"

"*Now.*"

"What happened?"

"Ever hear of Mugs O'Beer?" Shelby sat down on one of the old discolored wooden chairs.

"What about him?" Zola said.

"The last time he brushed his teeth was before he threw up."

"Well, every speak in Hell's Kitchen has to buy liquor from him or they get raided. Did your little plan work out?"

"We'll find out soon enough," Shelby said, looking out the window at all the hats walking down the street. "I never realized how corrupt our democracy is."

"Ohh—you mean that list of kickbacks and special-interest groups which I found in the wall of my rooming house?"

"Yeah, what a joke," Shelby said.

"Well, as Mark Twain once said: *We've got the best government that money can buy.*"

Robert Benchley stepped into Zola's office. "Miss Prevette..." Shelby stood up with open arms. He filled them and said, "I'm sorry I didn't meet you at Penn Station when you arrived in town, but I was out on assignment."

"His assignment was his wife," Zola said.

"And now that that's fulfilled, I'm all yours, Shelby."

"What's this about you sailing to Berlin?" she said.

"I'm doing an assignment for the magazine on all the craziness over there. You'll see me off this weekend?"

"You're sailing that soon?"

"There's too much going on there to wait," he said.

"I wish *I* were going," Zola said.

"You don't need to," Robert Benchley said. "There's enough craziness over here, which is why you're making a name for yourself."

"Yeah," Zola said. "One that no one knows."

"Which makes you even more exotic," he said.

"Sure, it does," Zola said, turning back to Shelby. "Hey, you were supposed to call me this morning about you know what."

"Well, don't. It's all set up," Shelby said, "Now, I've got to meet Virginia at Saks Fifth Ave for a little shopping." Shelby slipped on her coat.

Zola warned her, "You're not going anywhere until you tell me when I can put my hands on you know what," now on her feet too.

Robert Benchley said, "If you mean me, anytime," and followed them out the door."

27

Saks Fifth Avenue

Shelby dropped over a grand on jumper dresses, French lisle stockings, skirt sweaters, cape coats, belted blouses, hot off the shelf slave bracelets, skirts of wool and crêpe de Chine, hoop earrings, sweater outfits, broadcloth pajamas, gigolo hats, cloches, two-piece evening gowns, and a raccoon coat which smothered her. She told her personal shopper, "Send it all to 399 Park Avenue, Penthouse A." Virginia piped in, "Hey, don't forget my stuff."

Zola said, "Mine too," even though she hadn't bought a thing. She said to Shelby, "I can't take all this money," and went back to her office.

The personal shopper said to Virginia, "Would this be for your new show, Miss Swain?"

"Yeah," she said. "It's called *Spend Till Ya Drop*."

Virginia dipped her hands into the shoe display and tossed every shoe at the personal shopper. "Get each one in our size and make it snappy."

"What sizes would that be Miss Swain?"

"Size three for Miss Prevette and five for me. And don't you dare call me big foot."

Nettie Gimpel heard this from her hiding place behind a dress rack with her assistant who was taking it all down. Nettie planned on using the scene in her next ad along with Virginia's quips, but it was the other girl, the one whom Gideon couldn't keep his eyes off of at Tony Soma's, who made the real impression. Nettie had no doubt that some old millionaire with pea soup in his beard was putting her up. Nettie turned to her assistant, Alice, and said, "Didgya get me the dirt on her?"

Alice pulled out her notepad and folded back the cover. "Yes, Miss Gimpel. When Miss Swain called, we notified everyone that a celebrity was on her way."

"I mean the *other* girl."

"Oh, Miss Prevette..."

"Yeah, didgya look her up in the Social Register?"

"Yes, Miss Gimpel. It's on my desk right next to my telephone."

"I she *in* it?"

"Her father is and he's also in *Who's Who*."

"Who is he?"

"He comes from a wealthy planter's family that goes back before the Revolution."

"What else didgya get?"

Alice said, "He's related to one of the first presidents of the Continental Congress, he fought in Cuba, and is quoted as having said that only a dumb Yankee like Teddy Roosevelt would charge up a hill in his reading glasses."

Gideon came off the escalator. Nettie saw him and hollered, "Lunch was yesterday."

He bypassed her and headed straight to Shelby. "You wanted to see me?"

"Yeah," she said. "Ever hear of Artemus Cummins?" Sure, he had.

"Good, you're coming over for supper."

28

Hell's Kitchen

Mrs. Buchanan scoured the cold, pulseless streets as she dragged her lame leg down the stoop of her rooming house. She wrapped her arms around her gray, moth-eaten longshoreman's sweater, hastily thrown over a frumpy dress that had long lost its blue. Her newly bobbed hair, streaked with gray and misery, couldn't hide the creases and wrinkles which were increasingly lining her neck and face. She was getting old fast, and it scared her. When she could, she poured on the make-up and bleached her hair into a buttery blonde confection with tints of gorgeous make-believe red, and then did her lips in Valentine red so that when she blinked a lover might enter her life and pretend that loneliness and too much mascara had turned into love, but something more immediate confronted her as she cautiously crept down her building's stoop. She gripped the railing as if trying to pull it from its base and hollered in a voice meant to scatter people, not pigeons, "Get your ass outta here, boy!"

"I'm here on an errand, ma'am," Beau said, pulling out his papers. "See, I'm an employee of the Pullman Coach Company. Says right here. I ain't no vagrant."

"Then why ain't your ass on the train?"

"Well, Miss Nicholas, your tenant, she come from the same hometown as me and I brought her some things from her folks."

"Well, if it's money, I want it. She owes me rent."

"Sorry, ma'am, you can understand why I can't do that."

"No, I can't. And just what are you two up to—a nigger and a white girl?"

"I just explained, ma'am; gonna give her a few things from her kin then be on my way. And my name is Beau not nigger."

"Your name is what I give you. And I know all about white women getting sucked in by you nigger boys. Go back South where you belong. We got enough wops and bohunks up here as it is." She raised a pair of scissors that she'd been hiding behind her long coat and aimed it at him.

Beau stepped away as he tried to calm down the old lady. "Easy, ma'am. I never robbed nobody in my life."

"That's what *you* say, boy."

Zola walked out the door and quickly stepped past Mrs. Buchanan who hollered, "I want your ass outta here now or I'll get the coal boy to do it!"

Zola said to her, "I paid for the month, Mrs. Buchanan. You either reimburse me or I'm going to the police. And if you touch anything that belongs to me, I'll press charges against you."

"*Go* to the police. I already reported you as a dirty lesbian."

"I'm *not* a lesbian."

"Denying it only proves you are!"

"That makes no sense, Mrs. Buchanan."

"It makes all the sense in the world. Now get your ass outta my building!"

"I have to work tonight, Mrs. Buchanan. I'll leave in the morning."

"Why can't you whores work 9-5 like everyone else?"

"Mrs. Buchanan—I'll leave when I get home from work because I'm sick of living here. But I want my money for the rest of the month that you owe me or I'm going to the police."

"*Go* to the police and tell 'em to lock you up!"

"Sure, after I tell 'em what a crook you are."

Zola and Beau quickly headed west to Ninth Avenue for the elevated IRT Uptown train. Mrs. Buchanan went on with her harangue, but the cold air and wind swallowed it up.

Beau said, "Maybe ya oughta go back and get your things out while the goin's good."

"When I get back later."

"Might be too late, Miss Zola."

"No. The old lady sleeps late. I'll leave in the morning without her on my case. If I go back now, it'll only add to her anger, which is what she wants. Now, what about those Harlem clubs?"

"There's the Sugar Cane, ma'am, just opened. Not too many white people go there, yet. Might be right for your column."

"Let's go!"

29

The Sugar Cane Club

A negro dancing waiter inched his way through the jammed narrow dance floor crammed with saxophones, horns, and hot bottomed mamas. In the mix was a white boy in black tie, black boys in any tie, and a weightless white girl dancing loose and wild with anyone who caught her fancy. A visiting white couple from the South, still in their chairs, felt uncomfortable but nonetheless intrigued. The wife had yet to take off her coat as they considered the unthinkable for the first time. A waiter set glasses and soda water on Zola's table. Beau then spotted Officer Elgin Bumpus by the front door. "I'll be right back, Miss Zola."

Officer Elgin Bumpus said to Beau, "Nice lookin' girl you with."

"Ain't what ya think."

"Who is she?"

Beau said, "Writer for a new magazine causin' a stir downtown. Her job is to go to all the clubs and let the fancy folk know which is fairest of 'em all. I'm her guide tonight; that's it and no more."

Officer Elgin Bumpus said, "Well, the girl you lookin' for is over at Smalls Paradise right now."

"Doin' what?"

"She's a singer-dancer. Got an act goes on in an hour."

"What's her name?" Beau said.

"Carmela Knight. Ed Smalls, owner of the club, said for you to see Henry, the backdoor man. He knows everythin' and'll show you to her dressin' room."

"Does she know I'm comin'?"

"Told her to stay in her dressin' room till you get done talkin' to her."

"What's she like?"

"Like all girls long on ambition," Officer Elgin Bumpus said. "Can't understand why she ain't at the top 'a things."

Beau pulled out the photo, developed that morning, of the man with the monocle and black cigarette holder which Al had taken on Riverside Drive. "Is this the man we spoke of?"

Officer Elgin Bumpus put his flashlight to the photograph and said, "Oh, yeah. That's Artemus Cummins. No one else. Man always on the move. Got several homes. Speak to Henry about him. But you better hurry over before Miss Knight goes on."

Smalls Paradise could have been anywhere in downtown white Manhattan. The dance floor was spacious and, when filled, it pleasantly bulged. The long bar was backed up with a sparkling mirror where bartenders moved about with smiles that made everyone feel welcomed. They sported white hip jackets with little flat brass buttons and black bow ties similar to those worn by ocean liner stewards who served tea to slumbering elites reposed on upper deck lounge chairs or those sheltered in plush bars beside grand wall mosaics.

Beau went through the backstage door. Henry was sitting on a wooden stool under a blackboard with the list of the evening's acts staggered across it. He wore a Dobbs black derby high on his scalp. A blue striped shirt with a detachable stiff white color. A diamond studded horseshoe pin that dubiously sparkled on his purple tie. His vest pockets were stuffed with folded pieces of paper which had the names, numbers, and various showtime reminders along with a pocket watch that bulged out like a tumor. He bit into his cigar, wet and grimy from those deep life grip impressions. Some musicians let the backdoor slam, something Henry had told them not to do. They carried contraband in brown paper bags. They left one with Henry. He placed it under his chair. Then he looked up at the tall man standing before him. "…You Beau LaHood?"

"Yes, I am."

"Officer Bumpus said you was tall and you is."

"Where's Artemus Cummins?"

Henry sat back as if he'd been pushed. "I thought you was here to see that girl."

"I am. But Officer Bumpus told me that you know where Artemus Cummins can be found."

"I keeps to my own business, son."

Beau put two bits into Henry's hand. Henry didn't like the feel of it. Beau replaced it with a silver dollar. Henry slipped it into his vest pocket. "Could be on his boat tonight."

"What boat?"

"You know the 12-mile limit?"

"Yeah. You know the name of the boat?"

"Could be the name of a club," Henry said.

"Smalls?"

"You're close."

Beau tried again. "Smalls Paradise?"

"Could be. Ain't nothin' small about it though."

Beau held up another silver dollar. "What's the name of the boat, Henry?"

Several more musicians came through the back door carrying contraband.

Henry took the silver dollar and said, "*Pair-a-Dice.*"

"What's Cummins doin' on a boat out in yonder limit?"

"Entertainin' white folk. What else?"

Beau held out another silver dollar. "Keep on talkin'."

Henry took the coin. "Folks get done with shows downtown, they come up here to Smalls by way of them who run Broadway. If they got a special card, then they gets on the boat. White folk kill for that card."

"Why?"

"Cause it hard to get."

"So, Cummins and Broadway are tied together."

Henry waited.

Beau tossed him another silver dollar.

Henry said, "Tied like a knot, they is."

"How do you mean?"

"They and Cummins got some kinda deal," Henry said. "But it's a woman who runs everythin'."

"What's her name?"

"Like that mixed drink," Henry said.

"Which one?"

"Tom it's called."

"I suppose you want another dollar?"

"Give it a try."

Beau tossed him a silver coin.

Henry said, "Mary Collins."

"What she do?"

"Puts in a call here." Henry turned toward the candlestick telephone on the small shelf next to the blackboard behind him."

"Why she call you of all people?" Beau said.

"Because she and her boss, Gant, got all the girls on Broadway and they need a telephone to keep in contact and I'm here all night; so, it's my job to dispatch."

"You mean dispatch to Cummins."

"You said it. I didn't."

"And this is all connected to that *Paradise* boat?"

"Yeah," Hendry said, "but the one I'm talkin' about is spelled different and said like this: *Pair-a-Dice*. Man got two boats with the same soundin' name." Henry looked Beau up and down. "I thought police officers wore uniforms."

"Not always," Beau said, amused that Officer Elgin Bumpus had told Henry that he was a cop. "Anything else you wanna tell me?"

"Carmela's third door down thataway, iffen'ya still wanna see her.

Better hurry 'fo she goes on."

"You from Mississippi?"

"That I am."

"Where back home, Henry?"

"Calhoun County."

"You was born a slave?"

"That I was."

"You done well for yo'self."

"That I have," Henry said.

"Is Cummins out at sea every night?"

"Most nights," Henry said.

"Why?"

"Money. Why else? And that's all I'm gonna say."

"I suppose iffen I give you a sawbuck you could tell me a whole lot more," Beau said.

"You could give me double that, but I can't double what I don't know..."

Carmela Knight was slow to open the door, but her Eton bob highlighted her pretty brown eyes which were shy, distant, and wanting of approval. She held a worn silk floral dressing gown close to her chest. The burn on her forearm was plain to see as well as the effects of the grueling life of a hoofer on the vaudeville circuit where small-town folks went to bed early and often skipped the show. Her most recent act had been *Kiss Me Deadly* where she played a venomous snake dancer who crawled out of a Hindu magic box. She would call to a plant in the audience to come up on stage to get kissed. He would then drop dead with a highly erotic smile to let everyone know that he wasn't all that dead. The rest of the audience would then come up to try their luck with the requirement of leaving two-bits in a box her promoter held for funeral expenses, and it seemed a lot of men wanted to die every night. The act lasted until it got to Junction Ohio where the vice squad claimed it was a fraud because there hadn't been one funeral. Carmela Knight's white promoter then unceremoniously skipped town with the money box.

Stranded and broke, she found her way back to New York and once again pursued her dream of dancing in the famed Ziegfeld Follies despite the fact she was now into her fourth decade, but unlike the Cotton Club, in Harlem, where a colored girl had to pass the test of having skin lighter than a brown paper bag, in the Follies a girl had to be milk white and at a certain age color didn't even matter, but it didn't stop wannabes, aging starlets, or even rich old ladies from turning to the new plastic surgery to revive their careers and youth, despite the tug of war played out on a woman's face as plastic surgery pushed out old age and old age pushed back even harder. The seesaw of time and vanity was lost on no one, including Carmela Knight who could only afford Pond's Vanishing Cream.

She stood before the large round vanity mirror that was bordered by a circle of light bulbs. Her maquillage: face brushes, powder, mascara, lip paint, and a pint of bad whiskey, crammed the small table. A burning cigarette squeezed itself into the already overcrowded ashtray. A vaudeville trunk, lingering in the corner, was indebted with unredeemable outfits from closed and forgotten shows. Carmela turned to Beau and saw a man so black and untainted with the master's blood that she knew that he never had to deal with the burden of being *almost*.

"Officer Bumpus sent you?" she said, reaching for the stale cigarette stained with morning lipstick.

"Yes," Beau said, handing her the photograph of her and Addison Prevette. She immediately turned it over on her dresser.

"You're very pretty," Beau said.

Her eyes brightened. "Thank you."

"I ain't gonna waste your time, Miss Knight," Beau said. "What I need is information concernin' Artemus Cummins."

Carmela sat down at her vanity table, put a brush to her hair, and then gazed into a mirror which seemed to highlight only her flaws. She then walked away from herself and went through the drawers of her trunk, at the other end of the room, looking for something long lost. "I'm going to Paris when I get the money," she said, turning back to Beau to make her point. "Then to Berlin. Bertye Lou Wood is now there in the *Chocolate Kiddies* review. It's a big hit. But then, of course, she's only 15 years old." Carmela reached for her dancing shoes that were even older and scrubbed away the hard-to-get dirt with her fingernails. "I used to dance with Florence Mills. She's a lot older then Bertye Lou and has done alright for herself. Plays in the white clubs where white people go see negroes. But I'm not a negro. I'm white, and it's my ticket out of here and *no one* will take it," Carmela said, sitting down and moving the mirror so Beau would be out of it.

Beau tried again. "What about Artemus Cummins?"

"What about him?"

"How much money you need to get to Paris, Miss Knight?"

"Why do you ask?"

"Answer my question and I'll tell you."

"Five grand," Carmela said. "It's very cheap living over there because of the war. Five grand will last me for years. They appreciate colored girls. Look at Josephine Baker."

"You tell me where I can find Artemus Cummins and the negatives to this photo, and I'll see to it that you get 20 grand."

Carmela Knight looked at Beau like he was crazy. Her whole life she'd been promised the world by men who wanted her body and not her soul. She touched the silver heart shaped locket which hung around her neck and shut her eyes as if she were praying. "When can you get me the money?"

"First I need to know where I can get those negatives of you and this man in the photograph."

"Get me the 20 G's and a boat ticket to France, or you won't get a thing."

"Miss Knight, I don't walk around with that kinda money on me."

"Cummins does."

"Then go to Cummins."

"I've already been there," she said, jotting down a number. "Call me when you have the money and *only* when you have the money."

Beau gave her a 50-dollar bill which Al had given him for payoffs. She grabbed it and folded into her garter.

"Tell me about Cummins and the 12-mile limit."

"If you're trying to trick me, forget about it. I know how men work."

"Miss Knight, I need a little somethin' to get the juice flowin'."

"A little bit is all you're gonna get."

"I'll take it." Beau handed her another 50 and she hid that too." Carmela said, "Cummins keeps nothing incriminating inside the 12-mile limit."

"How do you know?"

"I was his girl until he got tired of me."

"What happened?"

Carmela looked at Beau like he was the dumbest person on earth. "He got someone new."

"Why did he burn you?"

"You're asking too much."

"Well, iffen you was his girl, why did he prostitute you?"

"Who said he loved me?" She dipped her comb into a jar thick of Brilliantine and slicked her hair back so that it would stay.

"Is this boat called the *Pair-a-Dice*?"

"Seems you know more than you let on," Carmela said, on her way to the door, feeling that she had already spoken enough.

"Are you sure he don't keep valuable stuff nowhere else?"

"I'm not God," she said, opening the door for Beau. "I only know what I know, but then it's a lot more than what you know. Now, if you don't mind, I have a show to do."

Beau said, "There's a man I want you to talk to."

"Who?"

"One who can help you with your dreams."

"I want the 20 G's first."

Beau wrote down Al Nachman's Biltmore Hotel number. "You

give this man a call right now and not a second later iffen you want the money."

"Who is he?" Carmela said.

"Man with the money."

"I suppose, I'm going to have to have sex with him."

"Miss Knight, I wouldn't allow that, and neither would he."

"I've heard that one before."

"Miss Knight—I once worked on the train as porter and a white passenger, in a compartment car, wanted me to have sex with him and he said that if I didn't, he'd report me and say that I tried to steal his money and gold watch on the table beside him."

"You had sex with him?"

"No, I slammed him up against the wall and told him the only man I fear is an honest one. He got the message. I hope you do too."

30

The IV League

Morningside Heights. Gideon exited the IRT uptown Broadway line and entered the campus of Columbia University. He was tired of always having to explain to everyone that his school was in the IV League and not the Ivy League, which didn't exist. He would enlighten them that I and V were the roman numerals which represented the football league of Columbia, Princeton, Harvard, and Yale back in the gridiron era. Still, all the foghorns insisted on spelling it like a plant; that's how deep in the pot they were.

Gideon carefully tacked the slippery wide steps of Lowe Memorial Library. He passed the huge figure of Alma Mata seated on her Athenian throne—another send-off to Phidias. Root Buckner was waiting by the grand entrance, his head tucked under his coat collar. He shouted through the dry icy air. "Hey, Remley. Ya hear about Farnham?"

"Yeah, I heard."

"They say it was your stuff that killed him."

"You're still alive," Gideon said, as he grabbed his friend's arm and pulled him inside. They went through the circular library, a vast round rotunda, and hurried downstairs to the lower ground floor. Root Buckner said, "I sold Farnham's golf clubs to Lindenhoff."

"How much?"

"Twenty dollars."

"Your dead roommate still owes me 150 for hooch," Gideon said. "What about his raccoon coat? Didgya sell that too?"

Root Buckner said, "I was gonna keep it for myself."

"Farnham paid 400 dollars for it. You could easily get half that. We'll split the difference."

"I'll see what I can do."

"Well, you better do it quickly, Root, because his folks are gonna be snooping around our fraternity soon enough to collect all his junk."

They continued on around the big rotunda and entered a room used by students between semesters. Gideon shut the door and said, "There's another reason why we're here."

"What's that?"

"I need to speak to your uncle," Gideon said.

"I got lots of uncles."

"Emory Buckner."

"Oh, I don't think he needs any liquor."

"Root—*why* the hell would I want to sell booze to the Manhattan District Attorney?"

"You sell it to everyone else."

Gideon gripped his classmate. "We're going down the hall to call your Uncle Emory. Then we're selling Farnham's coat."

"I think it's got his name in it."

"Rub it out then. "

31

One Good Fellow

District attorney Emory Buckner was a Nebraskan. A man all corn, alfalfa, and milk, and he mooed every time someone asked him why the government couldn't do anything about enforcing Prohibition. He would say that for every scofflaw caught, there were court fixers who counseled on bail or bribed jurors in the fifth-floor restroom of the Federal building in downtown Manhattan. He would go on about how the politicians of a certain party, who staunchly backed Prohibition, refused to spend the money for the army of enforcers needed to get the job done. He would tell them that the Lower Bay of Manhattan needed a fleet of at least two hundred ships on twenty-four-hour patrol to have any real effect on Prohibition and that for every bootlegger arrested there would have to be a juror trial, and with the current backlog, cases were staying out of court for years. When he told Congress what it would cost to build the new ships and courtrooms for all the future trials, they wrote him out a check, but it was for his train ride back home.

Gideon was led into Emory Buckner's study and seated in one of two opposing ancient brown wingback leather chairs that were just feet away from a roaring fire. The district attorney said to the young man, who was wearing a dinner jacket and black tie, "My nephew, Root, tells me you're one good fellow."

"Well, sir, Root and I go back a long way."

"He told me you're on the Dean's list."

"Been on it every semester, sir."

"Said you have a keen mind. That you have the rare ability to cut through the clutter and quickly understand the underlying meaning of complex issues and present them with clarity. Have you thought about going into the law?"

"Well, sir, I've been thinking about a lot of things. I mean you never know. I mean the point of an education is to teach you how to think, not react impulsively and get betrayed by your emotions."

"I most certainly agree and that's the whole problem with this world. It's sustained by ignorance, which invariably dismisses reality and truth. And since there's no filter to the human mind, other than self-interest and injury, the law has to intercede on man's behalf. But that's not why you're here. My nephew said you needed to speak to me urgently. Just what is the problem, son?"

"Well sir, you are a lawyer, and I would like to hire you, because, well, I need confidentiality."

"Concerning what?"

"Information concerning the murder of Ed Goulson."

"Really...? And just what information do you have?"

"I need confidentiality, sir."

"Well, I can't be your lawyer and serve the government at the same time. That would be a conflict of interest."

"I understand, sir, but I thought regardless that the attorney-client privilege, meaning just speaking to you, could be preserved if I confided in you, or am I wrong? Because now I'm getting the feeling that I am."

"You are; you're not a client, but a crooked district attorney might tell you otherwise. Now, if you *are* in any trouble settle up now before it's too late. You're a bright young fellow with a grand future ahead of you. A boy like you I'd immediately hire if you had your degree."

"Well, thank you sir, and I'll have it soon enough, but I think it might be better if I spoke to another lawyer first, to protect myself legally and then get back to you."

"What crime have you committed, son?"

"I haven't committed any crime, sir."

"What's this information you have concerning Ed Goulson's murder?"

I need confidentiality first, sir, but I'll tell you there was no gunman on the rooftop where Goulson was killed."

"We already know that."

"Do you know where the shot came from?" Gideon said.

"Do you?"

"That's why I need confidentiality, sir."

"Well, as I said, I can't give you lawyer-client privilege."

"Then it would be hard for me to talk," Gideon said.

"Have you evidence concerning Goulson?"

"I need confidentiality, sir."

"It would be immoral if you didn't hand over any information."

"With all due respect sir, I will not be a witness."

"Well, if you're not willing to be a witness, son, then why did you come here?"

"I thought you could protect me, sir," Gideon said.

"I can only do what the law provides. Now, do you have irrefutable evidence concerning Ed Goulson's murder or are you just talking?"

"I won't go on any witness stand, sir."

"Without a witness any litigation will be thrown out of court, and I've lost cases even with good evidence and a witness, notwithstanding jury tampering. Despite that, I'll do everything I can legally to protect you. In fact, the least that will happen is that your name might get in the papers."

"Pardon me sir, but I don't think *least* is the right word."

Emory Buckner rose from his chair. "Then there's nothing else to discuss."

Gideon followed the district attorney out of the library. "I hope I haven't wasted your time, sir."

"Young man, you have information and you're withholding it. Legally, there are things that I can do to get it."

"Yes, sir, but there are things that I can do to make sure you don't get it."

"Such as what?" Emory Buckner said, standing by the front door as if he might not open it.

"I'm sorry, sir, I think I've said enough."

Gideon was allowed to leave. The district attorney was then called to the phone. The voice on the other end of the line said, "Good evening, Mr. Buckner. I've got that colored woman who can help you indict Artemus Cummins."

"Mr. Nachman, I'll be right over......"

32

Bedroom in Arles

3 99 Park Avenue. Later that evening.
"Mr. Nachman's here," Caitlin said, knocking on Beau's door in the servant's quarters."

"Please let him in, miss."

Beau's small room was neatly furnished with a single bed, a dresser, sitting chair, and a small writing table. It looked more like the second version of *Bedroom in Arles* now on its way to the Art Institute of Chicago, except there was no view, just a brick wall across the back alley.

Al entered and said, "Carmela Knight came through."

"You made the deal with her?"

"She's giving a deposition to Emory Buckner right now. But I made it clear to her that unless she answered every question, she wouldn't get the 20 grand—which is a little steep, if I might add."

"I'm sorry," Beau said, "but I felt there be no way she could turn down that much kale."

"Well, we're not paying for it. But what's more important, she gave me a detailed description of that steam yacht *Pair-a-Dice* and it's priceless."

"What about the negatives?" Beau said.

"She said she had no idea where Cummins keeps them onboard."

"Don't he have an office onboard where he does his business?"

"Carmela said the only office he has is in the Knickerbocker Building on 42nd Street and Broadway, and that the Knickerbocker is known as the bootlegger's building, because so many floors are rented by them. But she swore that Cummins keeps everything aboard the boat, so we're going to have to find out on our own."

"You get a hold 'a that Gant fella, the one who's the Broadway producer been turnin' down Miss Knight?"

"Yes," Al said, "and since Virginia's starring in his play, I called her right after you called me and unless something happens, he should be on his way here now."

"What about that woman who runs everythin' for Gant?"

"Mary Collins? She's his gal Friday," Al said. "Virginia told me that she auditioned for her before being brought to Gant. Oh, one other thing."

"What?"

"When District Attorney Buckner heard I was from Mississippi he brought up Addison Prevette."

"Why?" Beau said.

"Turns out Prevette was involved in the recent mayoral campaign."

"*Here* in New York?"

"Yes."

"What for?"

"Influence," Al said.

"What kind?"

"That I don't know."

There was a knock on the door. "Come on in," Beau said.

Caitlin entered and said to Al, "Miss Swain is back with that gentleman. He's waiting impatiently in the living room."

Al said to her, "You shouldn't call him a gentleman, but then we tend to use that word for any kind of man today including criminals."

"Do you still want to see him, sir?"

"Tell him I'm on my way..."

Broadway producer Franklin Gant was more interested in meeting Shelby than Al Nachman. Harry Richman of the eponymous club said that she had not only taken his breath away but his heart as well. Emil Coleman said that when Shelby and her crowd came into his club, he only played what she wanted to hear and that was fine with him, because a girl who moved from the horse set to the nightclub set at a gallop brought along the best people. Gant now had to have her, and he had his own way of getting a woman. His first move was to get close to her, talk it up, shift his weight so that she'd fall right into him. Then he would paw, caress, and squeeze, and those gals wanting to be stars gave in pretty quickly.

Gant had learned, early on, that ethics and morals—so called decency—were just a façade and not everyone shared the same notion of what they were anyway, so he had to learn what was and what wasn't and for whom as he perfected his varying degrees of lying, pandering, cheating, sucking-up, coddling, and the art of verbal echoing. He quickly learned that power and access were measured against those who had nothing, and even if they had morals they would have to be measured against wealth in a world where people wanted things more than they wanted the truth. Gant's first move was on Wall Street where he sold bonds to literally anyone.

The banks had instructed him to stake out church picnics. Stalk retirees in their backyard for their lifetime savings. Sermonize the young about their future. Embarrass middle aged folks for still having nothing and having done nothing about it as he sold them bonds, which they believed were guaranteed by the rock-solid reputation of a banking industry that no one ever dared to question.

Soon he got rich and was known for his favors as he moved on to Broadway for the glam and the galas where he took businessmen to the side and spoke about their wives, as if he had had them five minutes ago. He'd then pay all the women grand compliments and let it be known that they were half his. He spent big. Threw swell parties. Invited Broadway stars and big shot artists who loved to have their photos taken at more than one angle. It was all about getting attention, that deep human need for praise and affection that he played to the hilt. Gant, the connoisseur—the emphasis on con—would tell people how wonderful and important they were while uncorking the champagne and singing along with the band, when sooner or later a certain kind of woman, who shopped for men as she did her clothing, would try Gant on for size and soon find out that he was always too big and had to be taken in—but by whom?

Gant looked up from his cigar. He didn't like waiting for anyone and he didn't like Al.

"Nice to meet you, Mr. Gant," Al said. "I hear your new show with Miss Swain is a big hit."

"Cut the bullshit, Nachman."

Al took it in stride. "I was told that you were recently assaulted by a colored performer."

"I'm assaulted by every dreamer in this town," Gant said, as he searched the long hallway for Shelby.

Al said, "Virginia Swain told me that when a girl auditions, she leaves you her address and telephone number to be contacted."

"You looking for a girl?"

"No, Mr. Gant, but do you keep their information on file?"

"I'm not a stenographer."

"Which show of yours did Carmela Knight audition for?"

"Why?"

"How many girls of color audition for your shows each season?"

"None," Gant said, "and where's Emory Buckner? You said he was going to be here."

"The D.A. got tied up, but he sends his regards."

"Bullshit."

"I'll let the district attorney know how you feel. Now, I was told that Carmela Knight has already auditioned for you several times this season."

"She's stupid," Gant said.

"You also got into an argument with her, more than once."

"The girl is delusional."

"How so?"

"Carmela thinks she's white."

"So, you're on a first name basis with her."

"What's it to you?" Gant sneered, impatiently looking down the hall for anyone.

"Ever hear of Ed Goulson?"

"Who hasn't?"

"Ever been to his supper club?"

"Everyone has," Gant said.

"Do you know that he was murdered?"

"The pope in Rome knows that he was murdered."

"Are you aware that Ed Goulson had something on Artemus Cummins.

"Such as what?"

"Information concerning Cummins's prostitution ring."

"That's his problem."

"And now it's your problem, Mr. Gant."

"Get to the point."

"Carmela Knight told me that Ed Goulson had tried to help her get into one of your shows, because he thought that she was an exceptional talent."

"Is this after he fucked her?"

"I have no idea, Mr. Gant, but I'm sure it was way after you fucked Miss Swain."

"I wouldn't remember. I fuck a lot of girls."

"Then see if you can remember this: Miss Swain told me that before she became a big star, she auditioned with two hundred girls for a show of yours and it came down to her and three others."

"Happens all the time," Gant said.

"Sure, it does, and you told Miss Swain that she and the other girls all had a lot of talent, but that you thought she had something special."

"That's why Virginia's become such a big star, Nachman."

"Well, if you knew she was so special, then you didn't need to sleep with her."

"I like pussy."

"What about the rest of a girl—or don't you give a shit?" Al said, pushing Gant back into the couch. "You're not getting up until I say so." The uncompromising rage in Al's eyes spoke of a violence reserved for insolence and stupidity and that Gant—a flocculent concoction of Wall Street, show business, fancy galas, and street corner bullshit—was going to do what he was told. "Artemus Cummins gives you kickbacks for the girls you supply him."

"Prove it, Nachman."

"You don't have to prove evidence."

"You said information, not evidence."

"In this case, it's one and the same," Al said.

"Well, if it happened outside the 12 mile limit your evidence is useless."

"Have you ever been on the steam yacht *Pair-a-Dice*?"

Gant reached into his billfold, pulled out a card, and gave it to Al. "Show this to McCreedy on the Grand Street Dock and you'll get a ride out to that boat. You won't pay a thing with this card, but it's only good for tomorrow night, because in a few days that dock will be empty again."

"You mean Cummins keeps moving the location?"

"Why don't you ask him?"

Al took the card. "I'll stop by your office tomorrow and speak with Mary Collins, your office manager."

"Nachman, you're wasting your time."

"Buckner doesn't think so."

"Tell Buckner he's fishing outside the 12-mile limit. Tell him there's not a thing he can do, and he knows it. That's why I gave you the card. I got nothing to fear. Get laid. You need it."

Al said, "What you mean is to discredit me by having my photograph taken in an uncompromising position."

"…Nachman, if you keep up this bullshit, I'm going to sue you for slander."

"Then you're going to need a lot of lawyers because *The New Yorker* is doing a profile on you in their next issue and—" Shelby entered.

Franklin Gant saw the dream of his life walk by and then the nightmare behind it: Dorothy Parker of *The New Yorker*. He said to her, "You're the bitch who trashed my show last week in that cheap rag of yours."

"Yeah," Dottie said, "and it's back in the trash where it belongs."

33

She's Cuckoo

Gideon entered Shelby's white-gloved building and gave his name to one of two doormen who called him up. He then proceeded down the long, elegant hallway—more like a Greek inner sanctum with its fine marble and long-stemmed flowers that dismissed the winter wind blowing outside. He entered one of three brassy elevators with collapsing gates and a side leather bench for its passengers. All were manned by a gloved operator who used a handheld pivot starter for moving the cage. Still, the building wasn't as exclusive as Gideon's, only by a slight margin, but enough to lose friends in New York.

The elevator opened into the penthouse private foyer which was designed with black and white marble flooring. He stepped out of the cage and noticed Braque's 1910 Mandola painting on the wall ahead. He wasn't sure if it was the real deal, but it was something that his mother would have liked and that his father would have thrown out. The flooring, on the other hand, made him think of his father's latest magazine ad where the perfect family gazed at their perfect new linoleum, the caption reading: *If your floor looks beautiful, so does your family.* Gideon, assuming there was a butler, waited for him. Meanwhile, Virginia hurried into Shelby's bedroom. "That boy is here."

"Has everyone left?" Shelby said.

"All gone, including Gant."

Shelby dropped her silk robe. Caitlin handed her a Callot Soeurs dark blue and silver sequined evening dress wild with red filaments that hemmed her dress into glittering strips. "Where are my shoes, Caitlin?"

"Over there, miss," pointing to 27 boxes just delivered from Saks Fifth Avenue.

Daisy, the cook, entered the bedroom and said, "That boy's waitin' in the foyer, miss, 'n supper jus'bout ready."

Shelby said to Daisy, "I'll be right there." Then to Caitlin, "Bring him into the living room. I'll finish dressing on my own."

"Yes, miss. Right away."

Daisy said to Shelby. "Which wine you want served, miss?"

"The Côtes de Rhône that just came off the SS *Paris*. Oh, and open it and let it breathe."

Daisy was off.

Virginia said, "I hope you get what you want from that boy."

"Oh, I will," Shelby said.

"Well, I gotta go, but call me at the theater if you get bored. I'm not on until the end of the first act." Virginia hurried off.

Caitlin, wearing a black maid's dress, white apron, and white head bonnet shaped like a tiara, met Gideon in the foyer. His eyes were ingrained with a reader's glow that made him look sleepy, but he awoke when Virginia rushed through. "Mrs. Prevette?"

Caitlin giggled. Virginia sent her off.

"I'm Gideon Remley, Mrs. Prevette. Are you going out?"

"Yeah," Virginia laughed, "and I'm running late."

Gideon helped Virginia with her evening coat.

"Still snowing?"

"Uh, no, not anymore, ma'am."

"Good. Shelby will be ready in a minute."

"Aren't you dining with us?"

"I'll grab something on the way," Virginia said.

The elevator door opened. Virginia stepped in and before she could turn around it closed.

Gideon was now all alone except for an assortment of expensive Parisian coats and opera cloaks which were stuffed inside the tall cloak closet. A powder compact of royal blue Guilloche enamel was on a slim contemporary table up against the wall, just under the Braque and beside a DuBarry compact with a teal and gray fairy painted over celluloid and foil. Shelby entered the foyer.

"Come," she said.

They made their way into the grand living room, facing Park Avenue, which was furnished with Shelby's Bauhaus furniture. The walls were painted white. The room was untouched by the impulsive purchase. Gideon took notice of the contemporary art stacked up against the wall waiting to be hung. "Where did your mother go? She seemed to be in a hurry."

".... My mother?"

"Yeah, she was off somewhere; looks like that actress."

"Which actress?"

"Virginia Swain," he said.

"I'll tell her when I see her."

Gideon walked over to the art. "So…it's just you, your father, and I for dinner, or do you have siblings?"

"Oh, I have siblings."

Gideon pointed to the paintings. "Your art?"

"Why would you think that?"

Gideon picked up one of the canvasses Shelby had recently bought from a Berlin artist and said, "My mother does this sorta thing."

"Really…?"

"Yeah."

"What's her name?" Shelby said.

"Whose name?"

"Your mother's?"

"Sarah Revenlöw Remley—when she's annoyed at my father, she drops the Remley."

"I've never heard of her."

"No one has," Gideon said, going down the line of paintings, thinking that the colors were washed out to a hazardous level. "I could swear my mother painted this stuff."

"She must be brilliant, then."

"Everyone thinks she's cuckoo."

"Why?"

"Because of what she paints," Gideon said, sitting on a sleek Wassily chair with canvass upholstery. He looked down the hallway and said, "The girl's parents usually come in about now and the old man asks me what I plan on doing for the rest of my life in case I should decide to support his daughter once he's done with her."

"It's no different back home," Shelby said.

"Back *home*?"

"Yes."

"This *isn't* home?"

"Oh, it is," Shelby said.

"You're sure it is?"

"Of course, I am," Shelby said.

"Then what did you mean by back home?"

"It's just an expression."

"What is?"

"That is."

Gideon turned away from the hallway. "…Where was your mother off to?"

"Oh, she's probably reading to little Martha right now."

"Little Martha…?"

"She's my younger sister," Shelby said.

Gideon took another look down the hallway.

"Something wrong?"

"Your mother just left," Gideon said.

"You saw her go?"

"I just told you I did."

"That wasn't my mother."

"*Who* wasn't your mother?"

"She wasn't." Shelby said.

"I'm talking about the blonde I met in the foyer," Gideon said.

"That was Virginia Swain."

"The *actress* Virginia Swain?"

"You said so yourself."

"I said she *looked* like Virginia Swain."

"Well, she and I live here," Shelby said.

"*You* and Miss Swain live here?"

"Yes."

"…How old are you?"

"Nineteen," Shelby said.

"You're an actress?"

"What makes you think that?"

"Well, I don't go to the theater, so I've wouldn't know."

"Why don't you go to the theater?" Shelby said.

"It bores me to death, unless you like watching people taking turns speaking. They just oughta give the script to everyone to read at home and save them the trip."

"Well, I'm not an actress."

"What are you then?"

"Someone who doesn't live a life written by other people."

"Well, I'm not so sure people in the theater would agree with that," Gideon said.

"Then tell the fools that there's poison that blinds you and poison that opens your eyes and that they're of the former."

"Just who are you anyway?"

The cook rang up from the kitchen. Shelby took the house phone and turned to Gideon. "Supper is ready."

Gideon followed Shelby through the living room arch and into the grand dining room that had a table long enough to ignore bad company.

After Dinner

Dessert plates. Coffee. Brandy. Salt and peppershakers became ships. A knife marked the 12-mile limit. The tablecloth was the Atlantic Ocean. Gideon said to Shelby, "These here are the motherships that the bootleggers buy liquor from and they're all outside the 12-mile limit."

"What's a motherboat?" Shelby said.

"Mother*ship*."

"What's the difference?"

"That's what it's called," Gideon said.

"Why is it called that?"

"A mothership is a supply ship, and the government can't bother it if it's outside the 12-mile limit and in international waters, but the Coast Guard often breaches it by saying they were chasing a ship which started within the limit although in court any evidence from outside the limit can get struck down."

"Have you been out there?"

"Where?"

"Beyond the 12-mile limit."

"Sure," Gideon said.

"So, you know how to find these ships?"

"If I have to."

"How do you know all this?"

"I was a swamper," he said.

"What's a swamper?"

"Someone who unloads liquor for quick cash."

"How do you get out to the 12-mile limit?"

"By boat. How else?"

"You have a boat?"

"Yeah, and now it's mine," Gideon said.

"What do you mean now it's yours?"

"My grandmother gave it to my father and then she gave it to me for Christmas, because he didn't know what he was doing with it."

"You don't like your father," Shelby said.

"I didn't say that."

"You intoned it."

"Put it this way: If he's not telling you what to do, he feels useless."

"A lot of people are like that," Shelby said, moving a saltshaker past the knife. "So, your grandmother gave you a boat to use for the 12-mile limit."

"No, she gave it to me as a gift."

"Do you know anything about boats?"

"I've been sailing since I was a boy."

"So, it's a sailboat."

"No."

"What kind of boat, then?"

Gideon explained, "I have sailboats out on Long Island for summer wind. But I've got a powerboat on the East River just a few blocks from here that I use all year round."

"A *few* blocks from here…?"

"Yeah."

"Good," Shelby said. "I'd like to see a real live mothership for myself."

"Maybe one day I'll show you."

"I want to see one now."

"…*Now?*"

"Yeah, now."

"It's too cold to go out now," Gideon said. "And it's pitch-dark anyway. Only a lunatic or a bootlegger would go out there in this frigid condition."

"How many cases does a mothership carry?"

"Why do you want to know?"

"Just tell me," Shelby said.

"Just how many do you plan on buying?"

"I plan on doing the opposite."

"What do you mean the opposite?"

"First tell me how many cases a freighter carries," Shelby said,

"Why do you need to know?"

"*How* many cases?"

"Well…up to 10,000."

"Where do these ships outside the 12-mile limit come from?"

"Why do you want to know?"

"Just answer my question," Shelby said.

"*Why* do you want to know?"

"We're having a conversation after dinner. You *are* free to leave." Gideon remained where he was seated. "…Now where do these ships come from?"

"…Mostly from Glasgow, Scotland, or St. Pierre & Miquelon southwest of Newfoundland, which is still French territory,"

"Why there?"

"Because it's French territory," Gideon said. "Foreign registration."

"So," Shelby said, putting her finger on the salt- and peppershakers, "these motherships just sit out here beyond the 12-mile limit for months on end getting resupplied and selling to bootleggers."

"There are schooners and ketches which pick-up liquor from the Bahamas, but they're no longer the main suppliers. The big ships have taken over," Gideon said.

"Why the Bahamas?"

"You get British registry down there."

"So, as long as you have foreign registry you may, in effect, sail in and outside the limit with impunity."

"Yeah, but even with foreign registry, you can't sell inside the limit. You may give it away, but you may not sell it."

"Which would mean," Shelby guessed, "that some or even a lot of it is pre-sold."

"Well, that all depends, but it's easier to stay outside the 12-mile limit."

"And they're out there now?"

"The motherships?"

"Yes," Shelby said.

"But more so during the holidays and warmer weather."

"And after the holidays?"

"A lot less," Gideon said.

"So, no one goes out there now."

"I didn't say that."

"What did you say?"

"Moneywise, it's actually the best time to go," Gideon said, "but if you fall overboard, you're dead in 12 minutes; that's how cold the water is."

"*Twelve* minutes?"

"That's all it takes."

"And yet, people go out and risk death."

"Bootleggers," Gideon said, "have to if they need to resupply."

"So, there must be a lot of bootleggers out there and weather really isn't an issue—or is it?"

"Well, it's an issue, but it doesn't stop people...Why are so you interested, anyway?"

"I'm from Mississippi. This is new to me."

"If it's so new to you then why did you say that you plan on doing the opposite?" Gideon said.

"I was speaking rhetorically."

"Baloney," Gideon said, staring at the blue-eyed beauty: she who knew things.

"How often do you go out to the 12-mile limit?"

"Why do you want to know?"

"Do you buy liquor?"

"Sometimes," Gideon said.

"So, then the cold doesn't bother you?"

"It does," Gideon said, "but there's less to worry concerning hijackers or the Coast Guard taking pot shots at you this time of year, since everyone's hunkered down, and prices are lower."

"Even though you have to be goddamn nuts to go out there in this kind of weather."

"Yes," he said.

"What about hijackers?"

"What about them?"

"Have you dealt with them before?"

"Not personally," Gideon said, "but pirates are a problem, which means you can't do business out there unless you're armed."

"Are you armed?"

"Have to be," Gideon said.

"You just said pirates and hijackers. What's the difference?"

"They're the same thing except pirates stay out at sea longer, whereas hijackers are looking for the quick hit."

"And how do they go about that?"

Gideon said, "They board a boat pretending to be buyers then pull guns out, steal everything, and kill you. Sometimes they just wait for the mosquito fleet to return back to shore and pick off one of the boats, steal its liquor, and then kill everyone onboard."

"They always have to kill everyone?"

"More often than not," Gideon said. "Bodies are washing ashore all the time bloated up and disgusting. I tried to pull one in last week, but the floater's arm popped right off."

Shelby pretended to be amused. "What's a mosquito fleet?"

"They're speedboats which buzz in your ears like a hoard of mosquitos and when they're massed into a fleet it's deafening."

"I want to go out there," Shelby said, getting up from the table.

"Out where?"

"The 12-mile limit. Now."

"*Now?*"

"Yes."

"You're crazy," Gideon said.

"The whole world is crazy."

"It's dark out there."

"You don't have lights?"

"Rumrunners don't use their running lights," he said.

"Why not?"

"Because the Coast Guard will see them."

"We won't be rumrunning," she said, "so you can use your lights."

"Yeah, but unless everyone else has their lights on, the danger isn't diminished, and if you try to use them near the armada you'll get shot out of the water."

Shelby didn't care. She left the dining room. Went down the hall. Grabbed her coat. Stepped into the elevator. Waited. Then pulled Gideon in.

Gideon's powerboat was docked off Beekman Place in the East River next to his grandmother's steam yacht: a grand old piece of machinery that required more servants and coal than passengers. The previous fall, he had installed two Fiat direct-drive 300 horsepower aircraft engines into his own mule, thanks to Granny. It could now easily hit 40 knots in calm water with way more to spare, but the real advantage was Gideon's understanding of coastal navigation and his ability to use a sextant for fixing positions in open water. He was also able to adjust currents in his head while most people took forever to work them out on paper. He understood nautical engineering and weight distribution. He had spent months in dry-dock rebuilding his powerboat and testing it before adding a newfangled radiotelephone along with a spark transmitter-receiver below deck, but since so few boats had this advanced technology he more or less talked to himself except when listening to that bootlegging ring whose transmissions he had sent to the Coast Guard as a joke, until one day they were all found dead in a lookout house off the northern New Jersey shore.

But that was then. He turned over the powerboat's engines. They hummed with a deep gurgling pitch. Shelby was bundled up on deck. He said to her, "You're freezing."

"No, I'm not."

"Then stop shivering."

She couldn't. She gripped the side of the powerboat as the East River current tried to yank it off its mooring just south of the 59th

Street-Queensboro Bridge whose arches rose high above the city like a colossal crown. Gideon undid the mooring ropes and then got behind the wheel. He steered the powerboat southward. Port-east was Queens, southwest the docks which collared the island of Manhattan. Gideon continued under the Williamsburg Bridge and then motored past the gigantic utility structures of the Brooklyn Navy Yard with its enormous hanger where the USS Arizona, later moored at Pearl Harbor, had been launched in 1916. Then they rode under the Manhattan and Brooklyn Bridges where the docks were jam-packed with fishing boats at the Fulton Street Fish Market right off the river. They went on past Gardner's Island, port-south, and into the Upper Bay of Manhattan and on to the Narrows, toward Lightship Ambrose in the Lower Bay, and then further out into the Atlantic Ocean where legit freighters were heading into port or out to sea in a long east and west line.

Gideon pointed eastbound toward the dark hazy winter vapor which hung over the ocean. "Here's what you've been looking for." It took Shelby a moment before she could see the blacked out bootlegging armada of freighters, schooners, and other boats outside the 12-mile limit. Its vast outline left a range of craggy mountainous edges fragmenting the skyline from end to end. When the armada had first formed, at the beginning of Prohibition, the limit had only been three miles out and was therefore very close to shore, so close it caused locals to hysterically call the authorities and claim that they were being invaded—they were, but by soldiers that were fifths and quarts.

Gideon pointed abeam to port. "You hear the speedboats ahead?"
Shelby listened.

"They're the contact boats and they're going ship to ship to ask the price of liquor until they find what they want. But I can tell you, it's easy to be fooled by so-called good product."

"Why's that?"

"Because there are several kinds of ships out here," Gideon said. "A few are distilleries. Others import whiskey from Glasgow. Others pretend to have real American rye whisky. But most of the liquor gets watered down and recapped for sale, because there's just too much money to be made for anyone to be honest. I mean, what's the incentive? Honesty—like greed—requires it." Gideon turned southeast and said, "But there's one great fleet out here which sells the best quality liquor, and the ships have a special mark on their bow."

"What mark is that?" Shelby asked.

"A flower."

"Which flower?"

"I don't know," Gideon said. "But that mark on your bottle means you've got gold."

"Can't it be copied?"

"You'll find yourself dead if you do."

A speedboat plowed right by them. Too close for Shelby's comfort. "I see what you mean about running lights."

He handed her another sweater. "Put it on and don't argue with me."

She did and was happy for the added warmth. "How do they fit all those cases of liquor into speedboats?"

"They're packed in burlap, six to a case, not the old honest twelve in a wooden box. But this way they can fit more bottles into the false bottoms of schooners, trawlers, or whatever. I've handled them myself as a swamper and I can tell you that it's the only way."

"Sounds like you enjoyed it."

"I loved it," Gideon said. "I was doing something real. Getting involved in the world and trying to learn everything I could, because I'd need it later. Look over there." He pointed port-north to Long Island's underbelly which was still rural and sparsely lit. "There are thousands of inlets, coves and sanctuaries that'll be soon be filled with swampers making a bucket line to unload the liquor into trucks."

"A what?" Shelby said.

"In the old days we had to line up and down Manhattan's streets with buckets of water to put out a fire."

"Don't the police know about these swampers?"

"They do, but the government would need an army to do anything about them," Gideon said, "and the local police are not federals. They're not mandated by law to go after bootleggers. In fact, most are more than happy to get paid off, including the Coast Guard. I mean a police chief out on Long Island can make 200 dollars a night turning his head the other way. You're talking over 70 grand a year if he turns it every night."

"Have you ever heard of a man named John Smith?"

"There are a million John Smiths," Gideon said. "Why?"

"He's connected to Artemus Cummins."

Gideon eased the throttle. "You mentioned Cummins at Saks Fifth Avenue this afternoon."

"Do you know John Smith?"

"Why?"

"If you do, it would be ungentlemanly of you not to tell me."

Gideon, still not sure what Shelby was up to, wasn't about to be fooled by the old gentleman dodge. He pointed to yonder sea and said, "There's a steam yacht out beyond the limit—" foghorns quickly punctured his words as the night got filled with long lingering brays from legit freighters chugging through the ocean with funnel stacks rising over wheelhouses which shadowed the sky, "and it's called the *Pair- a-Dice*."

"It belongs to Cummins?"

"Yeah," Gideon said.

"Let's find it."

He eased the throttle. "You like trouble. Don't you…?"

The 12-Mile Limit

Rumrunning crews loomed on decks with weapons brandished as liquor prices were shouted into the night. Gideon's powerful powerboat hummed through the armada at low idle and rocked in seesaw wakes made by other boats. Ships with deep water lines were the busiest for they were filled with liquor and were eager to make sales. Prospective buyers pulled alongside. Rope ladders were thrown over. Negotiations began. Shelby, feeling the excitement, said, "It's ghostly without lights."

"The sea is strange night or day," he said.

"What do you mean strange?"

"I meant that its vast emptiness is intolerable for most people," Gideon said, steering between two ships that were too close for comfort. "The mind wanders and imagines things that aren't there."

Shelby, as Gideon had expected, started seeing things which weren't there. She pointed to a ship and then another, and after several attempts at verification she realized that it was just her imagination. Then she heard the faint echo of distant music. Then an aggressive sound, coming from another direction, feverishly grew into a steady high-pitched buzz. "I guess I'm hearing things, too."

"What you're hearing is for real," Gideon said.

A noisy mosquito fleet appeared in silhouette and then lined up alongside a steam yacht that was backlit by light seeping out from its hatches. Guests disembarked and climbed up a ladder to the main deck. Gideon handed Shelby his Rodenstock-München Army field binoculars that he had bought in Berlin. She put them to her eyes and under the backlight saw dozens of landlubber revelers who were seemingly feet away, dressed to the nines, and ambling across the gangway only to disappear below deck. A single speedboat peeled away from the group. It headed toward them at full speed. "Why is that boat coming toward us?"

Gideon said, "The steam yacht, ahead, is the one you've been looking for."

"The *Pair-a-Dice*?"

"Yes," he said.

"But why is that speedboat heading toward us so fast?"

"They think we're hijackers."

"*Are* we...?" Then she heard a sharp sound tear through the centerline panel. The thud was deep. She lit a match and found a spent bullet jammed into the wood. Gideon quickly put out the match and opened up the throttle. He rode point-blank ahead to ramrod the chaser amidship. Shelby grabbed onto anything as Gideon's powerboat roared ahead burrowing through the waves. The men in the other boat were rapidly becoming more distinct. Two were aiming rifles. Then the boat gunned its throttle to cut away from Gideon, but its weight was all in the centerline, so it flipped over and wildly skidded through the ocean, landing hull side up. Gideon eased the throttle to a lull. He reached over for Shelby who was down on the deck.

He said to her, "You expected maids and chauffeurs?"

"I didn't expect this," she said, feeling sick and dizzy, taking Gideon's hand as she tried to get up. "I didn't know you were crazy."

"You didn't know what you were getting into."

"Take me home. I've seen enough for one day."

They left the 12-mile limit and headed back to Manhattan with its million lit windows. When they reached the Upper Bay, Gideon cut the throttle and stepped aside of the wheel. "You take us home."

Shelby thought he was nuts. "I don't know how to steer this thing."

"You're going to learn." Gideon said, as he brought her to the wheel.

Shelby gripped it and dared to peer down the powerboat's long sharp snout that threatened her inexperience. She put hand to throttle and at a touch the boat leaped a punishing mile. Gideon put his hand on hers and said, "No. Like this......"

34

Mary Quite Contrary

Broadway was shifting from its nighttime prowl of luminated billboards and marquees to its daytime crawl of trolleys, taxis, and motorcars. The early morning streets were now filled with accountants, stenographers, lawyers, shopkeepers, salesmen, bootleggers, and tourists who wanted to get a head start on the day. A man in black-tie stepped out of a nightclub with a woman asleep on his shoulder. School kids hurried past them. Al turned the corner of 7th Avenue and entered a long dark red brick alleyway which led to the stage entrance of a huge Broadway theater. He opened a nondescript door and went up a steep set of stairs leading into a hallway to Franklin Gant's office—already crowded with talent waiting to audition. The serious actresses, those who knew how to perform a kiss correctly on stage by sitting on the armrest of a chair with arms slack, face straight up to the ceiling, upstage foot forward, pretended not to see Al as he walked by. The talent who came from the small towns, where plays were done under clothes lines and behind barn doors, had no problem making themselves known, and when Al mentioned that he was just a country lawyer one cutie with sauce in her eyes said, "I'll take the fifth anytime you want," meaning a fifth of rye whiskey.

The reception area of Gant's front office was crowded with the talent that had gotten through the first call, and they were no less enamored of Al's potential power as he approached the railing which divided the front office in half. Behind the railing was a receptionist, and behind her a desk that belonged to a wiry dance man with big impatient eyes and nervous hands which mimicked every thought that came to mind. He was busy on the telephone, yelling at a dancer who had moved from chorus girl to understudy. "You'll never work in this town again if you don't dance in my show," he hollered. But it was all bluff. His job was to create drama without the playwright. He hung up and set his eyes on Al who said, "I'd like to speak with Miss Mary Collins."

"And who are you?"

"Al Nachman."

"Yeah, but *who* are you?"

Al said, "Call Gant if you have a problem."

"You an actor?"

"Do I look like one?"

The dance man wasn't sure. "Nachman, you say?"

"Yeah."

"What's the problem?"

"Who said there was a problem......?"

Mary Collins' office was filled with wall-to-wall wood filing cabinets. A large center table was stacked with headshots of dancers, singers, actresses and actors all divided into gender, hair color, age, height, attractiveness, and ethnicity. There was a huge trash bin at the end of the table stuffed with rejects. The dance man, who had brought Al in, sat by the window anxious to know if he was going to lose his job to the good-looking man with the Southern drawl.

Mary Collins said, "You must be Mr. Nachman," rising from her desk. "Please come with me." The dance man also got up. Mary Collins said, "I was talking to the gentleman, not you." She and Al entered a conference room with a long mahogany table in the center. She pulled out a file and showed Al the headshot of Carmela Knight. "Is this the girl?"

"Yeah," Al said, turning it over. A dozen or so telephone numbers were scrawled in fountain pen ink on the back but without addresses. "I noticed a trash bin filled with headshots in your office. I assume they're of talent that you've rejected."

"It doesn't please us," Mary Collins said.

"Has Carmela Knight ever been rejected by your organization?" Al said, holding up the headshot.

"I believe she has."

"Then why would you still have her photo on file?"

"Mr. Nachman, this is a business."

"I understand that."

"We tend to keep things."

"Not from what I saw inside," Al said. "That trash bin was filled to the brim with headshots."

"We have a select group of girls."

"For what?"

"Girls who on notice can provide private entertainment."

"What kind of private entertainment?"

"A little revue perhaps," said Mary Collins.

"Where?"

"Wherever. Not all gentlemen have time to go to the theatre."

"But they have time to go somewhere else—these *so-called* gentlemen."

"You'll have to speak to them about that," she said.

"Miss Collins, time spent in a theater or somewhere else is the same amount of time, isn't it?"

"Yes, but time spent differently."

"…Do you know Artemus Cummins?"

"No," she said, crossing her arms.

"He wears a monocle. Smokes a cigarette in a black holder. Rides a blue Isotta-Fraschini sedan."

"I wouldn't know."

Al pulled out his fountain pen, uncapped it, and took down Carmela Knight's phone numbers. "What about John Smith?"

"Who?"

"John Smith."

"There must be a million John Smiths in Manhattan, Mr. Nachman."

"Are there a million Colm Haydocks?"

She didn't answer.

"What about Michael Collins?"

"What about him?"

Al said, "Documents connected to the 1920 Wall Street Bombing have been found in a rooming house in Hell's Kitchen hidden behind a photo of the Irish nationalist…Do you know him?"

"Michael Collins is a common name."

"I know that, but Michael Collins was not a common man. He happened to have worked for the Guaranty Trust Company of New York in 1915, owned by J.P. Morgan, whose building, on Wall Street, was the target of the 1920 bombing. Some speculate that it was payback for Morgan having kept England financially afloat during the war and for having used that money to finance the Ulster Volunteers with caches of arms."

"The Italians and Russians blew up that building."

"You have proof?"

"Everyone knows it," Mary Collins said.

"Not everyone believes it."

"Why are you telling me this, Mr. Nachman?" her brogue now thicker.

"Because one of those documents belonged to you and, according to a certain landlady of Irish descent in Hell's Kitchen, Mary Collins once lived in her building." Al pulled out an old British territorial passport from his inside suit pocket and showed it to her. "When you left that rooming house, why didn't you take your passport?"

"Is this a trial, Mr. Nachman?"

"If it were, you'd be facing the electric chair."

"What I'm facing is a defamation of character."

"No, Miss Collins, since nothing has been published nor publicly said concerning you, all you're facing is me. Now, why did you leave the Webley Scott top loader, the money, the dynamite, and the passports in the rooming house—or should I guess?"

"I have no idea what you're talking about."

"Then I'll remind you," Al said, waving her old passport in front of her eyes. "You feared anyone who might talk or turn you in. So, you hid the documents knowing that Mrs. Buchanan could be bought anytime you wanted access to the apartment. But you didn't hide all the money there. What you left—something most people couldn't get themselves to do—were the stolen British banknotes which you couldn't easily convert along with the stolen U.S. bills. But what's more curious is that you put Michael Collins's photo on the wall. Your grievance was too strong to throw out his clipping, so in an act of defiance you hung up his picture, and if you ever did need the documents only you knew where they were, which gave you power over anyone else wanting them."

She lit her fist cigarette of the year.

"Miss Collins, you're going to tell Artemus Cummins that District Attorney Emory Buckner wants the negatives taken of Carmella Knight and that Mississippi gentleman to be sent to this post office box address by next Monday or Buckner is going to get access to all that was found in that apartment in Hell's Kitchen and I swear, not because it is my desire, you will burn in the electric chair."

"For what, Mr. Nachman?"

"For the bombing of 1920."

"Mr. Nachman, I never bombed any building." She was now standing. "I've only worked *here*. A girl takes a job she can."

Al, now out of his chair, said, "And that job is to supply whores to Artemus Cummins outside the 12-mile limit."

"You can't do a thing about what happens outside the limit. Everyone knows that."

"But I can do a lot with what happens inside it, Miss Collins."

"Do you work for the government?"

"District Attorney Buckner does."

"Then why haven't I heard from his office?"

"You will," Al said, "but first you're hearing from me. Those negatives are to be sent to this address by Monday, or things are going to get very nasty......"

35

Harlem

The robbery was at a luncheonette on the corner of West 137th Street and Broadway. Cigars, cigarettes, magazines, and newspapers were sold up front. The Detroit Safe Company vault was in the back room behind a desk. The man slumped over the desk was a bookie. He had been working on a point spread. Blood ran off the desk and into a pool which reached Officer Elgin Bumpus's foot. The safe behind him had been cleaned out except for a flat brown envelope and a cigar box stuffed with betting slips. He took out the cigar box and went through each slip. A woman said, "I'll take that." She handed Officer Elgin Bumpus $200.

"Who are you?"

"I just do what I'm told."

"Yeah, but who are you?"

"What matters is the $200," she said, leaving the money on the desk.

"You didn't answer my question," he said.

"Ever see one of these before?" she said, reaching into her purse and taking out a $500 11-K bill. She left that on the desk and took off with the brown envelope.

A black cop, who had been stationed at the storefront, walked in. "Elgin, some white girl just drove away in a fancy Italian automobile......"

36

Ransacked

As Manhattan turned to dusk, storefronts lit up and streaked the avenues with shifting shades of light, but it was in the side streets, where wrong turns were made, that the lighting turned loneliness into a dim vignette as you confronted your dreams at the end of the day and wondered how much longer you could go on.

The Biltmore Bar, on Madison Avenue, was no wrong turn. Located next to Grand Central Terminal, it thawed commuters, natives, and out-of-towners wanting to escape the winter chill for the thrill of jazz and speakeasies all inside a city still made of brick and mortar unlike the dressing down soon to come. The Biltmore lobby was crammed with luggage pasted with colorful international hotel stickers which made galleries of each side. Foreigners and out-of-towners easily stood out by the distraction of their novelty, but it was the children who were having all the fun in their new playground and in a variety of languages and games. Al and Zola made their way through the crowded lobby to the elevator bank.

"My apartment was just ransacked," Zola said to Al, "and you want me to live on the street?"

The elevator door closed. They squeezed into the crush of coats and stale tobacco which made the air noxious.

"Who gets home at seven in the morning?"

"New Yorkers," Zola said, "and why're you trying to make me sound guilty?" The elevator door opened, but it wasn't their floor.

"Where's your luggage?"

"In the lobby," she said.

"How much do you have?"

"Several trunks."

"You travel like your cousin."

"Just because I'm a poor girl doesn't mean I have to live like one."

"No, but it's cheaper and you'll live a lot longer."

"Well, I won't be poor for long," Zola said, without telling Al why. They left the elevator and went down the long hallway lined with plush carpeting that softened each step. They entered Al's room: a single facing east with a clear view of the Long Island City skyline that was still flat and went on forever.

"I want you to go back to that rooming house and canvass the building. Find out if anyone had seen the people who ransacked your apartment or knows them by name or face."

"Why don't you come along if you're so interested?"

"I would," Al said, "but I've got to meet Beau uptown."

"What about the bellboy?"

"What about him?" Al said.

"He's waiting downstairs to bring up my luggage."

"We're not married."

"…You don't like me?"

"No, but this is a first-rate hotel and I'm not getting kicked out."

"You're cruel, Al."

"Sure I am. What about your cousin? She lives in a palace. Call her up."

"I'm in no mood for teenage abuse," Zola said. "Now, it'll only be a couple of days."

"When does your next column come out?"

"…Why do you want to know?"

Al reached for the hotel stationery on the side table and spent the next several minutes writing. Then he handed her the sheet of paper. Zola read it: *Artemus Cummins has moved the red-light district outside the 12-mile limit where he entertains the best of society with hooch, women, and gambling. I've also been informed, by a certain lady, that photos are taken of wealthy husbands in compromising positions. It seems that Prohibition has not only helped the bootlegger but also the blackmailer. Of course, anyone who doubts this should visit that ship. Just ask for the Pair-a-Dice.*

Al said, "I want you to publish this in your magazine."

"I'll be killed as soon as it gets out."

"You don't use your real name. You use Lipstick. So, there shouldn't be any problem," Al said.

"I've got a better idea."

"What?"

"Actually two," Zola said. "The first has to do with Shelby. She happens to know a society boy who once worked for Cummins's gang, and he's got a boat faster than a bat out of hell and he can get you out to that damn steam yacht you've been talking about."

"What's a society boy doing with Cummins?"

"Ask him when you see him, Al. But the kid is brilliant. Behind that sweet blonde head of his is a demon equal to Shelby's."

"He knows where the *Pair-a-Dice* is located?"

"He and Shelby found it last night," Zola said.

"The hell were they doing out in the 12-mile limit?"

"Shelby's looking out for her father," Zola said.

"She told you that?"

"She didn't have to." The bellboy knocked on the door. Zola opened it. He set her luggage down, took his tip, and left.

"What's your other idea?"

Zola folded the paper which Al had given her and put it in her purse. "Emil Gauvreau."

"Who's he?"

Zola said, "The managing editor of *The New York Evening Graphic*, and he'll print this."

"Why?"

"Because it's the looniest tabloid in town. Their biggest act is running crazy contests for tons of dough and printing composographs that drive the prudes nuts."

"Could you get a hold of him now and set up a meeting?"

"Sure, Al, but first I have to do something."

"What?"

Zola kicked off her shoes. "*Mrs.* Nachman is going to take a real shower."

37

The Big Plunge

Virginia stormed into Shelby's bathroom with five New York dailies. "Take a goddamn look at the morning editions."

Shelby flicked a bubble off her nose and grabbed one of the newspapers. The lead was: *Soling Consolidated General Plunges.* "Gee," Shelby said, "I guess the market went down a bitty." She plunged back into the tub.

"A *bitty...?*

Shelby peeped through a bubble, "I told you that stock was worthless."

Virginia grabbed the newspaper. "Yeah, well now I have to sell this penthouse." Virginia left the bathroom in a hurry almost knocking over Caitlin who said, "You might want to hurry, Miss Prevette. Mr. Brush is waiting for you in his office."

"Call him and tell him I'm just out the door." Then Shelby shouted to Virginia, "How much is this place going for?"

Wall Street

Marbury Brush shut the door to his office and handed Shelby a folder. "You, my dear, are now worth 627,000 dollars in change. Spend it wisely." He gave Shelby another folder. "Give this to your cousin on the way out; it's her new account." He sat down and took out his pipe.

Shelby went through her folder.

"Uncle Marbury—"

"Yes?"

"Do you know of Ellis Remley?"

He reached for his tobacco jar. "Why do you ask?"

"Do you know him?"

"Why, yes, he belongs to my club."

"The Metropolitan?"

"The same one your father belongs to," Marbury Brush said, striking a match, sitting back, and looking for that perfect draw.

"So, then you know Sarah Remley—the former Sarah Revenlöw."

"I do…Why?"

"The Revenlöws are an old family of good stock."

"Very much so."

"What can you tell me about Mrs. Remley?"

Tossing the match, Marbury Brush sat back and said, "Sarah is a woman with superior intelligence. Very well read. Articulate. Charming. The flower of society when she came out. Her only flaw is that she thinks she's a man—what you suffer from."

"Suffer…? I've never felt better in my life."

"Yes, you've done quite well for yourself," he said, pointing to Shelby's new financial folder, "but, like you, Sarah Revenlöw Remley talks about the world as if she knows it like her home. Still, her innate decency and determination hasn't suffered from having been a Suffragette—only her marriage."

"And how has having been a suffragette affected her marriage?"

"Because," Uncle Marbury said, as he blew out a long soothing stream of smoke, "she took up silly causes, started painting, and made a good man miserable."

"How does art make someone miserable?"

"Just why are you so interested in her?"

"You must know her son, Gideon."

"Oh, yes, I do," Uncle Marbury said, now sitting up.

"You don't approve of him?"

"Stay away from him, Shelby. I warn you. He took Celeste up in a flying machine and it crash landed."

"Yes, she wrote me about that."

"So, then you know the boy."

"I had never met him until the other day," Shelby said.

"Celeste broke her leg that day and he'll break yours. He's reckless and has got a boat that he races back and forth to East Hampton like the devil. A reform school is what that boy needs."

"Then why is Gideon always on the Dean's list at Columbia if he's so irresponsible."

"He cheats," Marbury Brush said.

"Do you have proof?"

"I don't need proof."

"Well, if he's that stupid," Shelby said, "how did he rebuild that boat all by himself?"

"I'm sure someone else did it for him."

"How can you be so sure of something, when you don't have any proof?"

"Shelby…you don't mean to say you have something for that boy?"

"Uncle Marbury, I'm only giving credit where credit is due. If that boy can build a boat on his own that's faster and more agile than anyone else's, then he's no dummy."

"Shelby, I warn you. Don't go near him or you'll end up like my Celeste, maybe worse. Now, we expect you up at the country club this weekend. Everyone is excited to meet you, especially the boys, and they're all from very good families. I can already see several marriage proposals by Sunday night."

"I already told Celeste I'm coming."

"Good. Now, I just spoke to your father, and I told him what I did for you."

Shelby rose from her chair. "You said that you wouldn't tell him."

"You misunderstood me," Uncle Marbury said.

"You *betrayed* me."

"By doing what I'm supposed to do? Your father and I are old friends. I'd be betraying *him*."

"And that gives you the right to talk behind my back?"

"You're confusing the situation."

"I'm confusing nothing," Shelby said.

"Child, he wanted to know what were up to. Our friendship obligates me to be honest with him."

"What else did you tell him?"

"I told him that I was looking after you, as I had promised, and that includes what I've been doing for you. There's no betrayal in that. In fact, he thanked me."

"You could've told me first," Shelby said.

"I could have, but you're a young lady who's inexperienced in life and must be looked after."

"*Looked* after?

"Yes, Shelby, looked after."

"I'll have you know that rights are no longer generated by gender."

"But they are determined by gender."

"No," Shelby said. "They've been determined by the deceptive notion that physical strength is a prerogative to power. We've seen what mess you men made in the last war. Wait till the next."

"Yes, but that war has ended all wars and for good reason. No one will be in the mood for another one like that again. Yes, there may be squabbles, here and there; that you can't help. But men will look for other solutions than to relive the horror of the last conflict."

"We'll see about that," Shelby said. "Now there's a steam yacht I want to know about."

"Which steam yacht?"

"The one outside the 12-mile limit which men are known to visit for women and gambling."

"What about it?"

"It has a first-class restaurant and orchestra," Shelby said. "It's called the *Pair-a-Dice*."

"I know nothing of it."

"But you've heard of it?"

"As I've heard of Siberia," Uncle Marbury said.

"What can you tell me about Artemus Cummins?"

"Not a thing."

"He's very tall, wears a monocle, and always has a black cigarette holder in his mouth.

"I know nothing of him, child."

"What goes on in that ship?"

"I think you know more about it than I do."

"I can assure you that I don't," Shelby said. "What kind of man is Cummins?"

"I only know bankers not criminals."

"But you know that he's a criminal."

"I'm only putting two and two together. If a ship is anchored outside the limit, then it must be there for a reason." Marbury Brush got up from his desk and headed to the door. "Now you stay away from that Remley boy. He'll ruin a girl like you and be *very* careful with your money. Times are good now, but they won't be forever. I remember the Panic of 1910 and '11 when people were completely wiped out."

"As they were in the panics of 1873 and '93," Shelby said.

"I see you've done your homework."

"As others have done their mischief," Shelby said, heading out the door.

38

Hell's Kitchen

"We should be taking a limousine home not the damn subway," Zola said to Shelby as the train left the Wall Street IRT Subway station.

"I got a feeling you're going to blow every cent you have now that you're rich."

"Yeah, well you're the one always riding around in a limousine."

"I wouldn't call this a limousine, Miss Jealous," Shelby said, gripping the straphanger.

"What about that Gardner Coupe you bought for two grand last week which goes 85 miles per hour?"

"What about it?"

Zola said, "I saw you flying down Fifth avenue the other day and I nearly waved my arm off for you to stop."

"Well, there were a million other people waving their arms off."

"Shelby, your problem is you're too rich. My father barely makes 1000 dollars a year and you've already blown 10 grand this past week alone."

"Zola, your problem is that you compare everything to what you don't have. If you want to keep what you do have then compare it to what you once had."

When the subway stopped at Grand Central Terminal, Zola hurried out the double sliding door.

"Where're you going?"

"Hell's Kitchen," Zola said.

"I thought you were done with that hole?"

"It ain't done with me..."

The thought of Mrs. Buchanan gave Zola more than heartburn. The old lady had become a psychic wound. Always on the prowl. Digging through garbage cans. Looking for bathtub gin. Roaming the halls. Listening at tenant's doors or climbing the fire escape and inspecting the laundry lines which reached across the building, and if she decided your clothing was dry, she would pull it in and bang on your window with an onslaught of accusations.

Zola went up the stairs and knocked on tenants' doors. If they didn't open them, she would talk through them. Some tenants lied about the ransacking. Others spoke through the crack of their door to evade recognition. Those on Zola's floor, the fifth floor, said that they were at work at the time. She then tried the door of an elderly Ellis Island immigrant who lived down the hall from her.

She knocked. "Hello? Mr. Schultz?" She knocked again and waited. Then she heard footsteps approaching the door. "Mr. Schultz?"

"...Yah?"

"It's Miss Nicholas from down the hall."

"Yah...?"

"I'm sorry to disturb you, Mr. Schultz, but my apartment got ransacked last night and I was wondering if you saw any of the intruders and could tell me what they looked like or maybe who they were?" Zola waited. "I didn't get that, Mr. Schultz. Did you hear or see anything in in particular?"

"...No."

"Anything would be of help."

"Ich erinnere mich nicht," he said pretending to speak no English.

"Yes, but did you open your door and look?"

"No."

"I need your help, Mr. Schultz. You're one of the few people who were at home when it happened. I'm really trying hard to be nice." She then said it in German, but he did not want to talk in his native tongue.

Zola had to push open her apartment door. She then checked the rooms, the closets, and all the drawers. She worried that she had left something which could have identified her or that maybe Mrs. Buchanan, for a few dollars more, had told the intruders who she was since Zola had spoken to her about growing up in Mississippi, her rich younger cousin, and other things that resentful lips betray. Zola then made her way downstairs and warily knocked on Mrs. Buchannan's door. No answer. She checked the back of the building where birds grouped in bunches over laundry line lines, but the old lady couldn't be found. Zola then checked the coal chute, where Mrs. Buchanan was fond of hunting vagrants, and spoke to several tenants entering the building. Not one would admit to having witnessed the ransacking. She quit the rooming house and headed west to Ninth Avenue toward the elevated IRT train on West 50th Street. She found Mrs. Buchanan slowly making her way down the big broad iron stairway, bundled up in a long gray wool overcoat and tattered scarf which couldn't hide the pain that gripped her face. Her big blue velvet cloche with its brightly stitched flowers seemed long out of bloom. Mrs. Buchanan hollered, "I lost it all. *Everything*," including her voice. She peered down the stairway as if she were bracing herself against the ledge of a skyscraper with the wind at her back.

"What did you lose, Mrs. Buchanan?"

"He told me that he was there to help me choose safe investments, because of the complicated nature of security issues and bonds, and that it could only be done by experts like him and his bank."

"Who told you that?"

"That goddam lying banker told me that!"

"How much did you lose?"

"Everything!"

"You invested all your money in the market?"

"*No*. Just Soling Consolidated General. Then the banker shoves me out the door like I had robbed him and not the other way around. He wanted me to hand over my building to him now that I got no money."

"How much can you get for it?"

"Not enough," Mrs. Buchanan said as she reached out her trembling hand. "Help me down the stairway."

"Grab my arm," Zola said.

"Help me home."

"I can't, Mrs. Buchanan. Really, I can't. I have to hurry off, but I'll help you to the street. And you can keep the last two weeks rent that I've already paid."

"*Two* weeks? I've got glaucoma and cataracts! And my leg! How will I pay for my medicine? Where will I live? Who'll take care of me? I'm not a young woman anymore!"

"I'm sorry, Mrs. Buchanan."

"*You're* sorry!"

Mrs. Buchanan pushed Zola away and made her way down the icy path of Ninth Avenue. The punishing wind, coming off the Hudson River, had even less mercy.

39

Mott Haven Yard, The Bronx

Al Nachman weaved through the crisscross of train tracks, cleaning crews, and ice packing haulers until he found Beau by the yardmaster's old coach car, an 1890s fixture which had enough ornamentation to make Park Avenue look middle class. Beau said, "I see you got my message."

"I thought we were going to meet Officer Bumpus in Harlem. Why are we up here?" Al said.

"Need to show you somethin' first," Beau said, taking Al to the other side of the yard where trains heading north were bunched up in long columns. "There's a private car sittin' in the yard, way over, like nothin' you ever seen. Found boxes onboard with clothin', linen, and other fine things. The name of A. Cummins was printed on all of 'em. I got off the car when a party of folks was about to board. Yonder was the man with the monocle and cigarette holder. He come along with the yardmaster and somebody else. They talked some, boarded, and talked some more."

"Did you overhear anything?"

"No," Beau said, "but I checked the car's future log and it's slated to hook onto that new Orange Blossom Special Line ridin' between New York and Florida. Seems Cummins done purchased the private car in New Haven and brought it down here to be resupplied before gettin' rerouted to Pennsylvania Station."

"Why there?" Al said.

"New York Central don't run south. Just north and west."

"Do you know when Cummins's private car is leaving?"

"Day before I report back to work," Beau said.

New York Central Railroad detective Fred Heinz walked into the conversation. The last time he had seen either Beau or Al was on the 2:45 New Year's Eve 20th Century Limited ride to Chicago and what had happened that night hadn't soured him.

"Nachman, I thought you were back in Mississippi," Detective Heinz said.

"I was." They shook hands. "Maybe you can help me out," Al said.

"With what?"

"You know of a criminal named Al Cummins?"

"What about him?"

Al said, "I'd like to know if he gets billed by the New York Central for keeping his private car here."

"He'd have to," Detective Heinz said.

"Good, I need his billing address and the bank he uses."

"What's going on?"

"I'm working on a blackmailing case," Al said.

"Come on over to the yardmaster's coach. I'll get it for you."

When they were finished, Al and Beau headed down to Harlem.

40

C. K.

A bright red American LaFrance 1000-gpm Rotary Gear Pumper was busy putting out flames in a Harlem railroad flat just off Seventh Avenue and 132nd St. Officer Elgin Bumpus was inside the fire zone perimeter speaking to the hook and ladder chief. When the fire was finally put out, the chief took him, Al, and Beau up to the fourth floor. The air was thick with smoke. The knocked-out windows gave little relief as the men headed through the scorched rooms. They stopped at a melted charred body strapped to a stool in the middle of the living room. "Here she is," the fire chief said.

"How can you be sure this is a woman?" Officer Bumpus said.

The fire chief put his gloved hand under the melted chin and pulled out a silver locket. "Men don't wear this," he said, as he headed back downstairs.

Beau recognized the locket's engraved initials: C.K. He said to Al, "Carmela Knight was wearin' this here locket last time I seen her."

Al took Officer Elgin Bumpus to the side and quietly said, "I want her head."

"...You want her *what?*"

Al opened his billfold and took out several hundred dollars. "And just how you gonna get it outta here?" Officer Elgin Bumpus said.

Al went through all the closets. He came back holding a hatbox which hadn't been scorched in the fire. "This is how," he said.

Officer Elgin Bumpus put the money away and said, "Me and Beau gonna take a walk downstairs."

Al went into the kitchen. He found the cutlery in a charred cabinet drawer. He took out a long carving knife.

41

Miss Special

The Knickerbocker Building stood on the corner of 42nd Street and Broadway by Times Square. Ellen Wirth, stenographer extraordinaire, entered the lobby and made her way through the morning crowd holding a box up against her chest. She squeezed into an overcrowded elevator—something smelled. She knew what it was and so did everyone else. The elevator opened on the 8th floor. She hurried out and went down the hall to the offices of Transatlantic Imports. Rosie, one of the three stenographers, hissed as soon as the door opened. "Well, if it *ain't* Miss Special."

"Shut up," Ellen said, as she walked in and knocked on her boss's door.

Sally, the other stenog, looked up from her typewriter. "You bought our dear old boss a gift?"

Ellen said, "If that's what ya wanna think."

Rosie said to her, "I don't see why he trusts you so much to run errands all over the place."

"It's her cute little bob," Sally said.

Ellen, again, knocked on the boss's door.

Sally turned to Rosie and said, "They must be Eskimo lovers. That's why she's rubbing her nose like that." She and Rosie rubbed their noses and giggled.

Ellen said, "I'm rubbing my nose because something in here stinks."

Rosie said, "Well, I used to run him errands all the time and smelled fresh as a daisy."

"You *used* to," Ellen said.

"*Shut* up."

Ellen knocked again. This time she was allowed in. She set the box on her boss's desk and returned to the typing pool and rolled a sheet of paper into her typewriter.

Rosie walked over and dropped a file on Ellen's desk and said, "All outgoing communications gotta be done by noon."

"Why?"

"'Cause the boss says so," Rosie said, still looking at the boss's door. "Was that the new whiskey they're all talking about?"

Ellen began typing. "If it were whiskey, one of the men would've brought it up."

Sally said, "Louie Four-Stacks brought up a case of Glen Trool an hour ago and acted like I should lift up my dress for it."

Rosie, back at her desk, said, "Too bad no one knocked him off last night."

Ellen said, "What happened now?"

"What always happens," Sally said.

"He got very fresh," Rosie added.

Sally turned to Rosie and said, "One day I'm gonna grope him with a sharp knife you-know-where."

Rosie, seeing Ellen rub her nose, again, moved her chair back. "Hey, you're not sick or anything? 'Cause if ya are, stay away from me."

Ellen said. "I'm not sick."

"What was in that box?" Sally said.

"I have no idea, but it stunk," Ellen said.

"*She* knows what's in it," Rosie said with a nasty little sneer. "But Princess Wirth-less won't tell us because she thinks she's so special."

"You're the one who stinks," Ellen said.

"Oh, yeah? Haul your damn snout over here and take a sniff, Miss special; you won't smell a thing."

"I don't need to stand over a pile of shit to smell it."

Rosie shot up from her desk. "I'm gonna *cut* your tongue out."

"I'd cut yours out right now," Ellen said, "but you won't shut up."

It took Sally both arms to hold Rosie back who really wasn't going anywhere. Rosie parked herself in her chair with all her hurt.

After a lot of noisy typing and nothing said, Sally broke the silence. "Hey, what's the deal with Louie Four-Stacks anyway? He used to have to wait outside like the rest of 'em. Why the sudden lather?"

Ellen said, "He's the new boss of the mosquito fleet as of last night."

"That creep?" Sally said.

"Yeah, that creep," Ellen said. "Charlie Evans and his crew all drowned last night."

"Geezuz, what happened?" Rosie said.

Ellen said, "I wasn't out there, so I don't know, but I did hear that the Coast Guard found the boat upside down with the motor still running."

"Louie Four Stacks was supposed to be on that boat," Sally said.

"Too bad he wasn't," Ellen said, "because he invited me over to the McAlpin Hotel to dance the mamba with him like I was part of his new promotion."

"Did he put his hands on ya?" Sally wanted to know.

"He tried to."

Rosie wanted to know, "Did he try 'n kiss ya?"

"Nobody touches me," Ellen said, "and I didn't go with him."

Sally said, "You musta put him in a bad mood."

Ellen said, "Why should I worry what mood I put that groper in. It's my body. He can go fuck himself."

"*Oooh!*" Rosie covered her mouth. "Another naughty word from Miss Special."

Ellen ignored her.

Rosie turned to Sally. "I'd take a free meal at the McAlpin anytime."

Ellen said, "You mean a free hand."

"*Shut up*," Rosie hollered, halfway out of her seat.

Ellen said, "The truth hurts. Doesn't it?"

Sally intervened, "Anybody get that invitation?"

Rosie, still sore, said, "If *she* got it, I don't want it."

Sally said, "Well, whoever got it, it's for that yacht outside the 12-mile limit. I hear they getchya glad rags so ya can dance all night long and drink quality hooch with all the rich flat tires."

Ellen warned, "That wasn't an invitation."

"What was it then?" Rosie said. "A wake?"

Ellen said, "Sometimes you're really dumb."

"I got more brains than ya think," Rosie shot back.

Sally said to Rosie, "What she means is that you have to allow rich men to fondle you on that boat."

Rosie said, "If they're rich enough, I don't care. I'm sick of getting fondled by poor boys."

"You're not the only one," Sally said. "You read about that stenog who worked in that stock-jobbing outfit down on Wall Street?"

Rosie said, "Ya mean the one goes 'n marries her millionaire boss, and him and her lives happily ever after on Fifth Avenue right across the street from the Vanderbilt shack?"

"Yeah," Sally said. "Now she's got a house full of servants and maids to powder her nose whenever it needs a dusting."

"That was six months ago," Ellen Wirth said.

"Six months in this dump is an eternity," Rosie said.

"Two minutes with *you* is an eternity," Ellen said.

"You're lucky you're not worth slapping," Rose said. "Otherwise, you'd have ran home to Poughkeepsie a long time ago. And what was in that damn box anyway?"

"How many times do I have to tell you all? I *don't* know."

"I bet it's more of that Glen Trool whiskey no one can't get their hands on—the stuff you-know-who hates," Rosie said, pointing to her boss's door.

Sally said, "Betchya it's real American rye from before Prohibition. I hate scotch. It tastes worse than cod liver oil."

Rosie said, "Well, we're all stuck with it because of those damn long skirts and their goddam up the ass morals."

"Tell me about it," Sally said. "Those witches used to come to our town and stand in front of the saloon and sing: *In This World of Sin and Sorrow* all day long. They had so much God in 'em, heaven was empty."

Confused, Ellen looked up from her typewriter and said to Rosie, "Hey, I got a question about this Huber & Köhler food order requisition you just handed me."

Rosie said, "Ask Mr. Cummins, iffya got a problem."

Ellen got up from her desk and knocked on her boss's door. She waited a moment and then knocked again. Sally waved for her to go in, but Ellen wasn't sure about entering her boss's office without his permission.

"He ain't gonna bite ya," Sally said.

"Yeah, but you're supposed to wait for a reply after a knock," Ellen said.

Rosie got up as if only she knew how to do things. "*I'll* do it then."

"No, you won't," Ellen said, turning the knob and opening the door. She walked inside Artemus Cummins's private office and let out a scream that stuck to the walls.

42

Do You Mind?

In the early 1800s, anything north of the Lower East Side was rural. The Upper West Side, at 84th Street and Broadway, was where the old Brennan farm stood. Midtown East, by the East River, was where the Brevoort estate sat under puffy clouds and chestnut trees which favored a sleepy view of rural Long Island, and the only traffic was Mabel the cow moseying back to the barn at sunset. By the 1920s it had become a mélange of walkups, with a slaughterhouse, brand-new Sutton Place townhouses that edged along the East River, and the Consumer's Brewing Company on First Avenue which by law had to produce "near" beer and nothing more. The closest thing to a farm was Rosebush Farm Products on the southwest corner of 54th Street and First Avenue. West of that were the grand apartment buildings on Park and Fifth Avenues manned by doormen dressed in fancy faux military outfits that the wiseacres from the press made hay of in their columns, and despite the clamor from the straw-hat brigade, the fabulously rich continued on in their airy trot of pinched noses, dainty feet, and rolled R's.

Gideon and Shelby entered his apartment building on Fifth Avenue. His mother was in the hallway behind the butler who had showed them in. She said to her son, "Your father's gone for the evening again."

"When will he be back?" Gideon said, as if his old man was lurking in the corner.

"I don't know," Sarah Remley said, "He's entertaining out-of-town clients at his club. We're having dinner alone."

"What else is new?" Gideon said, as he turned to the flapper beside him. "Mother, this is Miss Shelby Prevette."

The introduction was late, but Shelby let it pass. She was more interested in the magnificent matron dressed in Dutch clogs and a paint-streaked smock—the woman whom Marbury Brush had said was brilliant and something else. But Sarah's eyes were kind, not tragic, and full of concern as she welcomed her new guest. "It's a pleasure to meet you, Miss Prevette."

Gideon said, "Please address her as Shelby, mother."

"Shelby it is, then. Always a pleasure to meet a friend of my son."

"It's very kind of you to allow me into your home, Mrs. Remley," Shelby said, intrigued by her long golden-brown bob that was swept up to the side.

"Shelby's from the South." Gideon said.

"I can hear."

"And she wants to see your art, if you don't mind."

Shelby corrected Gideon. "Mrs. Remley, the only picture I wanted to see was the beautiful one of you that your son had described, and I'm looking at it right now."

"That's kind of you to say, but I won't bore you with my dabbling. I paint for fun and only began to take it seriously when I found out how much it distressed people."

Shelby followed her down the long hallway. They headed up the grand staircase that slowly turned to the upper floors. "You must sell your art all over," Shelby said.

"Not at all. No dealer wants it. I've only had one sale and that was to someone my husband knew who had been looking for cheap art."

"It's good that your husband supports you."

"Oh, he doesn't support me at all, Shelby. In fact, he hates my art. I'll never forget the first time I showed him a canvas. I hoped for praise and love. Instead, I was the shame of having been his mistake. Love is a funny thing."

"How is that?" Shelby said, stunned by the woman's candor.

"It's only later when you find out that it was never really there."

They reached the second floor and proceeded down another long, elegant hallway.

"Mrs. Remley, do you mind my asking which painting you sold?"

"The one with the ships."

"Ships...?"

"Yes."

"Why ships?" Shelby said.

"We sailed to Hamburg a few years back to see my husband's family in Berlin. Some were having it very hard because of the war and the terrible inflation. But the other side of his family are great industrialists, and they still live in the grand manner. But I couldn't get Hamburg out of my mind. It was as if a premonition had struck me that something was about to happen involving me, and when I mentioned it to my husband, he looked at me as if I were crazy and said that I had no grasp of the world and that I knew only of my house. You can imagine how hurt I was. I had foolishly expected intimacy and once again got rebuked. The pain of realizing that someone actually finds you annoying never goes away."

"You speak from the heart, Mrs. Remley. So few can."

"It's my great fault. But to do otherwise is to have nothing but the pleasantries of affectation and the lies that go with them."

"What did your painting of Hamburg look like?"

"It's hard to say. An image, unlike words, is immediate, and therefore always a victim of first impressions; so, your art better come out of some life experience where the pain you're suffering isn't just some petty grievance, otherwise you insult those who are really in pain. But then there are those who are in art for the fame and glory, those things you can't share, which I guess is the whole point, isn't it?" she said with a laugh.

"Was the painting just of ships?" Shelby said.

"No, but I can no longer paint a face the way it is and be satisfied."

"What do you mean?"

"I mean that I'm always trying to reach inside and pull out some inner geometry as if I'm on the wrong side of looking in, but more than once I've come up with nothing but an artless twisted face, a fraud of my own making with all the clichés about the abyss of self or the questions of identity you hear from fatuous critics and curators. But there is no 'question'. We know exactly who we are, and we hate it."

"…Are you afraid of being a fraud, Mrs. Remley?"

"I am, but then the deep desire for attention distracts us from that peril, and if then we should look like fools it matters less because at least someone is looking," Sarah said, laughing at herself as if there were two of her there.

They entered the studio.

Shelby immediately went through all the canvasses. "Mrs. Remley, do you know the German artists Jeanne Mammen, or Hannah Höch, or maybe those men Dix and Grosz?"

"I know of no one. I make art out of exhaustion not inspiration."

"Yes, but I would think you go to the galleries and museums all the time," Shelby said.

"I never bother. But if they are from Berlin then I'm going to look them up. Fortunately, I speak German as well as French, as does Gideon—a boy too brilliant for his own good."

"Why do you say that?" Shelby said.

"To be so smart at such a young age is always seen as a conceit. It makes a boy restless and seemingly uninterested in life because he rejects the bourgeoise narrative that society ruthlessly enforces on everyone, especially women."

Shelby said, "You mean how men control our lives."

"Not just men, but mostly them."

"And your husband thinks you are too outspoken?"

"Everyone does," Sarah said. "As if I've strangled a baby and drunk its blood. But when we were in Berlin with our cousins, only Gideon and I were able to converse. His father sat there worried that we were saying things that would embarrass him. You see, Ellis—and many men like him—has this horrid thing about embarrassment and, amidst the folly and confusion of Berlin, it only got worse since his opinions of what should be done were much different than mine. I found the political scene fascinating and so did Gideon; of course, my daughters were too young to understand what was going on. So, I told my husband that I wanted to stay another few weeks in Berlin to absorb the madness of the long game of hard politics being fought out in the streets, rather than just go. But he forbade me. I think it was fear. That I had my own mind. So, we packed our trunks and sailed home."

"You should've held your ground."

"Young lady, you're not married. When a husband decides something, there's little you can do." Sarah reached behind an easel and said, "This is the sketch that I had done before painting the ships and if everything looks a mess, it's my own fault."

Shelby approached it and the canvasses against the wall and all the others across the room. "Do you mind if I look at them?"

"Go ahead if you want. But be prepared for disappointment," Sarah said, stepping aside to let the teenager rearrange the canvasses on the walls, including the sketches. Shelby walked around them as if solving a riddle. Then she stepped away and said in a voice that would forever hold, "I'll buy them all......"

43

Hell's Kitchen

Ellen Wirth exited the IRT Elevated train at West 50th Street and Ninth Avenue. She made her way down the heavy wrought iron stairway and through the clutter of shops and long shadows that lunged from the tracks above. She went east on 53rd Street and immediately caught sight of her landlady reaching for empty gin bottles in one of the building's ash cans that had been set out on the street for pickup.

"Is this yours?" Mrs. Buchanan hollered, holding up an empty soldier.

"No," said Ellen Wirth.

"You had another hot little party last night, didn't you? How many boys felt you up this week?"

"None. And *let go* of me, Mrs. Buchanan."

"What's this soldier doing in my garbage can?"

"How should I know?" pushing the old lady away.

"I heard you were home when they ransacked my building."

"I wasn't home, Mrs. Buchanan, and I live on the second floor not the fifth where it happened."

"I know where you live. I've had two potential buyers come by this morning who had read about the ransacking in the papers. If you and your friends were up to this, you're going to jail."

"I'm a stenographer, Mrs. Buchanan, not a criminal."

"That's what you say."

Ellen Wirth tried to get past the old lady who grabbed onto her. "And just what're you doing home so early? You never get home until past six. I suppose you've got a boyfriend waiting out on the fire escape."

"No, I don't, Mrs. Buchanan, and I'd wish you'd mind your manners," Ellen Wirth said, giving the landlady another push.

Mrs. Buchanan pushed back. "Then what're you doing home at this time of day?"

"We all left work early today."

"You mean you were fired. That's what really happened. They caught onto your dirty little small-town tricks. Well, you're going to run a few errands now that you've got nothing to do."

"I'm all done running errands for you on my free time," Ellen Wirth said, pushing away Mrs. Buchanan's tacky fingers, "but for a half a dollar I'll to go to the store and get you something then go back again because you're never satisfied with what I bring you the first time."

"Get out of my building right now you thief!"

"You're throwing me out *again*?"

"*Yes*. And this time if you don't have your crap out of here in ten minutes, I'm going to get my nigger coal boy to do it and he's not fussy about a girl's bloomers." Mrs. Buchanan went down to the cellar door and hollered for Harold. He came up and followed Ellen Wirth to her apartment and waited as she threw all her belongings into her one and only trunk and then watched her lug it down the stairs. Then she knocked on Mrs. Buchanan's door, "I want my money back for the month already paid, Mrs. Buchanan."

"Over my dead body, you little slut," Mrs. Buchanan hollered from inside.

"Then I'm going to the police."

"Sure, you are—to spread your legs!"

"*Mrs. Buchanan*, if you want trouble, you'll get it. Expect a visit from me within the next few days." Ellen Wirth heaved her heavy trunk off the floor and carried it out onto the cold street. The YWCA, on Lexington Avenue's 53rd Street southwest corner, was directly crosstown. She would have to hurry to get a room at this time of day. A man, halfway down the block, approached her. "Do you live in this building, miss?"

"Not anymore."

"Do you remember that box you picked up this morning in the lobby where you work?"

Fearful that the man was one of Cummins's henchman, Ellen Wirth hurried down the street as fast as she could with her heavy trunk.

He followed her. "Could you tell me about Artemus Cummins and the *Pair-a-Dice* steam yacht?"

"Leave me alone, mister, or I'll call for the police."

"You want me to tell them that you're the girl who brought the severed head up to Transatlantic Imports?"

She stopped. "...*Who* are you?"

"I work with the government."

"Are you the police?"

"You better hope not," he said. "There are some that arrest innocent girls for prostitution and force them to pay bribes or they serve time in jail."

"I've heard all about that. Are you one of them?" she said.

"No, miss. I'm not here to hurt you. I just want some information. Nothing else. Then I'll be on my way."

"What do you want to know?"

"Anything concerning Artemus Cummins and the *Pair-a-Dice* steam yacht outside the 12-mile limit."

"All I know is that Mr. Cummins has got an interest in some boat. But I'm just a stenographer." She hurried on.

"You mean he doesn't own the *Pair-a-Dice*?"

"I guess not," keeping several steps ahead of the man.

"Who does, then?"

"It's registered in England. Now leave me alone," she said, struggling with her trunk and not letting him help her.

"What's the name of the company that owns it?"

"I have no idea," Ellen Wirth said. "All I know is that they get paid a fee."

"Who gets paid a fee?"

"They do, in England."

"I've heard that Artemus Cummins keeps everything aboard the *Pair-a-Dice*, because the government can't search it outside the 12-mile limit."

"You heard wrong," she said, now dragging the trunk.

"What did I hear wrong?"

"Ask Mr. Cummins if you want to know."

"I'm asking you, miss," trying to help her with the trunk.

"And just who are you?" not letting him near it.

"A private investigator working with the government."

"Sure, you are, and if you're looking for sex get lost."

"I'm looking for something else," he said.

"Good. I hope you find it."

He got in front of her. "I'm looking for photographic negatives."

"Will you get out of my way?"

"I'm not in your way, miss," he said, stepping aside. "Do you have the keys or access to where they are?"

"Only Mr. Cummins has them—*if* there are any."

"Where they would be?"

"Look mister, I don't know anything other than that he keeps everything aboard some yacht."

"You just said Cummins doesn't."

"I changed my mind," trying to get away.

"Where on the yacht would he keep valuable things like negatives?"

"I already told you, mister. I'm just a stenographer."

"Have you ever stayed at the Biltmore Hotel?"

"Don't be funny. That's for rich people."

"I'll put you up there on my tab until you find another rooming house." He put 100 dollars into Ellen Wirth's hand. "All you have to do is sit down and answer a few questions."

"And give you sex."

"No, miss. Not all men are pigs."

"You're right. Some are just jackasses."

"Then keep the money and go on your way."

"I don't want it." She threw it at him and crossed the street.

"Do you know whose head it was that you carried up this morning?"

"I couldn't care less."

"It was Carmela Knight's."

Ellen Wirth stopped dead in her tracks. "…*Who?*"

"Carmela Knight."

Ellen Wirth tried to find something in the man's eyes that would convince her that he wasn't a madman, but it was Carmela's eyes, discolored by years of setbacks and failed dreams that wouldn't go away. "I didn't get your name."

"I didn't get yours….."

44

The Biltmore Hotel

"You said that we were going for a drive in your new Gardner 8 Cylinder Roadster, not get interrogated."

"This will only take a minute," Shelby said to Gideon who was deep into the hotel chair by the window.

He turned to Al and said, "So what did she tell you?"

Al said to him, "Miss Prevette told me that you have a skiff that is fast and equipped with a radio transmitter."

"What else did she say?" Gideon, eyes on her.

"I need to borrow it," Al said.

"No one borrows my boat and it's not a skiff."

"I'll pay you 100 dollars for the night," Al offered.

"No."

"Two hundred dollars."

"Five hundred dollars or nothing, and I'm helming it. You're just a passenger," Gideon said. "And what's this all about anyway?"

"Artemus Cummins is what it's about," Al said. "I may need you to pick me up on a boat out at sea."

"Which boat?"

"At the moment it doesn't matter," Al said, "but if something doesn't work out onshore then that's the next move."

"What's this is all about?"

"$500 is what it's about," Al said.

"Maybe it's about what Shelby said to you that I wasn't supposed to hear." Gideon turned to Beau who had heard.

"For $500 you don't need to know," Al said. "But for nothing and the use of your boat, I'd be more than glad to tell you. It's up to you."

The bathroom door opened. Ellen Wirth stepped out, hair wet, towel wrapped around her.

Zola then entered without knocking. She took in the pretty girl wrapped in the bath towel. "I see you've got company, Mr. Nachman."

"Miss Wirth lived in your rooming house," Al said.

"And now she lives here?"

"No," Al said, "but she got her room through someone in her office. I was wondering how you got yours?"

Zola took her eyes off the pretty stenog with whom she had crossed paths in the rooming house and said, "One of our bootleggers. He was moving out."

"Which bootlegger?" Al said.

"From the Knickerbocker Building where they're all located," Zola said. "Why do you want to know?"

"Ever hear of Transatlantic Imports?"

"No, Al, why?"

"They're in the Knickerbocker," he said.

"Still doesn't explain what *she's* doing here."

"I'll get to that in a moment."

"Sure, ya will. Meanwhile, take a look at this, Casanova." Zola handed him *The New York Evening Graphic*. The front page read: *Cummins's Fleet Goes to Pair-a-Dice*. "The editor and publisher loved your little missive," Zola said, tossing the competition's clothing off the bed.

Ellen Wirth grabbed her dress and said to Zola, "I'm waiting for my room to get prepared—*if* you don't mind."

"I don't think you can afford one here," Zola sneered, as she turned back to Al. "*The Graphic's* managing editor wants to speak to you in his office right now—that is, unless you and this girl are too busy making whoopee."

"Call him up and tell him I'll be right over," Al said.

Zola corrected him, "*We'll* be right over," then to Shelby, "What brings you here, little cousin?"

"I heard how desperate you are, so I thought I'd let you stay in my apartment until you find a new place."

"You mean Virginia Swain's apartment," Zola said.

"No, *my* apartment."

"Yours….? Whaddya mean yours?" Zola reached for the candlestick telephone on the night table beside the bed.

"What do you think I mean?"

"And just where did you get the money for a penthouse apartment?"

"Same place you did."

Zola stared at her cousin the way a poker player does who's holding a full house against a royal flush.

Shelby said, "You better make that call."

Zola did.

Meanwhile, Al pre-fixed the shutter speed and focal plane of his 35mm Leica A for night shooting. He showed Beau how to spool a roll of film until he could do it effortlessly. Then he gave him a sheet of paper with a hand drawn map that Ellen Wirth had made. Al said to Beau, "The speakeasy that Cummins has a piece of in the Meatpacking District is called Huber & Köhler Meat Purveyors. Wait for Cummins there."

"You think he'll show up?" Beau said, looking through the viewfinder, getting a feel of the camera.

"If he does, stay onto him until you run out of film. Then call me. We'll meet at Phil Levine's darkroom on Broadway and 49th."

Zola covered the telephone mouthpiece and said to Al, "Emil Gauvreau of the *Graphic* wants us downtown in half an hour."

Al put on his hat and coat. "Tell him we're on our way."

45

The Meatpacking District

January put out the day early. Washington Market, parallel to the Hudson River, was already starved of light, its streets clogged with crates that stocked the jumble of teamster wagons and motorized trucks that jammed the lower Manhattan piers where, under lamppost's glow, negro porters carried crate boxes, shoulder high, filled with produce right off the boats. A heave-ho was heard as each porter made his way through the stalls where nighttime street urchins were quick to grab a peach or pear that tumbled down, or pluck a carrot off a crate, pinch a yam or potato from the sky-high piles that looked more like Western Front munition dumps. Further up, along the Hudson River piers, ocean liners lulled in berths, knife-edged prows wedged the streets held to port by long stressed hawser ropes angled down from bows snaked around large iron cleats drilled into the ground. Tugboats up and down the Hudson River shoehorned big ocean liners in and out of piers that went all the way past Hell's Kitchen. Ships that let you dream were The Cunard Line, Hamburg-America Line, Scandia Line, Holland-America Line, White Star Line, Red Star Line, Clyde Line, Stonington Line, and Old Dominion Line. The piers swung easterly around the chin of Manhattan past Fulton Street Market where fishermen and bootleggers in schooners and ketches crammed into the edge of the East River right under the Brooklyn Bridge, gunwale to gunwale, with more sea yarns than a captain's quilt. Beau turned the corner of

West Street and saw the legendary Goulash Kitchen, a boxcar diner crammed with steamed windows and round-top stools where food was scarfed down on crowded wooden counters with calloused hands. He passed the standing railroad freight cars and then walked past the mouth of the Hoboken Ferry terminal where people entered and got swallowed across the river to New Jersey as seagulls circled above diving for scraps. Beau reached into his coat pocket for the map that Ellen Wirth had penned on Biltmore Hotel stationery and headed to the grimy and dense Gansevoort Meatpacking District where men in long white cotton cloaks were busy hanging slaughtered cows: brindled, or black and white, onto meat hooks to be skinned and butchered over waxy fat greased slippery cobblestone streets that stuck to the bottom of everyone's shoes including Beau's. He kept his eye out for Huber & Köhler, lodged somewhere between the tightly packed stalls of red brick and iron awnings, where Artemus Cummins bought his meat and had it shipped to the *Pair-a-Dice* through a deal made with Herr Adolph Köhler, a Bavarian of würst like proportions and thick dünkel brows.

"What deal?" Al had said to Ellen Wirth before Beau had left the hotel.

"When the bill comes in, it's considerably lower and that's because Huber & Köhler gets paid in something else."

"Liquor...?"

"I don't know. But there's always some in our office and quality stuff too."

"Which distilleries does Cummins buy from?"

"Glen Trool is one of late," she said. "The men say that it's the best ever, but Mr. Cummins hates it."

"Why?"

"Because the whole town wants it," she said. "See, it comes off another ship so he has to pay more, and he can only get a certain amount of it. Some claim that Cummins is forced to pay more than anyone else, but I wouldn't know. It's just hear what I hear."

"What about the *Paradise*? Doesn't it bring quality product to shore?"

"Mr. Cummins wishes," she said. "That ship is just a warehousing scheme for product he buys and stores and then drops off on Long Island when needed, but don't ask me where, because that I don't know. Though I have heard it's one of the many potato farms in East Hampton, but then there are so many, who knows which one?"

"Have you tried Glen Trool?"

"No," Ellen Wirth said. "I can only afford strike-you-dead gin. And I prefer American rye whiskey than any of that awful scotch."

"What about Huber & Köhler's speakeasy in the Meatpacking District?"

"When the men come into the office," she said, "they talk about where they've been the night before and the Meatpacking District has been high on their list for the past month."

"Why?"

"It's the new spot," she said. "But nothing stays for long. The men spend the night going from club to club, all over town, to see how business is doing and the next day they talk about all the girls they've had fun with, until the new cycle of speaks and girls appear and disappear."

"And you don't like the talk about girls."

"Should I?"

"Do you like Cummins?" Al said.

"He's all business. But if he wants you, he touches you in a creepy way."

"Has he ever touched you?"

"No."

"Why not? You're a pretty girl."

"He knows he's wasting his time."

"He could pressure you," Al said.

"He could put a gun to my head. It's not going to happen."

"So then why does he keep you? He could get a more amiable girl."

"Because I'm efficient," Ellen Wirth said, "and he prizes that more than anything in a girl, because he needs things done quickly and without error or he could lose a lot of money—or even his life."

"And that's why he picked you for all his errands?"

"Yes," she said, "but don't think I like him."

"Well, if you don't like him, why don't you look for a better job?"

"There *are* no better jobs for women."

Ten o'clock

Taxi cabs, private cars, and limousines were streaming into the Meat District. Beau kept an eye on all the swells who were lining up at the side door with the diamond shaped peekaboo window that abutted Huber & Köhler Meat Purveyors. A tough guy was stationed behind it. Customers who were admitted in were given long white smocks and boater hats so that if a raid went down they could pretend they were butchers. It was all a joke, and everyone knew it. Upstairs, the drinks were listed on the walls next to large illustrations of meat. Rye whiskey was a pastrami and rye. Mixed cocktails for the ladies were called skirt steaks, and a bottle of Champagne was a tenderloin. The waiters wore long white smocks and boaters, and so did the eight-piece dance orchestra, but the main attraction was the brick wall packed with big, framed photos of prized livestock and real cowbells that the customers rang every time they wanted a drink or a steak with more than a little sizzle.

Midnight struck and a steady stream of revelers crowded the Meatpacking District. Many were rejected at the diamond shaped window and many more argued with the tough guy, but to no avail. Then at one o'clock a group of hard looking men got out of a taxicab with something other than partying on their minds. Beau put the Leica A to his eye. *Click.* The men headed through the diamond windowed door. *Click.* Beau waited a half hour wondering if they'd ever come out. When they did, they were led by a man in a top hat, black evening coat, obligatory white scarf, a monocle, and a black cigarette holder. *Click.* A blue Isotta-Fraschini appeared. *Click.* They got into it. *Click.* It drove off. *Click.* Beau hurried down the street to the waiting cabs. He took the first one, showed the hack a ten-dollar bill and told him to follow the sleek Italian hardtop sedan wherever it went.

Twenty minutes later, the Isotta-Fraschini reached the East River piers just north of Grand Street. The city's outline had long changed from its day dress, a cascading topline, to its evening wear, an electrified outline that silhouetted the evening sky. There was a bluntness to the night as ferries and steamboats chugged their way between the black lagoons of jutting wharfs, skeletal masts, stout funnels, monkey islands, deck winches, and cargo derricks. Abaft the waterfront, the city's elevated trains flickered by as lit windows twitched above the roar of the rumble. The West Side piers may have had the Atlantic Ferry, the banana boats, the hunkering Cunarders, the Southern Pacific, the Atlantic Steamship, the Saugerties, the Catskill Evening, and The Royal Mail, but on Grand Street you had the ethnic tributaries of Rivington, Orchard, Eldridge, Hester, Pitt, Ludlow, and Delancey Street all crowded into the Lower East Side: the cuckoo clock of Manhattan.

The hack stopped short of the Grand Street pier where the Isotta-Fraschini had turned in and parked. Beau paid the fare and followed Cummins and his crew on foot as gentlemen in dinner jackets and ladies in splendid lamé dresses and silk patterned opera coats dazzled the nighttime tinsel under the glow of the Williamsburg Bridge: another stone in the city's necklace.

Beau aimed the Leica A at a Packard turning into the pier. *Click.* Then a Ruxton, a Studebaker. *Click.* A Cadillac, Graham-Paige, several Pierce Arrows. *Click.* He found speedboats docked on either side of the pier, six in total. *Click. Click.* They rocked as passing barges sent rippling swells quayside. The speedboats responded by switching on their engines that rumbled a roaring collective pitch of 2,500 horsepower shaking Grand Street all the way down to Yonah Schimmel's Knishery on Houston Street. Beau quickly took cover aside the faded red wharf master's shack in the middle of the pier that glowed from the soft interior lighting. Inside, he could see a trap door that led to the pier's base below. *Click*. Behind the shack were three of the six speedboats where smooth slippers were climbing down long iron ladders attached to the piers. A fall at 30 feet could be deadly. No matter. *Click*. This was the real thing, unlike the landlubber nightclubs with their glammy gimmicks such as Don Dickerman's Pirate's Den over on Christopher Street with its phony gangway by the entrance, where waiters greeted you in goofy tri-corner hats, wearing fake daggers, stuffed parrots on shoulders, and beards attached to ears. Their Semitic-hating eye-patched boss lorded over the shenanigans as if he were Blackbeard himself, but then motoring out to the 12-mile limit in freezing weather wasn't some floor show with a stuffed bird. Your religion mattered none and if a body washed ashore, it made no curtain call.

Beau crossed over to the south side of the dock where the Williamsburg Bridge spanned across Brooklyn and Manhattan. Its tower and main castle posted long fortress shadows into the East River below. Artemus Cummins's speedboat was longer and deeper than the rest. Workers were busy lowering provisions down the wharf master's trap door to the rickety river planks below and then onto the boat. Beau put the Leica A to his eye. *Click*. The wharf master's door opened. *Click*. Artemus Cummins and three men appeared. *Click*. Beau heard bits and pieces that had to do with Glasgow and a freighter named *Remus* that had a whiskey shipment on its way across the Atlantic, and then some talk about real pirates and real guns on the open sea as Artemus Cummins and company climbed down the long iron ladder to his speedboat. *Click*. The fleet shoved off. *Click*. The boats turned around the southern part of Manhattan. *Click*. The blue Isotta-Fraschini pulled out of the pier. *Click*. Beau watched it park several blocks away by the Grand Street Ferry that ran across the East River to South 8th Street in Brooklyn. Its black chauffeur, dressed in livery, entered an all-night diner, once a Pullman train dining car, just off Broome Street. Beau followed him inside. The chauffeur seated himself at the far end of the counter. Beau took a stool beside him and said,

"Guess this here's the colored section."

"It is now," the chauffeur said. "Where're you from, brother?"

"Mississippi Delta," Beau said.

"Long way from home."

"Tell me."

"Lookin' for work?"

"Tryin' to figure out where I am first."

"Lower East Side, brother."

"I got lost in the subway," Beau said.

"Where're you headin'?"

"Harlem."

"You way off, brother, but that's where I'm goin'. Need a lift?"

"Got a motorcar?" Beau said.

"Can't ya see the way I'm dressed?"

"Now that I'm lookin', yeah. You leavin' soon?"

"Not for hours. Man I work for pay me to stick around. Could be four in the mornin', maybe six or eight. Who knows?"

"That's a long time to wait," Beau said.

"Got no choice. Man's out at sea. Can't drop a nickel."

"He a sailor?"

"Hell no. Big shot."

"Seem like you got a good job goin'," Beau said.

"I don't know about good, but soon as I get enough jack I'm gone."

"What's holdin' you up?"

"Ten G's what's holdin' me up."

"Lotta jack to be held up," Beau said.

"Need it for my race car."

"Really…? How much you got so far?"

"Two grand."

"Look like you gonna be workin' a long time," Beau said.

"Well, I got several partners all puttin' their assets together. See, we buildin' us a winner for the comin' season." The chauffeur put out his hand. "Name is Sugar Winslow. Sugar, 'cause I drive sweetly. But don't never look me up in the American Automobile Association."

"You ain't American?" Beau said.

"I ain't white."

"Be glad you ain't," Beau said, "Not a race to be proud of the way they treat people. When's your next event?"

"The 100 Mile contest out at the Indiana State Fairgrounds this August. Gonna get a big crowd—that is, if the Klan don't try 'n bust it up again."

"Well, good luck" Beau said, "but there somethin' like five million Kluxes all over now and most of 'em from Indiana where you headin'."

"I know," Sugar Winslow said. "The head of the Klan's from there and is on his way to jail for fraud and murderin' his girlfriend with poison, if that ain't enough."

"You'd think white folk would disown the Kluxes for that."

"As long as the Klan don't disown nigger hatin', don't make a difference what its leaders do," Sugar Winslow said.

"You're right on that," Beau said. "That foreign vehicle outside. That the one you drive?"

"That she is."

"Boss must be real rich."

"Rich ain't the word," Sugar Winslow said. "He got a swell townhouse over on West 20th Street right off Tenth Avenue fixed up with a lawn jockey and beautiful trees. Then he got this boat where all the real action is." Sugar leaned over. "Can you keep a secret?"

"Who's here for me to tell?"

"Ever been to the West Side docks?"

"Wouldn't know where they is," Beau said.

"Well, the man's Chelsea house is just a stone's throw from Piers 60 and 61."

"That good or bad?"

Sugar Winslow said to his new friend, "You ever hear of the Red Star Line?"

"Can't say I have."

"You have heard of an ocean liner?"

"Sure, but I ain't never been on one," Beau said.

"Well, them limeys on the boats is paid off to deliver whatever whiskey and champagne's left from the trip across the Atlantic right to his truckin' company garage over on Eleventh Avenue, just down the block from him, and you wouldn't believe what it's called."

"What's it called?"

"Milk & Cream," Sugar Winslow said.

"Oh, I get it. This fella what they call a bootlegger."

Sugar Winslow slapped Beau's shoulder and laughed, "Just what in hell're you doin' in New York, brother? Lookin' for a lost cow?"

Now it was Beau's turn to confide. He leaned into Sugar Winslow and said in a low voice, "I'm a policeman lookin' for a killer. That's what I'm doin' here." Sugar Winslow's big smile quickly faded. "And when I find the son of a bitch, he gonna be lookin' at his last day. Now can *you* keep a secret?"

"Who's here for me to tell, brother?"

Beau said, "Son of a bitch tied a sister to a chair up in Harlem, poured gasoline all over her and set her afire."

"I heard about that," Sugar Winslow said.

"You know Officer Bumpus?"

Sugar Winslow could see the nightstick with all the notches. "Sure, everybody know Officer Bumpus."

"Good," Beau said. "He was my partner before I moved up in the department. Now, I want you to tell me the name of that boat where your boss is headed out tonight, or I just may have to speak to the white boys above me and they ain't as friendly to black folk as I am."

"Well... there's two boats."

"I'm listenin'," Beau said.

"The *Paradise* is the tender."

"The other one?"

"Called *Pair-a-Dice* too, but spelled different," Sugar Winslow said.

"You ever been on them boats?"

"Only the smaller one when I drove Mr. Cummins to Florida."

"You mean the one spelled the other way?"

"That's right."

"And this Cummins' fella," Beau said, "he on both boats every night?"

"Maybe once a week on the tender; just about every night on the smaller one, the *Pair-a-Dice.*"

"Tell me about them boats," Beau said.

"Well, the smaller one used to be a millionaire's steam yacht."

"What is it now?"

"Still a steam yacht," Sugar Winslow said. "Once belonged to some commodore fella, but since then been refurbished with gamblin' tables, beautiful dinin' area, and real nice rooms. See, Mr. Cummins bought it at a federal auction for nothin' when the Coast Guard hauled it in for contraband, then he turned it into what it is today. Coast Guard can't touch it now 'cause it sittin' outside the 12-mile limit."

"What are those nice rooms in the *Pair-a-Dice* used for?"

"Well," Sugar Winslow said, "man pays enough gets a girl."

"What about the big ship? One spelled the other way."

"That's a tender," Sugar Winslow said. "Sits out there all year round. Waits for a ship to come in from England to get stocked up."

"What's the name of the ship from England that does all the stockin' up?"

"The *Remus* is the one on the way this time around. Should be steamin' in any day."

"You mean the one got problem with pirates?"

"Well, they all got that problem with pirates," Sugar Winslow said. "...How'd you know about that?"

"My job to know them things. Now what else can you tell me about the 12-mile limit?"

"Ever hear of the Gray Ghost?"

"The who?"

"The Gray Ghost," Sugar Winslow said.

"What about it?"

"His gang hits hard and fast and kills all aboard," Sugar Winslow said.

"He a pirate?"

"He a lot of things."

"Steals boats?"

"Do whatever he want," Sugar Winslow said, "and nobody know who the Gray Ghost is except my boss and they at odds with each other. See, the Gray Ghost got many ships and Mr. Cummins, he only got one and it's just half the size of any of the Ghost's."

"You mean the Gray Ghost is a pirate and also a ship owner?"

"I'll tell you what he is," Sugar Winslow said. "He's so fearsome they got him to be ten feet tall."

"You know his real name?"

"I just told you: Gray Ghost. Ain't no other name," Sugar Winslow said.

"Why they call him that?"

"You're talkin' sea lore, brother. It's a different world out there in that damn ocean. But you mention Gray Ghost to a seaman, and he get a look in his eye like a cottonmouth viper crawlin' up his leg."

"Whaddya mean different world out there?" Beau said.

"Some say the Gray Ghost is a dead sailor with revenge against the pirate who killed him. That's what happen if he been murdered. He haunt the ship and you know it when you see the albatross fly over because that's him. Other folk say they seen the Gray Ghost when the clouds part and he come out instead of the sun, and then there some say he the biggest, baddest bootlegger in the world who don't like any kinda competition, but whatever he is don't be where he is, 'cause you won't be there for long."

"You know anybody who seen this Gray Ghost?"

"Only people is Louie Four-Stacks and Mr. Cummins," Sugar Winslow said, "but they don't say nothin'."

"Louie who?"

"Eye-talian boy grew up in a Long Island fishin' village and he know the ocean better than a fish." Sugar Winslow leaned into Beau and said, "He the kinda fella laughin' when everybody else is cryin'."

"Does Cummins got anymore boats than the two out there already?"

"Like I said, just the one tender and the steam yacht, but the Gray Ghost he got four, sometime six, huge freighters parked outside the 12-mile limit and each one got a flower on the prow and when pirates see that flower, they all get scared, 'cause when the weather gets iffy the Gray Ghost gets itchy. But he got the cleanest whiskey on the market and if you get a bottle with the flower on it, then it like you won the grand prize, but then there's gangs try'n to copy that flower, but to their own no good."

"Whaddya mean?"

"Well," Sugar Winslow said, "there was this well-known gang did just that and they was all found dead in their lookout house on the Jersey shore. Somehow the Coast Guard got information on them and so did the Gray Ghost at the same time. Some say it was a radio done 'em in. Louie Four-Stacks says there's a spy in the water, so nobody uses their transmitters no more, see, but even so, bodies still keep rollin' up to shore bloated up that scare the bejesus outta townsfolk up and down the coast of Long Island and my boss don't want 'em scared or they won't swamp no more. But worst of all is the curses and ain't no one can do a thing about 'em."

"Curses?"

"Sea goin' curses," Sugar Winslow said.

"You mean like when you hear the Screechin' Owl?"

"Oh…you know that one?"

"I'm a country boy, Sugar. Ain't an owl, bug, snake I don't know its pappy.

"Well, seamen ain't no different and just listenin' to one give ya the willies every time, 'cause it's a spooky world out there in that damn ocean."

"Then why do men go out to sea if all they get is trouble?"

"Man needs a job," Sugar Winslow said. "That's why. Like I need this here job."

"What about the *Remus*?"

"Like I said, the *Remus* ain't in yet, but it's due any day and the gang I work for can't wait 'cause they is short and dry."

"What about all their liquor dumps on Long Island? They dry too?"

"Bone dry," Sugar Winslow said.

"You know the locations?"

Sugar Winslow shrugged the way a man does who's been deaf all his life and can't hear what's being said. "I just drive where I'm told. You tell your Chief of Police that I ain't got nothin' to do with illegal activates. All I do is drive that Eye-talian sedan around to earn a livin', so I ain't guilty of nothin' but survival and I got me a driver's license so he can't go after me for not ownin' one."

"I'll let him know," Beau said. "You ever hear of Ed Goulson?"

"Sure—who hasn't?"

"Tell me what this Cummins fella had on Ed Goulson."

"That Goulson fella's dead."

"I know he is. What got between 'em?"

"Someone is what got between 'em," Sugar Winslow said.

"A woman?"

"No," Sugar Winslow said, turning to where the ocean would be. "Them boats with the flowers is what got between 'em. See Goulson bought all his booze from Mr. Cummins. Then he went with the Gray Ghost and everybody else followed, because what Goulson does the world does—or *did*; so, my boss had to put a stop to it, because it was puttin' a big dent in his business."

"You mean he killed Goulson," Beau said.

"You said it. I didn't."

"You seem to know a lot, Sugar."

"I hear everythin' in the front seat."

"Ain't there no partition?"

"In the limousine model there is. But that model ain't as nimble as this one."

Beau put twenty dollars on the counter. "Leave me a number where I can get a hold of you."

Sugar Winslow picked up the small fortune and wrote down his number.

"You'll be hearin' from me," Beau said, stepping out into the cold night air that blew of sea brine and far-off places. He made his way down the dark grimy streets toward the right-hand drive Isotta-Fraschini. Beau tried the doors, but they were all locked. Then he felt a tap on his shoulder. Sugar Winslow said, "Had a feelin' you wasn't done." He opened the driver's door and removed the papers from a leather pouch that was part of the interior door cover. Each paper was a map and a list of drop-off locations on Long Island for smuggling liquor. "You got a pencil and paper on you?"

"I do," Beau said.

"Go over to the ferry terminal and sit under the lights. When you done, come back here."

"You stickin' your neck out, brother," Beau said.

"Maybe, but I work for the man five days a week. Other two days I spend on my car for the upcomin' race. I come back to work one Monday and Sal Montero's bitchin' about this white boy been fillin' in for me on my days off. Turns out the white boy was gettin' twice what I was gettin'. That hurt. *Really* hurt. I coulda had my race car done in half the time and not be standin' here waitin' all night long....so, you go do wuch'ya gotta do then come back with them papers."

"...What was the name of this boy?"

"Gideon, I believe, and he quit 'cause he said he wasn't gettin' paid enough."

Beau put a 100-dollar bill in Sugar Winslow's hand. The look on his face would last the night. Beau then took the maps to the ferry terminal where offshore ship bells sounded out the hour. He then spread the maps out under a lamp light, took out the Leica A, and got to work.

46

Like a Genie

The New York Evening Graphic took up the whole fourth floor of 25 City Hall Place in downtown Manhattan. Its lumbering freight elevator got started by yanking a leather strap and then pulling a wire rope for it to stop, and if it didn't, well, it plunged to the basement with you in it.

Stepping out of the elevator you entered a firing squad of pre-tempered steel typewriters whose little bells constantly rang as the carriages were reset. Reporters constantly slammed doors and hurried from one flashpoint to the next. Oxygen was rare. Chain smoking a sport. Cigar smoking a bout. The sweat and grime from the composing room, down below, made a man thin in no time, plus it was thick with carcinogenic printing ink and columns of lead piled high against Linotype machines that punched out the news, which was then stacked and tossed into trucks that took off like a hook and ladder battalion. The headlines were all Category 5: *WHAT IS AN AMERICAN?; CLEAN BOOKS BILL; WHITE CARGO; I LIKE TO MAKE MY HUSBAND JEALOUS; DOUBLE LOVE DOUBLE MURDER; KIDNAPPED HEIRESS* followed by glamourpusses, cheating wives, purity hounds, dumbbells who got rich, gang-queen dope outfits, or priests and banks who financed rum rings. The paper's one and only goal was circulation and most of it was high blood pressure.

The publisher of this bingo basket was Bernarr MacFadden. His real first name was Bernard, but when it had been accidently misspelled by a typo he kept the double "r" because it sounded manlier when rolled off the tongue. He even stretched "Mc" into "Mac" to complete the metamorphosis—but those were his minor peculiarities. He was a bona fide crackpot whose notions of fitness included hiking barefoot, every morning, from his home in Westchester, all the way to his Manhattan offices at 1926 Broadway, which meant walking over miles and miles of cement, dirt roads, and a lot of thorny litter, but his real obsession was smearing the medical profession and ridding it of inoculation. His cure for all diseases was fasting, which had some merit. He claimed that exercising in the nude, in extreme weather, would reinvigorate the humors and doing it in the snow, stripped down, stimulated the glands, and cleansed you of biotic imbalances regardless of what saw you: bear or housewife.

Despite these quirks, he knew the publishing business, and as soon as he got wind of the story about the fancy yacht out on the 12- mile limit, he hurried downtown to tell his managing editor to hire Zola away from *The New Yorker* and pay her double because of the story that she, or really Al, had written about Artemus Cummins. Emile Gauvreau, the Managing Editor, didn't want any of it, and since he couldn't chain smoke any faster, he put two cigarettes in his mouth and double puffed as he said in Brooklynese, "But they'll moider us all!"

Bernarr MacFadden disagreed, "What we have here, Mr. Gauvreau, is a gold mine. *You* can only see the darkness in the shafts. The toil of men stripped down to their waists. The long hours of dimly lit tunnels and the fear of cave-ins and suffocation. There is gold at the end of this tunnel that will shine light on vice and indecency. Our readers will rise up against this Artemus Cummins and all criminals as circulation increases." Bernarr MacFadden turned to Al and Zola, who were sitting near Emile Gauvreau, and said, "Artemus Cummins burned to death a poor young beautiful white girl and every citizen will be enraged if it's the last thing I do."

Emile Gauvreau interrupted his boss. "The girl he burned alive was colored and we already mentioned her on page 16."

"That's a different girl. We'll do a composograph of the murder with flames rising into the air and we'll print captions galore of her shrieks for help—get that stenographer Miss Dingley, the one with bleached blonde hair, to be Miss Knight."

"We could also make Miss Dingley colored if you'd like."

"You'll do as I say, Mr. Gauvreau, or I'll get Miss Nicholas to take your post as Managing Editor right now. I want Miss Dingley dressed up in a dance outfit with a four-foot-high Ziegfeld Follies feather headdress and a banner headline: *CUMMINS'S FOLLIES.*"

"You mean you want her naked in the center spread."

"With taste! Always with taste!"

"Yeah, but the Post Office censor won't like it one bit, Mr. MacFadden."

"We'll pay him off."

"He says he can't be bought."

"He's negotiating. Give him *more* money," the great publisher yelled, showing a row of teeth fortified by a strict vegetarian diet with a lot of cracked wheat. "Now, about this contest." Suddenly the building shook as the printing presses started the evening run. "We'll offer 10,000 dollars for the negatives that Cummins is withholding for blackmail to be brought to your desk and, upon verification of said amount, it'll be dispensed to the qualified person."

"Why not bring it to your desk?" Emile Gauvreau said.

"Because *you* are Managing Editor, Mr. Gauvreau, not I." Bernarr MacFadden turned to Al. "You do have a photo of this Cummins fella?"

"I'll have one for you later, sir."

"Better yet, make two composographs, Mr. Gauvreau."

"What's the second gonna be? Colored?"

"You have no imagination," Bernarr MacFadden said to his managing editor. "The second composograph will be of Artemus Cummins pushing a beautiful white girl off the observation tower of the Woolworth Building. I want her dressed only in a silk teddy with her arms flailing and next to that I want an insert photo of her parents watching her falling to her grisly death. You can photograph Mr. Beasley from accounting and Mrs. Grimes, our Home Editor, as her parents watching in horror." Mr. Beasley and Mrs. Grimes were sitting in the corner couch and now looking at each other. "And I want this done *every* day until the whole town is seething with hatred for this Cummins beast."

"Yeah, but no girl nor anyone, for that matter, has ever been pushed off the Woolworth Building," Emil Gauvreau said. "Don't you think we're going a bit too far with that, Mr. MacFadden?"

"Not as far as the girl going out the window is!"

"But, sir, you're stretching the truth."

"Mr. Gauvreau—we're stretching the image *not* the truth."

"Yeah, but there's a difference between stretching it and making it up altogether."

Bernarr MacFadden approached his managing editor like a vulture diving in on a corpse.

"Mr. Gauvreau, how can you make up the truth?"

"Oh, it's very easy. We do it all the time and no one gives a damn."

"I don't care. You'll do as I say, or you're fired."

"—Yessir."

"Good," Bernarr MacFadden said, closing in on himself and looking tragically absent as he spoke in the poetic octave. "I am just a small, weak man under the broad umbrella of stars that shine upon this tiny earth. And as thoughts come and go, so do the people who think them." He took off his shoes and socks and headed to the door. "I must take leave now," he said. "For it is a long walk to Westchester. A pleasure to meet you, Mr. Nachman, and don't forget my little offer, Miss Nicholas." He departed the building like a genie.

Emile Gauvreau, waited, then said to Al and Zola, "I told ya he was nuts."

47

The Darkroom

A red soft glow filled the darkroom that Al had rented at Phil Levine's Lab just off Broadway. The "red light" had only one purpose and that was to keep photographic paper from getting exposed. "You'll get used to it in a second," Al said to Beau, as he removed his suit jacket and tucked his tie into his shirt. Al placed several strips of developed 35mm film, which Beau had shot downtown, onto a sheet of Kodak Velox 6.5 x 8.5 photographic paper and secured it inside a wooden contact- sheet printing frame. Al moved it under the enlarger and adjusted the f/stop on the lens that was attached to an adjustable head. He switched on the enlarger bulb, housed over the lens, and exposed the photographic paper for nine seconds. He did it with two other rolls. Then he put the exposed contact sheets into the first tray, the developer liquid, that sat in a long deep sink. He waited for images on the sheet to come up. Then he put the sheet into the second tray, the stop-bath, and then the fixer tray and lastly into the washer before pulling them out wet. Frame by frame, Al followed the path of Beau's journey from the Meatpacking District to the Grand Street Pier, the wharf master's shack with its trap stairway, the six speedboats waiting in the East River, the climbing down the steep vertical iron ladders, the speedboats taking off, and then the maps Sugar Winslow had given Beau that revealed every drop-off point of Artemus Cummins's bootlegging operation on Long Island. There was a knock on the door. Al secured the unexposed paper.

Gideon entered. The door was relocked. Al fitted a 35mm negative strip into the negative plate holder and exposed it. He removed the photographic paper from the easel and into the developer tray. They huddled over it and watched the paper turn from white to real.

Gideon immediately recognized the location and said, "That's the Meatpacking District downtown on Gansevoort Street. The stocky guy is Sal Montero, the last one leaving the speakeasy."

"The tough looking guy?"

"Yeah," Gideon said, "and he's been practicing that look ever since he wanted to be somebody." Gideon pointed to the tall man with the monocle and the black cigarette holder, the first one out the door, "That's Artemus Cummins."

Al pulled the photograph out of the developer tray, stopped it, fixed it, and then set it in the wash tray.

Al said to Gideon, "You never told me how you got mixed up with these people."

Gideon said, "Our stable master's kid worked as a swamper so he got me a job out on Long Island."

"Why?"

"To learn how to become a bootlegger," Gideon said.

"Where out on Long Island?"

"Sag Harbor, north of East Hampton."

"Why all the way out there?"

"It's a deep port town and my family has an estate in East Hampton, which isn't far away."

"So, your parents decided you needed a job hauling in booze instead of sailing all summer?"

"They didn't decide anything," Gideon said.

"How did you end up working for Cummins's gang?" Al said. "Because he knew me from the society columns in all the magazines and newspapers. He figured he could get his gang access into all the right social clubs through me. So, I made a deal. I would become his face and get paid to make connections and, in return, get quality liquor to sell."

"Why aren't you still working for Cummins?"

"Because they started using me for other things, which I didn't like," Gideon said, "and then Sal Montero and I had a little spat."

"What can you tell me about Artemus Cummins?"

"He's losing the liquor war."

"How so?"

"He's getting squeezed out."

"By whom?"

"By someone way smarter," Gideon said. "That's why Cummins killed Ed Goulson to send a message, but it backfired. Then this morning they found a safecracker named Smith floating in the Hudson."

"*John* Smith?"

"Yeah," Gideon said.

"Did you know him?"

"Yeah. Recently took him to Penn Station."

"Why?"

"He had a job to do down South," Gideon said.

"What job?"

"I don't know, but they were having an argument about money."

"Smith and Cummins?"

"Yeah," Gideon said. "See, Cummins is in trouble."

"How so?"

Gideon said, "His days are over, and Smith knew it."

"And the money argument?"

"Smith wanted his money before something happened to Cummins," Gideon said.

"What do you mean?"

"There's a new man in town" Gideon said, "No one knows who he is, and he operates like no one else."

"How so?"

"He's very deadly, but without all the gang drama," Gideon said, "The thugs aren't used to that, so it scares the hell out of them."

"How much money was involved between Smith and Cummins?"

"Smith said that he was owed 25 grand from a jewel heist that he did for Cummins on Canal Street. Cummins told him that 30% cash under premium was the maximum paid out to anyone. Then Cummins goes and lies to Smith and tells him that if he fulfills his assignment, he'll get the money."

"What was the assignment?"

"I don't know," Gideon said. "But Smith's train was heading south."

"How do you know Cummins lied to Smith?"

"Because," Gideon said, "when we drove out of Penn Station, Cummins was laughing so hard I had to ask him why and he said that the best jokes are the ones no one tells and the lies no one knows. But the real joke was on him. As Smith said, Cummins's days are numbered."

Al placed another 35mm film strip in the negative holder. He exposed the paper, removed it from the easel, and then set it into the developer tray. Gideon leaned over and watched the image come up.

"Something wrong?" Al said.

Yeah. Gideon's father was in one of the speedboats and the woman he was kissing wasn't his wife.

48

It's No Secret

The *Remus*, eight days out of Glasgow, carried 25,000 thousand cases of whiskey that set the freighter deep into the water off Long Island. Speedboats looking for product quickly took notice but were waved off. Captain Hamish Smyth, of the *Remus*, left the bridge and entered the navigation room where First Mate Edwin Leeds was marking two intersecting lines on the nautical chart: one off Patchogue, Long Island, and the other off Montauk. The cross point was where the tender *Paradise* should have been. First mate Leeds moved the parallel ruler and drew another line. He said, "Had the *Paradise* drifted, it would have been over here, but it's not."

Captain Smyth said, "The Coast Guard checked our registry when we entered Montauk, so it's no secret that we've arrived."

"Well captain, until we get transmission that the *Paradise* has moved location, we might have to consider remaining here."

"Have you heard from Sparks?"

"Yessir, I told him to stay in the Radio Room until we get word."

Captain Smyth heard another group of speedboats approaching. "Wave them off, Leeds."

But they kept on coming.

49

Slugs

The Milk & Cream garage on 20th Street and 10th Avenue was just south of the elevated West Side freight line and Pier 61 where the English Red Star Line berthed on the Hudson River. The garage manager, Thom Burke, made his way through the rows of white trucks and lubricating oil that smothered the air. He checked the red crates with bottles painted white up to the neck—the white crates held real milk. One of the drivers approached him and said, "Most of the reds are still empty, Thom. What do I tell our customers?"

"You just deliver what's there," Thom Burke said. "Anybody asks you where their order is, you tell 'em it's on the way, and if they say they're gonna go somewhere else, tell 'em it's winter and that the seas are rough, and ships sink."

Thom Burke returned to his office in the back of the garage where spare parts and rows of Fisk tires were lined up against a long red brick wall. Inside the office, a big insurance company calendar hung on the wall with cross marks on dates passed. One of the two full-time mechanics stepped into the office and said to Thom Burke, "Look what I found in trucks 16 and 15." The mechanic held out a handful of .45 slugs. "Same what I found in trucks 20, 21, and 22 that cover Midtown where the best speaks are."

Thom Burke took the slugs and let them roll in his hand. It was the fourth day in a row that trucks came back shot up. He sat down behind his desk and reached for the dispatcher book and looked up the names of the drivers who covered each neighborhood. Then he picked up the telephone and dialed the Chelsea exchange and waited. A voice soon came on the line. Thom Burke said, "That little Midtown problem hasn't stopped. We got deliveries this afternoon. What do I do?"

"What happened now?"

"More slugs," Thom Burke said, "and I got trucks sitting here empty of reds. We need product, Artemus."

"How many trucks got shot up?"

"Five. What about the *Remus* from Glasgow?"

"There was bad weather, so it sailed in late. You been showing anyone your dispatcher book?"

"I got it hidden," said Thom Burke.

"I hope so, because whoever's doing this to our trucks wants that book."

Thom Burke said, "I told you there'd be revenge for killing Goulson."

"I own Midtown, Thom, and if I have to make a point of it, I'll do it again. You keep that book locked up."

"Fine, but what do I tell our customers?"

"Thom...did you hear what I just said?"

"I always hear you, Artemus."

"Then stop feeling the customer's pain. Make them feel *your* pain."

"Yeah, Artemus, but there's a lot of thirsty people out there and we're always short of product. Where's the *Remus* now?"

"It's in, Thom. How many times I have to say it's in? You wanna ask me again?"

"No, but you've got to get a bigger supplier, because people are now turning away from us; some are not even picking up the phone."

"You mean the nightclubs?"

"You can't kill any more people, Artemus. You gotta do something other than killing people. Maybe talk to 'em."

"You don't talk to people, Thom. You give them a choice and there's only one choice. This is not an election. It's a business."

"You mean racket."

"Whatever. You tell everybody the ship is here and the product is so good they'll pay more for it. You tell them that, Thom. You always do the talking. They do the listening. You learn from me, Thom, and you'll do alright in this world. So far, you're not doing alright. You're always calling and complaining. I just may have to fire you." The line went dead.

Thom Burke then looked up from the telephone. Two unfamiliar men had entered his office. They stood before his desk in long overcoats and black Stetson derbies—the same kind Ed Goulson had worn. They told Thom Burke to stand up. They told Thom Burke to give them the dispatcher book. Thom Burke said that his boss would get angry if he did that. The men looked at each other. Then they emptied their pistols. Thom Burke hit the floor hard. The killers pulled the dispatcher book out of his hands. Thom Burke reached for it, but the unfinished business of dying reached him first. The killers walked out. The mechanics and drivers were hiding behind the milk trucks and listening to what they couldn't see and waiting for what they didn't know. Then the phone rang. It rang and it rang.

50

Doing God's Work

The tabloids headlined with *MURDER ON MILK ROW*, but the serious broadsheets took up the cause of a single stock plunge: Soling Consolidated General. One financial ace wrote that its newly patented generators had always been worthless—he had forgotten to write about that before the plunge. A rabbit eyed bald banker, who looked like the class squealer, said that his bank had been doing God's work when it had issued the worthless securities and, therefore, he had no blame. Then there were the wiseacres who had the nerve to suggest that the whole mess was the result of the banking industry's successful resistance to financial legislation after the Panic of 1910-11 that had left everyone running to the hills, but that was nonsense—ask any banker.

Virginia hurried into Shelby's bedroom and said, "I spoke to that lawyer." She shook Shelby in her bed. "Hey, it's time to get up, girlie. Celeste Brush is downstairs honking her horn so loudly they can hear it in the Bronx."

Shelby rubbed her groggy eyes. "What time is it?"

"Almost noon."

"What did that lawyer say?" Shelby said.

"Said he'll get the paperwork done by the end of the day and then my apartment will be legally yours. He just wants the check sent over now."

"Good." Shelby went back to sleep.

"For you, Miss Bubble Bath. Not for me. It means I'm going to have to do a lot of shows no one in their right mind would do."

"Well, you're still living here as before," Shelby yawned. "It's not as if I'm throwing you out on the street."

"Yeah, but somehow it reminds me of when I got kicked out of my room on the Pelican midnight sleeper last December. Now *get* up and write that check," Virginia said, ripping off the bedcovers.

Gideon entered.

"*Turn* around," Shelby said, getting out of bed naked.

"I didn't know you were—"

"*Turn* around."

He did.

Virginia on her way out said, "I'll leave you two high-hats alone. But don't forget that check," and was gone.

Caitlin entered wearing her black dress, white apron, and white doily head cover. She looked as if she had lost the baby. "I'm sorry, Miss," staring at her buck-naked mistress, "but you said to send him in."

"I said to send him into the living room *not* my bedroom."

"It won't happen again, miss. Please forgive me, and Miss Brush called again from the lobby."

"Tell her I'm on my way out the door."

Caitlin quickly left the bedroom.

Shelby said to Gideon, who was facing the wall, "Don't move your head until I say so."

"Celeste Brush is downstairs?"

"Yes."

"How do you know Celeste Brush?"

"I've known her longer than you have," Shelby said, heading to the bathroom. Stepping into the shower.

"Yeah, but you're from Mississippi. How would you know her?"

Shelby turned the water on and shouted, "Marbury Brush and my father went to college together."

"Who else do you know in this town?"

"None of your business," Shelby yelled, rinsing herself off, grabbing a towel, leaving the bathroom, pulling dresses, skirts, teddies, and tops from her huge closets, and putting them on her bed along with an assortment of shoes to mix and match.

"You *just* turned your head," Shelby said, reaching into another closet.

"It's not easy looking at the wall."

"No one's forcing you to stay."

"You told me to come up for lunch last night," Gideon said.

"I never said anything of the sort."

"We had drinks at the bar downstairs and you—"

"*And* I told you that I had to get up early, but you don't listen."

"You said come over for lunch. I had to be listening to hear that."

"Not if you're making it up."

"I'm not making anything up," Gideon said. "And why're you getting up so late if you had to go to bed so early?"

"I get up when I damn please." Shelby said, thinking about her appointment with Celeste, because there was nothing worse than joining a group of friends dressed the wrong way. Shelby dropped her towel and brought out more blouses and stockings of different designs and put them on her bed. Gideon heard the softness of her bare feet touching the floor, her quickness undeterred by whatever he was feeling. She slipped her arms through the straps of one of the silk teddies. She went into another closet and came out with a Chanel belted black skirt that she matched with a black cashmere sweater. She put her tennis gear in a leather grip and closed it.

"Are you done?" Gideon said.

"You don't ask a girl when she's done. She's done when she's done. Your job is to wait."

"I didn't know that."

"You do now," Shelby said.

Gideon heard the silky rub of stockings getting pulled up her legs. The taut snap of garters. The tug of her skirt. Sweater over shoulder. The muffled noise feet make when slipping into brand new shoes. The brushing of hair. The mist of perfume. And the striking of a matchstick. Shelby picked up the house phone. "*Caitlin*—I need you in my bedroom right now." Then Shelby said to Gideon. "Turn around." She reached for her lipstick and compact and put them in her clutch bag. "Last night out at sea, you weren't distracted by all the little sexual insecurities boys at your age suffer. You were fearless and it wasn't some stupid act to show a girl how manly you are. I want you to be that person all the time. Not the fool who thinks he's cute walking in on a girl stark naked. I'm sick of stupid sexed up boys." Shelby picked up her tennis gear and headed to the door.

Gideon stood in her way. "I *wasn't* trying to be cute."

"You want to see me naked? You can see me naked anytime you want. Just call up. Sit over *there*. I'll put on a show for you."

"I don't want any show," Gideon said.

"Then what do you want?"

"You, I thought."

"Because we kissed last night?"

"I've never kissed a girl like that before."

"Then you need practice," Shelby said.

"I'm ready for it any time you are," he said, approaching her.

Shelby stepped back, "Not so fast, young man."

"Celeste can wait another minute."

"You'll have to wait even more," Shelby said, feeling his hands on her and the grip that comes before the kiss.

Gideon said, "You and I have something in common and you know it."

"Then you don't understand," she said, turning away from him.

"What don't I understand."

"Life is complicated," she said.

"Why can't you look at me?"

"Last night was last night."

"And today is just a few hours later."

"It's another day," Shelby said.

"Every day's another day."

"I never invited you up here."

"What happened since I saw you last night?"

"Nothing," she said.

"I don't believe it."

"Then get it through your head that last night was last night," Shelby said.

"I'm still the same person."

"No. You left him on your boat, and I left her outside my door."

Caitlin then entered with several newspapers and said to Shelby, "Beau was reading them this morning, miss. That's why I couldn't find them."

"Well, at least someone around here reads," Shelby said, taking them and reading the headlines about the tanking of Soling Consolidated General.

Caitlin pulled the sheets off the bed and said, "Miss Brush called again from the lobby, miss."

"Did you tell her that I was out the door?" Shelby said, going through each newspaper.

"Yes, miss," Caitlin said. "I told her you were on your way."

"I told you to tell her that I was out the door *not* on my way.

"I'm sorry miss. I won't make that mistake again." Caitlin pulled out a black sock from the sheets. Gideon fixed his eyes on it. He was sure it was a man's sock.

Shelby looked up from a newspaper. "Seems a bootlegger's speedboat flipped over in the ocean."

"What about it?" Gideon said, his eye still on the sock.

"Five men drowned," Shelby said, handing him the newspapers and heading out the bedroom door.

Gideon waited then whispered to Caitlin, "Who else slept here last night?"

Caitlin puffed the pillows. "Why Mr. Remley, shame on you for even asking."

51

A One Step Ladder

Sugar Winslow pointed to the cracked window high above the old horse stalls where hay was once lowered from a long pulley. He said to Beau, "See the crack in the window up where the hay pulley is? Thieves was tryin' to get in last night."

"That's pretty high up," Beau said, turning back to the bright yellow race car up on blocks.

"High or not, they gonna be back again," Sugar Winslow said, holding up his big wrench to show what he would do to anyone who tried to steal his race car.

"I guess people really want it iffen they willin' to risk breakin' their neck to come down from all the way up there," Beau said.

"Word is long out, all over Harlem, how I spent money 'n time and there's folks see it as work done for them. They got a thing or two comin' if that's their frame 'a mind."

Beau lifted up the cowl and looked under the hood of the race car.

"You know somethin' about engines, Beau?"

"Well, before I come up here, I was a bellhop and driver for the hotel back home. Did all the work on the engine and everythin' else. Got so good there was no place for them to put me."

"Whaddya mean no place to put you?"

"Only so far a brother can go up a one step ladder. So, I got on the train—I mean come up here on the train that is." Beau stepped around the race car. "How far you got to go before you be ready for the big race?"

"Maybe longer than I thought."

"Somethin' happened?" Beau said.

"My one big investor pulled out all his jack this mornin' and set me so far back that I won't make the race this summer unless I get another source of money fast. Otherwise, I'm just playin' with this here wrench pretendin' I'm goin' somewhere and I'm damn tired of goin' nowhere…I don't know how much longer I can take it, Beau. Sometimes I get crazy thoughts in my head that no man should."

"Then just remember good days will come and go, and bad ones will seem to last forever, but the courage to keep on goin' is all that matters in life—and where you go afterwards."

"I hear you, Beau. I hear you. But it's still hard."

"I know it is. You ain't the only one. Now, what about this job you went and arranged for me?"

"Well, they always needin' waiters on the *Pair-a-Dice*. And since you an undercover man, might be a place for you to poke your nose."

"You mean that steam yacht out beyond the 12-mile limit?"

"Yeah, not the tender. That's the *Paradise*," Sugar Winslow said, reaching into his pocket, taking out a card. "This is why I asked you to come here. Show this to the man on the Grand Street Pier and he'll put you on the boat. But it could be a month before you ever see land again. They work you to the bone and pay you nothin' and there ain't no doctor out there should you take sick. They got a cure, but you don't want it. And anybody gets outta line ends up swimmin' with the fish." Sugar Winslow slid back under the racecar with his long wrench. Beau put the card away and headed downtown.

52

Five-Legged Horse

District Attorney Emory Buckner welcomed the Mississippi lawyer into his office. "Mr. Nachman, I've heard good things about your work as district attorney."

Al took the seat across from Emory Buckner's desk and said, "Thank you, sir. I think no matter where you work it's a challenge. Each district has problems unique to its geography, industry, culture, as well as its history."

"I completely, agree," Emory Buckner said. "Now what's this idea you mentioned on the telephone?"

"Well, sir, you know as well I that the reason Prohibition is so difficult to implement is that the government won't allocate funds for enforcement. There are only 2,500 agents to cover the whole nation and that's like trying to spread a stick of butter from New York to California. Then there's that other problem of national resistance getting stronger by the day, and with it the rise of collateral crime. The targeted murder of Ed Goulson, and the payback killing at the Milk & Cream garage in Chelsea yesterday, are just the latest toll."

"…What are you suggesting, Mr. Nachman?"

"That a war has been started in this town and a calling card has been left."

"Calling card…?"

"A derby," Al said.

"A *derby?*"

"Yes. The Goulson derby is seen as a sign of resistance against Artemus Cummins. Two gunmen wore them when they killed Thom Burke."

"What has that got to do with what we spoke about on the phone?"

"Well, sir," Al said, "it concerns the documents that have all of Cummins's drop-off points, which include inlets, coves, beaches, and ports that he uses to bring contraband ashore including several potato farms in East Hampton, and since there are so many potato farms out there it would be hard to find his without a map. I also have truck routes and other information that in the right hands could have a devastating effect on his operation."

"I'd like to have those documents as soon as possible."

"There's a problem, Mr. Buckner."

"What problem?"

"The only way for these maps to have any effect on Cummins's operation is to coordinate a strategic plan that pounces on him all at once. You can't have agents picking off trucks and swampers here and there as has been done in the past, because you'll only continue the war of attrition that has no end in sight. The government, in my opinion, must step up to an operational level—but then that would bring another problem."

"What?"

Al said, "A strategic effort might cause untold civilian deaths, meaning those men and women known as swampers who, for highly desired compensation, hire themselves out to bring liquor to shore and to its final destination. Should the government come down too hard and inadvertently kill these civilians, the criminals will come out as victims and the government as the perpetrator."

"You're suggesting we do nothing then, Mr. Nachman?"

"I'm suggesting we give it to a third party."

"Which third party?"

"Mr. Buckner, I want to put these documents into the hands of criminals who can't wait to take Cummins down. They'll finish him off then they'll kill each other over the spoils."

"And then we'll be back where we started."

"Yes, Mr. Buckner, but politically, when the public has had enough of them killing each other, the government can then step in and be the white knight—as long it doesn't overplay its hand."

"Well, I like your first idea, but it's politically impossible, because the government has no desire to employ an operational offensive, but I would still like those documents. They could be the backbone of a trial against Cummins and his thugs."

"Sir, if you don't mind my saying, by the time you get Cummins into court it'll be years down the road and by then the documents could be worthless."

"I'll take that chance, Mr. Nachman. But we're not going to war, and I don't want this information in the hands of criminals."

"So, you're just hoping for a conviction?"

"Mr. Nachman, you have to understand the situation that I'm in. The Volstead Act, from the outset, has always been morally complicated. One of the unforeseen effects of it are overcrowded courtrooms with cases backlisted for years. Our rate of prosecution is stymied by this factor alone."

"What did you mean by morally complicated?"

Emory Buckner said, "I mean that the argument for Prohibition is specious. There has never been a legitimate case made that prior to Prohibition the United States had been drunk in the trough and heading for ruination and that corrective legislation was needed to save the country. If you look at national productivity and technological advancement over the past fifty years, the numbers are off the charts. U.S. exports in 1870 were 392 million dollars and by 1900, they were up to 1.4 billion dollars, proving that our economy was on the way to take over world production a generation ago, and yet, despite these hard facts, the Anti-Saloon League deliberately created its own distorted reality and supported it with deliberate lies that liquor was ruining the American family without any evidence whatsoever. Congress might just as well have passed legislation that five legged horses were needed to keep blacksmiths in business. But then we're not dealing with logic here, arc we, Mr. Nachman? Just the mindless brutality of people incapable of seeing anything other than their own petty grievances and puerile self-interests."

"I agree, but if your thoughts about the Volstead Act should ever be made public, they'll come back to haunt you."

"Mr. Nachman—frustration spoke, not I."

Al rose from his chair. "Well, thank you for your time, sir. And mum's the word about what we just said."

Al left the district attorney's office. He found the first telephone and called Gideon. "Ten o'clock, tonight, as planned…"

53

Yonder Home

The Will O' The Wisp tearoom was a clapboard house in Greenwich Village's Sheridan Square, built in the early 1800s, that had napped through time and had lost its original shape, but it remained unsullied by the lie that newness is an everlasting aesthetic. It was accessed through a slim narrow path that wound through an old courtyard. The matron of the tearoom, Kitty Morton, greeted you at the tearoom's Dutch door. Her long lavish hair was outdated, but she said that she hid a bob underneath. There was nothing stiff, distant, nor elitist about her. Though you were her visitor she was yours as well. And when she poured you tea from her kettle, long discolored and sweetened by use, it was the sound and greenness of the flow that made you want to forever escape the uptown march of the moneyed class rheumatic from all its social climbing, galas, awards, and pats on the backs.

Shelby stepped out of a taxicab and made her way through the courtyard. She could see through the open Dutch door the wooden tables with no top covers. The raw walls. The big arch fireplace with a spit that cooked meat over an open flame as the snapping grease flavored the air. Next to the pit rested a pile of firewood and behind it the secret door that led upstairs to the nighttime bohemian salon that she presided over. Kitty Morton opened the bottom latch of the Dutch door and let Shelby in. "Obie just called."

"What happened to him? I couldn't reach him," Shelby said,

taking off her coat and sitting down at one of the tables.

Kitty Morton poured her tea. "He said to tell you that he couldn't make it tonight, but that he hopes to see you in a few days to do that skit you so adore." Kitty Morton had prompted their friendship, because she loved nothing better than bringing disparate people into an intimacy disallowed by convention. Obie was a negro circuit performer well known for a vaudeville act about a tramp who is always in debt and out of luck: one day the tramp gets sick and tells the Man above: *I'm ready to die*, to which the tramp is told: *Son, you're not yet ready to leave this earth.* The tramp, high in fever and shaking to the bone, cries: *But I've had enough of life's misery. I want to go to yonder home.* The Man from below rises up from the flames and warns the sick tramp: *You have to cross my path first...* But soon the tramp recovers and is back out on the street with pockets turned out, pants rolled up, hat in hand, and singing to everyone passing by: *You have to cross my path first.* Shelby, having understood the spiritual payment for living in this world, became fast friends with Obie and made eyes, if not love.

"Did something happen to him?"

Kitty Morton said, "He got a job on a boat."

"Which boat?"

"The one out on the 12-mile limit."

54

The 12-Mile Limit

Freighters cast light that skimmed the water's surface as ship horns blew and lookout sailors scanned far and wide for oncoming prows and tall black funnels. Those that kept in lane kept the peace. Those that drifted baited death. Gideon steered away from the ships and then put his boat in neutral. He went below deck and moved a parallel ruler over the nautical chart that was on a drop-down table. He said to Beau, "This is where Shelby and I found the *Pair-a-Dice*."

Beau said, "Ain't as far off as I thought."

"Well, with this boat it isn't… Here's the course that Cummins's fleet will follow tonight."

"Where the *Paradise* is waitin' for the *Remus*?"

"No, that's over here toward the eastern end of Long Island."

"Why's that?"

"A lot of reasons," Gideon said, "but Cummins's real problem is that the *Paradise* is his only freighter and it's small."

"Why don't he get more freighters?"

"Because freighters cost a fortune to buy or lease," Gideon said, "and Cummins can only get so much product from distillers who supply a whole network of bootleggers and they need to keep the price up, which makes it difficult for Cummins to expand. That's why he's on the warpath. He believes the distillers should be thrilled that he can buy more quality product, but what he forgets is that this country is so thirsty there's no need to pander to any one bootlegger and so everyone has to pony up and pony high."

"Why don't he make his own liquor?"

"He does," Gideon said, "but his distilleries are always getting raided and, anyway, they can't produce quality liquor and quality is the game now."

"What about the maps I copied from Sugar?"

"I know nothing about them," Gideon said."

"They was in that leather pouch in the front seat door. You drove for Cummins. You *should* know."

"I'm not saying there weren't any maps, but I know Long Island like the back of my hand, so I don't need a map."

"Maybe Cummins was keepin' somethin' from you," Beau said.

"What do I care?"

"What about all the hideouts on Long Island that was on the maps I photographed?"

Gideon leaned over the nautical chart and drew a straight line through the underbelly of Long Island. "Over here is Far Rockaway. Here is Jones Inlet. Then Bay Shore. Patchogue and so on. Every one of these locations are drop-off points for bootleggers and not just for Cummins. See, in every village there are contact people who round up swampers when the call comes in. You don't need documents to know that. Just pay someone off and you'll be told what you need to know. Pay them off enough they'll take you right where you want to go. But what matters most is distance—always the distance."

"Why?"

"Look at the chart," Gideon said.

Beau did, but for nothing.

Gideon explained. "Jones inlet is closer to Manhattan and the local police take advantage of that. See, the closer you are to the city the locals demand more money for protection, because the cut in time for a smuggler reduces risk from hijackers or federals waiting on the roads."

"You'd figure it would be the other way around," Beau said.

Gideon pointed to the town of Patchogue at the eastern half of Long Island. "Last month, a truck convoy was stopped east of Patchogue and a gunfight ensued, but the hijackers took off with nothing. A few miles down the road, heading west, the same convoy was hit by another gang and this time it took off with the convoy. So, the risk grows the further out you are and that's why gangs are willing to pay the cops more for the shorter run."

Beau said, "Seems like you get the bum's rush either way."

"I would prefer to call it rational allocation," Gideon said, stepping away from the nautical chart and looking at his watch. "It's almost ten o'clock."

They headed up the ladder to the deck and waited. Soon they heard the mosquito fleet. Gideon switched on his engines. "All we have to do is follow those lights to the *Pair-a-Dice*."

"You sure it's Cummins's fleet out there?"

Gideon said, "Cummins keeps his lights on whenever he's carrying passengers. He can't risk anyone getting hurt. It'll kill business—if ya know what I mean."

A half hour later, Gideon cut the throttle and grabbed his binoculars. Up ahead the *Pair-a-Dice* left a warm inviting glow like that of a log cabin deep in snow on a cold winter's night. Gideon panned the yacht that had been registered in Saint Pierre et Miquelon, the last existing French territory in North America. The tricolor streamed astern. Lookout men huddled over the rails. The guests braced themselves against the wind as they climbed up the yacht's narrow ladder. The last one up turned back and met Gideon's eyes in the compression of the bifocal lenses. He then climbed aboard.

55

Keep the Change

A l headed toward the *Pair-a-Dice's* afterdeck and said to the couple with whom he had shared the ride out from Grand Street Pier, "We made it."

Dr. Le Veen, bald, with a curious habit of holding his breath and puffing out his cheeks if annoyed, patted Al on the back. "So, what do you think?"

"Some yacht," Al said, taking it all in.

"Maybe we got too pessimistic," Dr. Le Veen said.

"Maybe," Al said, "but everyone in the speedboat quieted down once we lost sight of land."

"I suppose the loneliness of the ocean got to us," Dr. Le Veen said.

"No, I think it was when you said that a man doesn't have more than 12 minutes to live before drowning that got us thinking."

"Sorry," Dr. Le Veen said. "As a doctor, I'm always giving a diagnosis."

"I'll second that," said the doctor's wife, the former Miss Betty Bernstein, a spring-loaded Boston girl still beaming from the hail of thrown rice. "But then I'm always getting diagnosed," she quipped.

Dr. Le Veen took his wife's hand and said to Al, "Nice to meet you. The wife and I are going to do some dancing now; see, I owe it to her from all the hours I put in at the hospital, but if you ever get sick, here's my card. I'll bring you back to life." They went on down the ladder to the supper club deck where the music was hot, the surface slick, the feet quick, and the waiters swift with trays of ice, soda water, bottles of whiskey, French wine, and champagne. Al went down to the lower deck. A passing steward informed him that the restrooms were abaft and that he could leave his coat with the hatcheck girl in the adjoining compartment. Al continued on past the stokehold all the way to the lastage. He opened the door, stepped inside, and found himself above the third futtock. All about him were hawsers, tools, and sundry items stacked on shelves and corners that had accumulated years of dust and nautical musk. Faded wooden navy surplus boxes with leather strap handles were piled high and covered with thick canvas for protection against moisture and salt. On both sides were tools and ropes in boxes of metal and wood with gauge numbers and naval markings. Al separated a column of wooden boxes. He took the detonator and dynamite—a little gift from Zola— out of his coat pocket and set the timer. Then he buried the explosives in between the boxes and checked his watch. In exactly twelve hours, when the ship would be empty of guests, the dynamite would go off. Al left the lastage and stepped back into the passageway. He caught sight of a tall angular man wearing a dinner jacket, white vest, white bow tie, black patent leather shoes, and a monocle. A black cigarette holder was tightly clenched into the corner of his mouth as if it were part of his jaw. His thinning brown hair—you could almost count each one—was slicked back and held fast by a double dose of Brilliantine that left a shoeshine gloss. His long Teutonic face exaggerated the grimness in his shifting eyes. He didn't bother with Al. His attention was on the cigarette girl dressing in the shallow compartment. Her back was to him as she stepped into her work dress: a sleek silver beaded dress that shimmered under the lights. On the chair beside her was a cigarette tray that she wore with a leather strap around her neck. "Good evening, Mr. Cummins," she said, turning around with a smile that went against how she felt. She handed Artemus Cummins several packets of cigarettes. Then he reached over, touched her arm, and pressed his thumb deeply into her flesh. He whispered something into her ear then moved on down the passageway and back up the ladder to the supper dance deck. Al walked over to the cigarette girl and said, "I guess Mr. Cummins is staying onboard for the evening."

She put the leather strap over her head and angled the cigarette tray just below her chest. "He never stays long anywhere," she said. "Need any smokes?"

Al handed her a dime.

She said, "Smokes are two bits on this crate."

Al gave her a dollar. "Keep the change."

"Thanks, mister."

"Are you a showgirl?"

"I'm trying."

"Any luck?"

"No."

"What makes a girl stand out above all the others?"

"If I knew that, mister, I wouldn't be doing this." She went down the passageway and then looked back. "Hey, you're not some Broadway producer? Are you?"

"No, I'm a country lawyer."

It wasn't what she wanted to hear. She quickly headed up the ladder with the cigarette tray sticking out in front of her like she was due any day. Al then noticed a waiter exiting a private cabin with an empty tray. When the waiter was gone, Al went inside. It only took a moment for him to realize that he was in the same room in which Addison Prevette had been photographed with Carmela Knight. There was the bed with plush pillows and the same fixtures on the wall that he now realized were standard on ships—something that he had missed. He found a closet, which had been out of the photograph, which led to the next room where a joiner and a double mirror had been installed to secretly take photographs. The whole cabin was set up for the single purpose of blackmail, but it was almost ten o'clock. Al had no time to waste. He hurried topside where lovers were spooning under the stars.

He stepped over the gangway, went down the ladder that was aside the yacht and waited by the edge of the nippy sea. At precisely ten o'clock Gideon's boat advanced at a cruising speed. As it rode by, it briefly slowed down. Al leaped aboard. Men above aimed their rifles at the boat and demanded that Gideon stop, but the Fiat aeronautical engines kicked in and catapulted the boat into the blankness of the ocean as errant shots missed its evading maneuvers.

56

Lipstick

Manhattan's 10,000 speakeasies were crumbs scattered across the city and one of them was stuck in a factory loft off Tenth Avenue that came alive after nine o'clock. It offered lousy booze but had a scrappy band that played too loud and too fast. The kids loved it. Zola thought the speakeasy looked more like a high school cafeteria at lunchtime—all the better. She was there to write a story about teenage girls, the original flappers who spearheaded the Jazz Age. She wanted to know how they played, worked, socialized, and how they felt about the world they would soon inherit. Deep into the crowd, Zola noticed an incredibly beautiful girl with dark red hair and bright blue eyes that got deeper the longer Zola looked into them. She would be the flapper for her next column in *The New Yorker*. Zola squirmed through the crowd and made her way to the magnet and introduced herself as a movie scout: one of Zola's many fronts that she used for her anonymously named column: *Lipstick*. She pulled out her flask and said to the flapper, without introduction, "I'm told everyone here is from the Bronx. Is that true?"

"Why? Do you need a visa to come to Manhattan?" the dark redhead beauty said, pushing away Zola's flask as her friends surrounded her.

"No," Zola said. "I happen to be a movie scout looking for a new star."

The dark redhead said, "I hate the movies."

Zola tried to ease her. "Look, I'm here to change all that. We're looking for a real flapper who'll do more than put on a beaded dress."

"Well, I'm not taking mine off," the dark redhead said. "And if you got a boss with that in mind, tell him to go to hell."

"I most certainly will. Now, were you born in this country?" Zola said.

"The Lower East Side. I'm all-American."

"How old are you?"

"How old are *you*?"

"Thirty," Zola said.

"Does your husband know you're out of the house?"

"I'm not married."

"So, you're an old maid."

"My fiancé died," Zola said.

"Didgya kill him?"

"*No*," Zola said. "Now, do you want to be a movie star or not?"

"No."

"But every girl wants to be a star," Zola said.

"I'm not every girl."

"What kinda girl are you then?"

"I'm in college and what's it to you anyway?"

"Where do you go to school?"

"The Bronx Zoo."

"I'm trying to be serious," Zola said. "What are you studying?"

"Anything that'll keep me from getting married."

"You've got something against marriage?"

"My mother's all for it and my father thinks he's getting robbed by my not going to some goofy stenographer's school, which somehow in his brain is a better place to spend his money until a husband comes along to rescue him."

"What subjects are you taking?"

"The ones I like," the dark redhead shot back, still not looking at Zola.

"If you don't tell me the ones you like then I can't put them in our next movie."

"Who're you kidding? I've seen all your dumb movies and I'm always an hour ahead of the story."

"Then write our next one," Zola said.

"Not if I have to work in Hollywood. I got better things to do than get bored all day."

"Such as what?"

"Trying to find out why people are nutty," the dark redhead said, meaning Zola.

"You mean psychology?"

"That's what they call it, but nutty is easier to spell."

"Can you tell me what you've learned in school so far?" Zola said.

"It'd be very hard to do that," the dark redhead said, stepping away, wondering when the old maid would get lost.

"Why would it be very hard?"

"Why are you such a snoop?"

"I told you," Zola said. "We're looking for our next movie star."

"I think you're a slunge looking for something else."

"No, I'm looking for someone like *you*. Now, why would it be very hard?"

"Because," the dark redhead said, "what they teach in school is dry, clinical, and irrelevant."

"Why is it dry and clinical?"

"Because who cares how many parts a human throat has?"

"Maybe it's necessary to know all that," Zola said.

"If you're a dictionary."

"Well, there must be something you like about the subject?"

"Yeah," the dark redhead said, "for some reason I'm interested in why people, during rush hour, when there's another train coming right along, keep on pushing themselves into the train they can't get into. And don't tell me it's because everyone's running from the cops or is having a baby. There's a reason for this kind of behavior that has powerful forces concerning the choices we make in life."

"You're a smart girl," Zola said.

"Who said I was dumb?"

"Most girls couldn't care less about science."

"Then you know the wrong girls."

"Have you always been interested in the human mind?" Zola said.

"I have no choice. It came with my ears, unlike yours."

Undeterred, Zola went on. "Were you always interested in psychology?"

The dark redhead's friend said, "Rachel was an artist until her father refused to buy her paint because it cost too much."

Rachel said to her friend, "The reason why he didn't buy me paint was because I did funny pictures of him."

"Were you a good painter?" Zola said.

"Did I have to be?"

"No," Zola said, "but maybe you should go back to art. I mean, don't you think pushing yourself into a train is no different than y'all squeezing inside here?"

"No, this place isn't making any stops and we're here to see boys other than the one's we're used to, and boy are we used to them."

"Are you Jewish?" Zola said.

"You're gonna kill me for it?"

"Not at all," Zola said. "Jesus was a Jew. If it was good enough for him, it's good enough for me, and anyway I was once engaged to one."

The dark redhead didn't believe her. "What's a Southerner doing all the way up here anyway? And don't tell me you all of a sudden fell in love with the Bronx, because the only people who love the Bronx are the landlords and the rats, and it's getting harder to tell the difference."

"As I said, I'm looking for a new star," Zola said.

"Baloney."

"Alright," Zola said, trying to square herself with the flapper. "Ever hear of *The New Yorker* magazine?

"No. What about it?"

"I write for it," Zola said.

"So, you're not in the movie business."

"No," Zola said. "I'm writing an article about flappers and what they think of our changing world."

"Why didn't you tell me that from the outset instead of all the usual Hollywood bullshit?"

"Because no one knows who I am, except for you now."

"I still don't know who you are," Rachel said.

"Look, I do a lot of reviews and they're not all positive. A lot of club owners and eat joints would like to shoot me," Zola said, "But getting back to you—you're never going to get married or were you kidding me before?"

"I wouldn't say never, but I'm not gonna sit around all day like my mother waiting for my lunatic father to come home and have to deal with his problems."

"What kinda problems does your father have?" Zola said.

"The kind that makes a person moody and a pain in the neck."

"What's your full name?"

"I don't have one."

A freckled boy with an apple face hollered. "It's Rachel Pschorr!"

Zola held fast to Rachel who was about to pounce on the boy. "Is your surname really *Pschorr?*"

"I'm *changing* it tomorrow."

Zola gripped Rachel. "Do you know who Bartel Pschorr is?"

Rachel separated herself from Zola as if she'd been stung by a scorpion. "How would *you* know Bartel?"

"Because the boy I was engaged to was Bartel Pschorr, but he was from Berlin, not the Bronx."

"Bartel is dead," Rachel said.

"I *know.*"

"*Say*—you're not the girl who was that surgical nurse during the war?"

Tears came streaming down Zola's cheek. "Yes."

"Well, I've got news for you."

"Bartel's *not* dead?"

"Oh, he's dead, alright."

"Then what?"

Mugs O'Beer stepped in. He was sure that Zola was one of those new female Prohibition agents used by the feds to sneak into speaks before making a bust.

"Get your hands off me," Zola shouted as she got dragged across the floor. She yelled across the factory loft, "We have to talk, Rachel! Please call me!" Zola fished into her bag. "Here's my card," but it fell to the floor as Mugs O'Beer threw Zola out and hollered, "Tell Coolidge he's not welcomed in Hell's Kitchen."

57

Into the Setting Sun

Run Gideon run
The street's a blur
Pedestrians dim
The sky's a haze
The sea's ablaze
Run, run, Gideon run

Gideon entered his building, went up the elevator, into his apartment, down the hallway, up the stairway, and into his mother's studio.

He handed her the extra edition of the *New York Daily News* with the list of *Pair-a-Dice* dead. "So, that's where he spent the nights......"

Al didn't run. He had to push himself past newsboys who were hawking extra editions that headlined the explosion out beyond the 12-mile limit. Male floaters were identified by their billfold papers, women by their shoe sizes. The *Pair-a-Dice* had completely vanished except for a cigarette tray floating off Long Island that a seagull had hitched a ride on. Al took the elevator to *The New Yorker's* floor and entered Zola's tiny office: a squeeze of stale cigarettes, clutter, and a large striker typewriter. She watched her fellow Mississippian drift by and drop into a chair. "The hell happened to you, Al?"

He looked down at the floor and found his feet. "…When was the last time the Navy sold ordnance to the public?"

"I didn't know that it did."

"Cummins had been stealing it," Al said. "He stored it in the lastage."

"The what?"

"Below deck."

"I still don't understand."

"I didn't realize it at first," Al said.

"The ordinance?"

"Yeah," still looking at his feet. "You see, the detonator went off early."

"What do you mean?"

"It was faulty," Al said.

"What I gave you?"

"Yeah, and when it did, the dynamite and the ordnance blew the yacht to kingdom come."

"Didn't you set the clock right?"

"Yeah," Al said, "but the mechanism was defective. I didn't think of that. You don't think of those things until it's too late. Like I should've known that the photograph was taken aboard ship." Al stared out the window in a way that Zola didn't like.

"When did it go off, then?"

Al watched a pigeon land on the ledge and move its feet in time with its bobbing head as another pigeon landed beside it. "Hours earlier, when everyone was still on board…I think I should turn myself in."

Zola got up from her desk and stood over him. "Al, you're not doing anything of the sort."

He looked into her eyes as if he had just woken up. "I'm not…?"

"You *didn't* kill all those people."

"I didn't…?"

"No."

"You mean they're *not* dead?"

"Oh, they're dead."

"I don't get you," Al said.

"Last night you told me that only the crew would die since they were complicit in the game. Okay. It didn't work out that way. But you have to understand that good men are not bad men because inadvertent things happen."

"...You're sure about that?"

"Look, Al, if Mrs. McCreary's children get asphyxiated in her railroad flat because of a negligent gas leak, it's a tragedy. When a locomotive explodes because the fireman didn't properly feed the coal into the firebox, it's a tragedy. When we flew up from Mississippi in that flying machine, last December, we thought it was the cat's meow until we heard that it crashed on the way back killing a good pilot and innocent passengers all because of unexpected bad weather—that's life. But when Artemus Cummins burns a girl to death it's not a tragedy; it's a crime. People who don't know the difference live in a world of ignorance."

Al got up and headed to the door.

"*Al—*"

He kept on going.

Zola grabbed her coat and followed him. "Look Al, I'm the one who gave you the dynamite, so blame it on me."

As a favor, he did, and headed down the hallway thinking of Dr. Le Veen and his pretty bride and how all good things face the same fate.

58

Pennsylvania Station

A middle-aged man of good breeding stepped off the Northeastern Limited train and tipped Joe Dawson, the Pullman porter who had served him on the way up from Bristol Station. "Why, thank you, Mr. Prevette."

Two Red Hats took Addison Prevette's trunk and waited as he greeted his daughter coming down the platform. "I missed you, child."

Shelby didn't embrace him. She said nothing.

Joe Dawson tipped his hat and said, "Say hello to Beau for me, Miss Prevette."

"I will, Joe."

Addison and Shelby went down the platform with the Red Hats in tow. "Something wrong?" Addison wanted to know.

"We have much to discuss and much to do," Shelby coolly said.

"You have a motorcar waiting for us?"

"Yes."

"I heard you bought a nice little roadster for yourself."

"...Yes."

"Uncle Marbury wired me and said that you bought the summer cottage next to his in East Hampton."

"Yes, but it only has 20 acres, and the barn is a reach out the front door."

"I'll call him tonight and get you more land."

"You can't."

"Why?"

"He's dead."

"...*Dead?*"

"Yes."

"What happened?" Addison put his hand on Shelby's shoulder. Shelby brushed him off and walked on.

"What happened to Marbury, child?"

"What happened to *you?*"

"I'm not the one who's dead," Addison said, trying to keep up with his daughter.

"No," Shelby said, still ahead of her father. "But you put a sadness in my heart forever, and should mama ever find out what you did it will crush her, because losing trust in someone is like being left to die and that's what you did to us with that whore."

They entered the concourse, headed to the carport, and into the waiting limousine.

59

The Prize

Sacks of letters, postcards, and telegrams were piled high in the contest editor's office at *The New York Evening Graphic*. People from all over were claiming that they had found the missing negative, and they were demanding the 10,000-dollar reward prize on the spot. Managing editor Emile Gauvreau had to hire five more stenographers to handle the flood of mail. He even kicked his star reporters out of their offices and put them back on the line to hammer out their stories. One overwhelmed stenographer walked in and said, "Look Mr. Gauvreau, we've already been through some 800 pieces of mail since eight this morning and every flub swears he knows where the negative is or has it in his or her possession. How are we supposed to know if anyone's even close to the truth if we ourselves don't know what the truth is?"

Emile Gauvreau told her, "If the flubs don't mention how many people are in the negative, exactly what they're doing, and what the people look like, you can toss the letter."

"Yeah, but if you don't tell us what they're doing, how are we to know what to toss?"

"You don't need to know what they're doing," he said.

"Well, if ya put it that way then I can only imagine what they were doing." The stenographer turned around and crashed into Officer Elgin Bumpus. "Hey, someone oughta give ya a ticket for blocking traffic."

Officer Elgin Bumpus ignored her and closed the door behind him.

Emile Gauvreau, smelling a story, got up and offered the big leather chair to the tall imposing flatfoot. "Have a seat, friend."

Officer Elgin Bumpus pushed the chair away. He pointed to the newspapers on the editor's desk that had the composograph of a beautiful white girl getting drenched with gasoline as a sneering gangster in white tie struck a match to her. The next shot she was all aflame. "Carmela Knight *ain't* white."

"Ohh, gee. I thought she was," said the editor.

"You gonna change the goddamn cover of your newspaper and put a colored girl on it."

"Gee, officer, I'd love to do that, but the paper is already out on the streets and if we did that it would be terribly confusing."

"I'll terribly confuse your white ass if you don't change it. Everybody uptown is mad as hell and they all gonna come down here 'n demonstrate in front of this here buildin' with signs that y'all're a bunch a goddamn lyin' sons a bitches and then run your dumbass newspaper outta town."

"Well, officer, I'd love to change the composograph, but the morning and afternoon editions are already out on the street, and it would be a big mistake if any changes were made, because then no one would believe anything; so, with the white girl, we can at least hold onto some of the truth."

"Bullshit. You change the color of the girl back to black or your ass gonna be a joke." He aimed his notched nightstick at the editor. "I'm gonna call you later 'n you better pick up the phone 'n tell me you done made the changes or there be hell to pay."

Officer Elgin Bumpus left Emile Gauvreau's office and headed up to Harlem where he met Beau on 135th Street. A somber crowd had gathered around a garage. Officer Elgin Bumpus spoke to the white cop by the door. Then he and Beau went inside. Sugar Winslow was strung up on the hay pulley, life having left him before he could shut his eyes. Below him were a smash of tools, tipped over oil cans, his yellow racecar upended and smashed. A tan leather automobile pouch, emptied of its maps, was just beside the car on the concrete floor.

Officer Elgin Bumpus said, "Cummins did this."

Beau pointed to the tan pouch on the floor. "Sugar must've tried to sell the drop-off maps I told you about. He needed money bad for that race in Indianapolis."

"Well, we know one thing, Beau. Cummins wasn't on the *Pair-a-Dice* when it exploded."

They left the garage and headed several blocks up to a walk-up that was crowded with tenants and police. They went up to a third-floor apartment. The bedroom was in the back. A police photographer was taking overhead flash shots from a ladder of the corpse strangled on the bed. A white detective stood by writing on a pad. Office Eglin Bumpus had a word with him then left the apartment with Beau and said, "Tammany Hall's gettin' into this, now."

"Why's that, Elgin?"

"The wrong people's dyin', and I don't mean Henry over there."

60

Until Love Sours

Flanders Fields
Eight years later
The girls who had jumped
And ran with voices high
Have come with flowers
For the boys in kilts
Long laid in dirt
Not as they dropped
But where they were dragged.

Addison turned away from the painting and said, "You wrote that?"
Shelby said, "Yeah, I gave it to Mrs. Remley."
"And she put it on her painting?"
"Why not?
"It's just that—"
"Who says you can't put words on a canvas?"
"…How much did you pay for all her art?"
"A grand," Shelby said.
"Do you plan on reselling it?"
"I plan on holding onto it."
"And how did you come up with a value?"
"Art has no value. It has only its lovers and they'll pay anything."
"Until love sours," Addison reminded her.

Caitlin came in with a Western Union Telegram and gave it to Shelby who read it and then said to her father, "Mama fears for her life. She wants you home now."

"I know, and I've already apologized several times, so stop looking at me like that."

"It's easy to say you're sorry."

"And it's easy not to forgive." Addison gently took Shelby by the arm. "Now come along. We're running late. The mayor will be here any moment."

"I suppose he wants more money."

"Just show him into the study when he arrives."

"He won the election," Shelby said. "What more does he want?"

"It's what *I* want, child. Now hurry along."

Caitlin brought Al into the living room. Addison took him into Shelby's newly decorated study that was filled with books yet to be shelved. The room was painted country white. A big soft couch was tucked under a wide tall window. Framed photos of her family were crowded around a corner table where stalks of flowers spilled from vases. Daylight flooded the room and left a sleepy stillness that dispensed with the notion of time. Al seated himself across Shelby's English maple desk. "So, what did Cummins tell you?"

Addison, sitting behind the desk, said, "He wants the quarter of a million brought to a converted Pullman dining car on Morris Avenue near Mott Haven Yard. I am to stand outside and wait for the pickup."

"There's no need for that," Al said. "The *Pair-a-Dice* is no more."

"I know, but you're out of this now."

"…What do you mean out of this?"

"You've done fine work, Mr. Nachman."

"But you don't have to give Cummins a thing. He's on the run."

"Here's the check for the other 25,000 dollars." Addison signed it and pushed it across the desk.

Al slowly took it and said, "You're still going to give Cummins the ransom money?"

"The matter is in my hands now."

Shelby opened the door and said to her father, "The Mayor just walked in and he brought Colm Haydock with him as well."

"Did they see you?"

"No," Shelby said.

"Good. Tell Caitlin to send them in and then I want you to leave through the service entrance. Now hurry." Addison turned to Al, "Stay a moment and meet the mayor."

Caitlin came down the long hallway and showed in the two guests. Meanwhile, Virginia, having just come home, walked into Shelby's bedroom and said, "Where're ya off to?"

"I can't talk. I'm in a hurry."

"Well, you better tell your cousin Zola to hide and *fast*."

"Why?"

"You know that landlady she's always moaning about?"

"You mean that crazy Mrs. Buchanan?"

"Yeah," Virginia said, "they just found her dead in the back of her building."

"What happened?"

"Thrown off the rooftop is what happened."

"How did you find out?"

"Some creep hanging around downstairs told me on the way in," Virginia said. "And *somehow* he knew we lived here."

Shelby thought for a moment then said to herself, "The old lady talked, thinking it would save her life."

"What do you mean *talked*?"

Shelby said, "The other day Mrs. Buchanan made a nasty comment on my way out of Zola's rooming house. She must have gone right to Zola who told her that I live with, you, Miss Famous. So, she figured Zola's now living here with us."

"The old lady knew our address?"

"Someone else did," Shelby said.

"You mean Gant's people?"

"Who else?" Shelby left her bedroom and headed to the service elevator that was out through the kitchen.

Virginia followed her. "Where're you going in such a hurry?"

"To pay my condolences to that boy's family."

"Well, that creep downstairs wanted to know if I'd seen that boy."

"Which boy?"

"Take a guess…"

61

Lord Ribblesdale

Friends and family gathered in great solemnity as they vainly tried to match each other's grief with more deep sighs and furrowed brows than in a movie. Sarah Remley and her daughters wore black. They sat close to each other on the center couch receiving mourners. Gideon watched the spectacle from his corner armchair, his grief chilled by the reoccurring image of his father kissing that woman—tongue-licking and all that.

"You're supposed to marry a girl after seeing her for a year otherwise you've disgraced her," Root Buckner quietly said under the intrusion of whispers and murmurs that added to the solemnity of the moment.

"Nettie said that I disgraced her?"

"In so many words."

"Where is she now?"

"On her way up," Root Buckner said.

"What else did she say?"

"Said she's done playing tennis with you and has got someone else who's much better."

"Who?" Gideon said.

"Chester Pinehurst."

"That idiot...?" Gideon quickly stood up, pretending to be absorbed by the consoling words from a middle-aged couple whom he did not know. They moved on. Gideon sat down and said, "All funerals are the same."

"How's that?" Root Buckner said.

"The conspiracy of every mourner is to tell the living what they would never tell the dead." He turned to the huge portrait of his father in his long black hunting coat, top hat, pinque riding britches, canary vest, and ivory tipped riding crop, all in the manner of Lord Ribblesdale. The grand portrait had been brought into the living room and hoisted onto one of Sarah's easels and draped with an overflow of black bunting. Nettie entered. She headed straight to Sarah and her daughters to pay her respects. Then she hiked over to Gideon, who was obliged to stand. She heaved her thumb back and said in a voice too strained to be quiet. "Your *friend* is here."

Shelby entered.

Gideon saw her and then turned back to Nettie. "How's your tennis game?"

"None of your business," Nettie said, nose up in the air.

"I thought you came here to pay your respects, not be a pain."

"I've been paying my respects too long concerning you," Nettie said, "and I've come here to let you know that I'm finished with you, once and for all."

"Yeah, well Celeste told me you can't stand Chester P. one damn bit."

"Celeste meant you. I can't stand *you*," Nettie said. "And I'm visiting her next, so watch what you say."

"Yeah, well you're the one who better watch it. Celeste and that girl over there are best of friends and they're not gonna want *you* around."

"*Gideon*, you're the one they don't want around with your big ideas and criminal pals. And get this through your thick skull, everyone argues and sooner or later you're going to argue with Miss Stuck-up."

"Well, with you it's always sooner than later."

"You're an idiot," she said.

"And Chester Pinehurst is a genius?"

"He's a damn sight better tennis player than you are."

"That's because you're so lousy."

"I'll tell you what's lousy," Nettie said. "That girl over there is so full of herself that she took up the whole damn elevator. You sure know how to pick 'em."

"I picked you."

"That's because, every once in a while, a dumb boy gets lucky." Nettie left in a great bug huff usually saved for plays needing to make a point where there wasn't any.

Gideon went over to Shelby, grabbed her by the arm, and took her down the hallway so quickly that she had to run to keep up with him. "I find it odd that you of all people are here."

Shelby pushed him away. "Keep your hands off me."

"You mean keep my hands off the killer who blew everyone to Kingdom Come including my old man and Celeste's. Maybe we oughta go back inside and tell everyone you're the one behind all the funerals in this town."

"You're as much to blame as I, Master Remley, and I came here to see your darling mother not you, ya big creep," giving him an angry kick, which had no effect on his grip.

"Beau told me *you're* the one who put the idea of blowing up the *Pair-a-Dice* into Nachman's head."

"When did Beau tell you that?"

"Out at sea," Gideon said.

"Well, you're the one who picked up Nachman after he left the *Pair-a-Dice*, so you're a co-conspirator and equally as guilty under the law. And anyway, I can't go to jail for just saying something that happened outside the 12-mile limit. That would really be stupid."

"They can still electrocute you."

"Says *who*?"

"Don't worry," Gideon said. "They'll figure out a way."

"Well, it's not my fault people take what I say and go crazy."

"Baloney," Gideon said. "And Beau told me that you spoke to Nachman like a general giving orders: *Blow up that boat.*"

"Well, at least I'm inventive."

"*Inventive?*"

"Yeah," Shelby said, "and that bomb was supposed to have gone off twelve hours later when no one was aboard. So, it's *not* my fault."

"It was *all* your fault."

Shelby kicked him again and this time she freed herself.

Gideon went after her. "*Hey*! Where're ya going?

"*Home. I hate* you."

62

The Algonquin Hotel, Manhattan

Waiters and busboys were busy setting flatware in the Rose Room for lunch service. Zola was seated at *The New Yorker's* reserved round table. Willy, the maître d' quickly came over and placed a glass of club soda beside her. "A little early, today, Miss Nicholas. We're not open for another 15 minutes."

"Want me to go?"

"Absolutely not."

"Thanks, Willy. See, I'm meeting someone before lunch, but I also need to have a word with you."

"With me...?"

"...Mind if I ask you a question?"

"Why of course not."

"Who provides the meat for this hotel?"

"Why one of the downtown outfits do," Willy said.

"Which one?"

"Huber & Köhler."

"Is their meat any better than the other purveyors?"

Willy lowered his voice as if the room were filled with patrons. "You're not going to write about this in your column, are you, Miss Nicholas?"

"Willy—you seem to forget that I don't write a column."

"My mistake, Miss Nicholas. I'm confusing you with someone else."

"You most certainly are. Now, why are some hotels using Huber & Köhler instead of the other outfits?"

Again, Willy looked sideways as if the room were filled. "Because the house gets a discount on its liquor that way."

"You mean Huber & Köhler are bootleggers?" Zola said.

"Well, it's not for me to say what they are, Miss Nicholas, but lately it seems that meat purveyors are moving product into hotels."

"And y'all have to buy the product they're selling along with the meat?"

"It would seem to be," Willy said, "but then it would be hard to stay in business if one didn't also buy from other purveyors as well. Not everyone has the same taste."

"Have y'all had any problems with Huber & Köhler?"

"Well…there has been some tension," Willy admitted.

"What kind of tension?"

"There's this other outfit," he said.

"Pray tell, Willy."

"It has excellent product and they're not thugs."

"They're not bootleggers?"

"Oh yes, Miss Nicholas, they are, but they were honest before Prohibition."

"Well, I have something to tell you, Willy."

"I hope it concerns the weather."

"Oh, it does. There's a storm brewing."

"When's it coming ashore?"

"Oh, it's already here," Zola said. "Ed Goulson used to buy his meat from Huber & Köhler. Then he dropped them as a supplier."

"I did hear about that."

"I'm glad you have, Willy, because he was killed. You do know who Artemis Cummins is?"

"The name does ring a bell."

"Good, because I got a tip from one of the club owners last night that someone else is in Cummins's sights. It seems that Cummins is making a move to consolidate power in the next few weeks and those who don't go along with him will go somewhere else."

"Should I take that in mind?"

"I would if I were you, Willy. I happen to like your boss."

"So do I."

"He's a good fella."

"I agree, Miss Nicholas"

"Knows how to treat people."

"He'd be glad to hear that," Willy said.

"Good, because I wouldn't want him dead like Ed Goulson."

"I'll let my boss know."

"Oh, he already knows," Zola said with half a smile.

Willy smiled back as best as he could.

Al entered the Rose Room.

Willy left the table.

Zola reminded Al, "You're *late*."

Al sat beside her. "It's 11:30."

"I said 11:15."

"I got here as soon as I could."

"We have a little problem," Zola said.

"How little?"

"Shelby went to Gideon Remley's Fifth Avenue shack to pay her respects and when she left, she noticed that her motorcar wasn't there. Another was in its place."

"An Isotta-Fraschini?"

"None other," Zola said. "Shelby, not being stupid, immediately got suspicious. It seems that someone had told Virginia Swain that my landlady had been murdered and that this someone was also looking for me and the Remley boy, and now Shelby."

"When was Mrs. Buchanan killed?"

"This morning. Thrown off the rooftop. They had to scrape the old lady off the pavement."

"Where's Shelby?"

"She went back up to the Remley shack to hide," Zola said, "and guess who was one of the mourners?"

"Who?"

Zola said, "That fella with the monocle and black cigarette holder. Seems he and Ellis Remley were acquainted, to say the least."

"Is Shelby still there?"

"She better be," Zola said. "I told her and that boy to remain where they are until it's safe to leave town."

"Well, I have news for you."

"What?"

"You're going to have to leave town too."

"*Me—?*"

"You," Al said. "On the train up to New York I told John Smith that a certain girl lived in Hell's Kitchen who had found some unusual things in her rooming house. He must've told his people who are now looking for you. They got your address from Mary Collins, who once lived in your apartment. Then they got your name from Mrs. Buchanan. She's now under arrest."

"*Mrs. Buchanan?*"

"Mary Collins."

"Why?"

"For running a prostitution ring."

"I thought Gant was."

"No," Al said. "He just got the kickbacks. She was the real boss."

"How did you find this out?"

"Carmela Knight gave a deposition to District Attorney Buckner right before she was burned to death."

"Then why didn't Cummins come after me sooner?"

"It wasn't Cummins who ransacked your place," Al said.

"Who was it then?"

"The same people who threw Mrs. Buchanan off the rooftop."

"Who?"

"Your old district leader, Colm Haydock. He believes you and Shelby have the documents that he wants. So, you'll have to get out of town now, until things cool down."

"I can't," Zola said.

"What do you mean you can't?"

"I just put a down payment on an eight-room Park Avenue apartment and I have a meeting with a decorator and furniture maker this afternoon, and then I'm interviewing a cook, a maid, and a goddamn butler, because Shelby's getting a fancy English one starting tomorrow."

"Zola…look at it this way."

"What way?"

Al got up from the table. "You'll have a place to come home to…"

63

The 12-mile Limit

Captain Ellsworth Marsham stood before the shipmaster's cabin dresser mirror and fixed his dark blue silk tie. He then slipped on a navy-blue double-breasted jacket with shiny brass buttons and yellow sleeve braids. He reached for the blue captain's hat with black leather visor and set it on his head. He squared it just above his eyes. Then he looked into the mirror that was over the dresser. He was getting grayer, softer in the cheek, fuller in the throat, heavier in the eye. He looked back at his life spent at sea, since the age of 14, and all he could see was water. He left the cabin and headed up to the top deck. He climbed the ladder to the bridge and greeted his first officer. "Is the *Paradise* secure, Mr. Shoney?"

"Yes, Captain Marsham."

"Good. Come along."

They entered the navigation room and studied the navigation chart.

"Is this our new fix?" Captain Marsham said to Mr. Shoney as he moved the parallel ruler.

"Yessir, I just plotted it, sir."

"Good," Captain Marsham said. "Is everything in order now?"

"Yessir, everything is back in order, sir."

"The dead?" Captain Marsham said.

"They're deep."

"The provisions?"

"The *Paradise* has been outfitted to stay at sea for months and the *Remus* is full of whiskey, sir."

"Good."

"Sir...?"

"Yes, Mr. Shoney?"

"Do you know when the party is arriving from shore?"

"No, Mr. Shoney, but be on alert."

"Yessir, I've given orders."

"Good," Captain Marsham said, heading out to the bridge.

"...Captain Marsham?"

The captain stood at the door. "Yes, Mr. Shoney?"

"I—was a little nervous at first."

"You did well, Mr. Shoney. You did well."

"Thank you, sir. Thank you......"

64

Mott Haven Yard

The grunt of steel on rail filled the evening yard as a lizard scorcher in a white chef's uniform came around the northbound tracks with several kitchen mechanics who carried tools and swinging lanterns. One of the mechanics said, "You scorchers always pick the dead of night when we can't see nothin'." They hung their lanterns up and then took apart the coal oven where they found a frying pan stuck inside. One of the mechanics looked up from the stove and said to the scorcher, "How the hell did this get in here?"

Beau, outside, said, "Some porter sick of bean sandwiches. That's how."

The lizard scorcher hollered through the open kitchen window, "Where the hell you been, Beau?"

"Hidin' like that pan of yours, brother."

Beau headed across the yard to Morris Avenue. The converted Pullman dining car, now a diner, lit up the whole corner. Its windows were fogged from oven haze. Deep funky smells of long roasted onions and garlic saturated the air. Beau entered the diner and took the middle stool. The counter boy, from Mulberry Street, poured one black and set it before Beau. Then he said to Beau in his crazy broken English, "Whatza-ya gonna eat?"

"Whatza-ya-got, Luigi?"

Conductor Liston Truesdale, sitting next to Beau, said, "Luigi, bring him what I'm having," then he said to Beau, "I hope you had fun the past three weeks. We're heading out tomorrow afternoon."

"I'm more than ready to ride, sir. You got that information on that private car for me?"

"It's going up to Harmon tonight at eight to get switched south to the Orange Blossom Special going to Florida."

"Did the yard master get the papers for it?"

"Got it this morning. There's something else, Beau," the conductor said in a quieter voice.

"What?"

"That lawyer, Steuer, who grilled you last December, is making some kinda fuss with the big brass and from what I hear it's been settled out of court with the Greenwich kid's parents."

"Why they doin' it outta court?"

"The train don't want publicity."

"Then they won't get it," Beau said, taking out his flask and pouring Conductor Liston Truesdale a drink while someone down the counter watched.

"I'm just letting you know what's up since you've been away. That's all," Conductor Liston Truesdale said, as he turned towards Jessica Jill Turner of Undercover Unit 6 who was sitting on the last stool and more than interested in Beau's suitcase. The conductor said to Beau in a low voice, "She'll be riding out with us tomorrow."

Beau could see her standing outside the 20th Century Limited in the snow the previous New Year's Eve on their way to Chicago, and she hadn't forgotten what had happened. Neither had he.

65

The Dandy

District Leader Colm Haydock left Shelby's study with parting words for Mayor Jimmy Walker: "Some Italian once said that if you do injury to a man, it better be so severe that vengeance need not be feared."

The mayor said, "An Irishman once said: A man who is easily insulted is easily played."

"I'm Irish and I never heard that."

"I know—I just made it up," Mayor Jimmy Walker said.

"Well, you can't play me."

"Then I cannot insult you and therefore we should have no problems. Glad you stopped by," the mayor said.

The district leader was escorted down the hall and out the front door.

Mayor Jimmy Walker, excessive in his bespoke striped black suit, starched collar, gray buckskin spats, and slick wooden cane with a golden handle and brass tip that shined like the silver dollars in his pocket, turned back to Addison with a self-satisfied smile. Addison thought that the dandy of New York had only one crease and it was the impatience in his eyes.

Addison said to him, "You were a bit rough on him."

"He thought I was a pushover."

"Yeah, but you insulted him."

"Look, Addison—"

"If you want to control a man then he can't see you as an adversary."

"Addison, I'm a lot smarter than you think, and I appreciate all that you did for my election campaign—including that very generous donation—but I've heard all I want to hear about Haydock. I'm mayor now and I'm going to show everyone in this town how things are done. Now, I don't mean to wag my finger, but every smooth slipper and rough collar is all riled up about that steam yacht getting blown up outside the 12-mile limit. So, I'm letting the press know that I'm going to hunt down the killers and electrocute the sons of bitches in Sing Sing, and I'll pull the goddamn switch myself just to set an example for all the other harebrained lunatics out there who think they can get away with murder—you do see what I'm getting at?"

"You mean that's what you're telling the public."

"I have no choice, Addison. I've got longshoremen refusing to unload ships thinking that any one of them will blow up in their faces. Citizens who are afraid to take ferries across the river for the same reason. Why they can't even look at a glass of water without getting the jitters. And on top of that, I've got an administration that's facing a loss of confidence after having only been in office for two and a half weeks. So, I don't want any argument from anyone. We're gonna do things my way."

"You're not getting an argument from me," Addison said. "But your problem is Colm Haydock. Not the public. Haydock just said to you that he's been running Hell's Kitchen long before you ever were elected, and so imagine what he'll be telling you next month or next year, if you don't deal with him now. He's testing you and early. He wants control of this city, and he doesn't give a damn that you're now mayor."

"I know what he wants."

"Yes, but you don't want *him* to know it and *now* he does."

"Don't you worry, Addison. I know how to deal with his likes."

"You forget that Cummins is at war with Haydock and not just because he blew away the *Pair-a-Dice*."

"Haydock swears he didn't."

"Then who did it?"

"Well, whoever did it," the mayor said, "better watch out, because when I pull the switch in Sing Sing, no one will ever question my authority again."

"Yeah, but Haydock controls the port," Addison reminded him, "which means he controls the city and the only competition he puts up with is the paying up kind. That's why Cummins has to truck in all his product. You heard Haydock say so himself—and with pride. Soon, he'll have you paying him off just to enter Hell's Kitchen."

"I'd like to see him try that," the mayor said.

"I think he's already put saw to wood."

"That's why I gave him a piece of my mind."

"All you had to do was listen to him and let him feel like an equal. There was no need to get into his face. Now he's got his eye on you. He'll have people following every move you make."

"I promise you, Addison, when we get done with this other matter, I'll take care of Haydock for good. And stop worrying about your little friend Miss Etta Jape. I won't let Haydock get near her."

"He better not," Addison warned with a coldness that the mayor had never seen before.

"My word is my bond, Addison."

"Mr. Mayor—where I come from, the nature of power isn't defined by words, but by actions." Addison grabbed his hat. "It's getting late. Let's go."

66

Mott Haven Yard

The nighttime yard was alive with the din and rub of steel and rolling wheels. Brakemen swung bird cages at ash cats. Bakeheads waited for pickups to Harmon, New York, where coal engines hunkered down for linkage west and north, but this mattered none to Beau, still sitting in the diner. He waited for railroad agent Jessica Jill Turner to leave. Then he stepped out of the diner and stood on the corner of Morris Avenue with the suitcase in hand. He stared up at the stars and wondered how far out in space you had to go before you got anywhere. The Isotta-Fraschini 8A-4 Sedan pulled up to the curb. Louie Four-Stacks stuck his head out the window. "Who the fuck're you?"

"Man couldn't make it here," Beau said. "So, I'm in his place." He handed the Italian the heavy valise. "It's all in there."

Louie Four-Stacks gave it to Artemus Cummins who opened it and made a quick check of the payoff. Then the sedan took off and stopped further down at the railyard's western entrance. A yardman guided them over the tracks to the buzzard's roost where papers were signed, and the private car was released. They were then led through the mass of train cars to the other side of the yard where they boarded Cummins's private car. Once inside, they turned on the lights and were greeted by a lineup of policemen with shotguns and pistols. Cummins took the cigarette holder out of his mouth and said to them, "Who put you up to this?"

They didn't answer him.

67

Beekman Place Mooring

The morning sun rose from its eastern shelf as an orphaned squall died just short of the old brick Domino Sugar Refinery that dominated the Brooklyn waterfront where at water's edge squawking sea gulls parried overhead as ship horns blew long heavy notes in shifting fifths across the East River.

Shelby came on deck wearing a naval peacoat that she had found in a footlocker where Gideon kept the high seas gear.

He said to her, "I thought your cousin was coming."

"You thought wrongly," Shelby said, reaching for the thermos of hot black coffee on the dock.

"What happened?"

"Nothing."

"...I kinda like her."

Shelby ignored him as she watched him fit his rifle beside the gunwale, near the wheel. He then handed her a 1911 Colt .45. She took it from him and popped the clip to make sure that all seven rounds were loaded. She then chambered an eighth round.

"I see you know how to use that," Gideon said.

"I see you have certain notions about girls that need to be changed."

"Maybe... What about that eight-room apartment your cousin just bought?"

"That's her problem," Shelby said.

"Where did she get money for Park Avenue?"

"She robbed a bank."

"I bet you planned it," Gideon said, reaching for a paper bag and offering Shelby a fried egg sandwich. "I suppose you're going to be mad at me the rest of your life."

She ignored him.

Gideon poured her coffee. "I still don't understand how Zola is going to live in an eight-room apartment all by herself."

"Ask her, if it bothers you that much," Shelby said, looking out into the East River where the soot gray from the jumble of factories, slaughterhouses, and skyscrapers discolored the finite space of Manhattan.

"Girls are long married by her age."

"She knows that," Shelby said.

"She's pretty. Why's she an old maid?"

"My cousin's love life is like the rent; it's always late," Shelby said, wishing Gideon would go away. She tried lighting a cigarette by kneeling below the gunwale. Gideon lit it for her. Then he undid the lines from the cleats and let his boat drift into the East River. He turned the engines over. The boat came alive with a hungry growl. Shelby, out of respect for the double Fiats, moved away from its housing.

Gideon said, "Maybe your cousin should buy a bird to keep her company."

"Hopefully one that doesn't parrot her," Shelby said. "When will we get to East Hampton?"

"I'll let you know."

"By lunchtime?"

"Before anyone who's after us," Gideon said, steering his boat under Manhattan's southern bridges crammed with tall ships of sprawling masts, coal steam freighters with cranes and smokestacks, small but nimble white schooners edged between the arched wooden sheds that housed the squat ferries that crossed the river between Brooklyn, Staten Island, Manhattan, and New Jersey. He cruised past the Star of Bombay, the Gong Gong, the Nomadic, the Cap Anselm, the Red Sphinx, the East Liverpool, the Prince Comet, and the freighters Janis Arnold and Stanley N. Greene: both of whom would sink in the following weeks and never be heard from again. Crewmen kept their eyes on Gideon's powerful boat as it slipped under the Brooklyn Bridge, past Governor's Island, into the Upper Bay, through the Narrows to the Lower Bay, past Lightship Ambrose, and then out into the great Atlantic Ocean where the swells rose into a smothering wall.

"We're heading into a storm," Shelby said, clinging on to her coat. The boat then heeled so that everything inside it scrambled to the side, including Shelby.

Gideon calmly helped her up. "The storm's moved out."

Maybe, but Shelby clutched her seat as she fearfully watched the eastern seaboard quickly submerge below the horizon. She was not used to the ocean. She did not understand how quickly it could change and that in temperament it was as childish as it was shrewd, but in time the sea did grow calmer as the darkest clouds drifted off. Shelby went below deck and returned with a hand-held compass. She took readings as Gideon had taught her. Then she went below to draw intersecting lines from two points on the nautical chart while correcting for speed, current, and drift. Then she went back up deck and said, "We're now past the 12-mile limit."

"You'd make a good sailor," Gideon said.

"You mean captain."

Of course, she would say that. "You have the keys to your new house?"

"Yeah, and there's a set that was left in the barn," Shelby said, staring out into the endless ocean thinking that the universe to earth was like land to water, with someone else looking down ad infinitum.

Gideon said to her, "I looked really dumb in that doorman's outfit."

Shelby got beside the wheel and shared Gideon's view of the ocean. "Well, at least I came up with an idea to get us out of your building. I saved your life—not that it was worth saving."

"Well, had I not been so scared, I'd've died laughing."

"From what?"

"You dressed as a maid, of all things." Shelby did not think it funny.

Gideon, unfazed by her new dislike for him, said, "Well, at least no one will find us in East Hampton with all those potato farms." He pointed north to the underbelly of Long Island. "See that Coast Guard cutter port-abeam?"

He gave her his binoculars. She stared into the haze. "How did you know that it was the Coast Guard without these?"

"By the ship's profile," Gideon said. "It's leaving the 12-mile limit."

"Why?"

"It's heading home, but it's spotted us and wants to know what we're doing out here in the freezing weather all alone."

"Will they pursue us?"

"I don't think so," Gideon said. "The Coast Guard works in shifts. Everything is scheduled like clockwork in the military."

Shelby aimed the binoculars toward the bow and searched beyond the 12-mile limit. "I see big ships ahead."

"That's the armada," he said.

"Those two on the left. They're very big."

Gideon took the binoculars from her and adjusted them. "One is an English tender getting restocked. The other is its sister ship. And the third, the smaller one, is empty. See how high it sits off the water?" Gideon handed her the binoculars.

Shelby focused the three ships into view. "I want to get closer."

"…Looking for more trouble?"

She said, "This isn't something you see every day and I've only been out here at night." Then she froze.

"…Something wrong?"

She handed him the binoculars. "You tell me."

Gideon searched the water and then found the problem. He changed course. A few moments later, he shifted the engines into neutral, grabbed the swamp pole, reached over, and poked a floater face down in the water.

"He must be from the *Pair-a-Dice*," Shelby said.

Gideon pushed the floater away. Twenty yards ahead was another one, then three more appeared bobbing up and down, all wearing dinner jackets. The bodies were frozen stiff—no decomposure. Gideon aimed the sharp end of the swamp pole at a floater with large patent leather shoes dipping in and out of the water. He dragged the corpse to the side of the boat and stared into the frozen blue face that was resilient with the numbness of death and the painful slowness of drowning. A black ribbon with a monocle floated off one ear. Gideon pushed the floater away and said to Shelby, "They're not from the *Pair-a-Dice*."

"Where then?"

Gideon said, "You remember that man with the monocle and black cigarette holder who had come to pay his respects in my apartment?"

She looked into the water. "...What's he doing out here?"

"We're going to find out," Gideon said. "Give me the binoculars."

Not so quickly. Shelby had her own ideas. She put them to her eyes and focused the three ships into view. She panned the main deck of the first English tender and then the ship beside it. The name on the prow was *Remus*. Crewmen were busy transferring cases of liquor to a third, much larger, ship. Shelby panned back to the first ship. On the prow, she saw *Paradise* in white block letters wet of its own sweat and grime. A group of men, in city dress, were on deck speaking to Captain Ellsworth Marsham as if they were on a street corner in Manhattan. Then Shelby heard the buzzing grind of speedboats. She followed them to the ships and watched them slide between the freighters. She moved the binoculars back up to Captain Ellsworth Marsham and the man to whom he was talking: her father. The mayor was beside him. The captain was handed an envelope. Then her father and the mayor climbed down the ladder into the lead boat and rode back to Manhattan. The rest of the mosquito fleet stayed on to take cargo. Shelby kept the binoculars on her father's boat until it was out of sight. Then she turned around and panned the deck of the big freighter where she met a sailor who had been watching her with his field glasses. She coldly smiled back.

She panned on and stopped. There it was: the magnolia flower of her home state on the prow. Shelby said to Gideon, "That ship. I found it."

"Which ship?"

The one you said that you didn't know what kind of flower was on its prow." She handed him the binoculars for him to see. Then she said, "We're going back to Manhattan."

"Why?"

"I don't want to be late......"

68

Pennsylvania Station

Shelby hurried through Pennsylvania Station's architectural snapshot of the Roman Baths of Caracalla, but without the water. She went up the sprawling stone stairway that led to a sky-high Corinthian arch fronting an arcade, as composed as the Galerie du Passage in Paris, which led to the main concourse that was integrated with a vaulted glass ceiling crisscrossed into a galactic spool of ironwork where far below Pullman porters, Red Hats, traveling salesmen, vacationers, soldiers and sailors, itinerants, and families all waited for their trains as children ran back and forth with playground fervor. The time-board numbers flipped, and everyone looked up.

Shelby hurried down the staggered stairway to the Northeastern Limited train's platform that was staged under a sky-lit canopy. She climbed aboard the Edendale car and knocked on the first door: Drawing Room A. Addison opened up and said, "I was beginning to think you weren't coming." A little girl on the platform pressed her nose up against the drawing room window. Addison pulled down the blind. He turned back to Shelby, "What took you so long?"

"Tell me what happened aboard the *Paradise* this morning?" Shelby said with cold impatient eyes.

Addison was equally impatient. "Why don't you sit down?"

She ignored him. "I found Artemus Cummins corpse bobbing dead-up in the ocean."

"What were you doing out there?"

"I was on my way to East Hampton," Shelby said. "Now what were you doing on that yacht?"

"Sit down, child."

"What were you doing on that yacht?"

"Taking care of business," Addison said.

"*Bootlegging* business?"

"…If you must know, yes. Now, sit down, child."

"How long have you been a bootlegger?"

"How did you find me out in the ocean?"

"I'll find you again, if I have to," Shelby said. "Now, how long have you been a bootlegger?"

"…A while."

"*How* long?"

"I'd been selling used bourbon barrels to Scottish distilleries to make their whiskey."

"And…?"

"I began investing in those distilleries—before Prohibition."

"Why?"

"Because farming had radically changed, and I had to look for new investments," Addison said, "but that's not what matters now—Colm Haydock is looking for you."

"I told you on the phone what I planned on doing."

"Yes," Addison said, "but I wouldn't count on that idea of yours to work, as clever as it is."

"Well, I'm not about to crawl under a bed."

"You're missing the point."

"I'm not missing anything."

"Your bootlegging days are over," Addison said.

"*Over*…?"

"Child, when I converted my distillery into a barn, it was not for you to become a bootlegger."

"We made a bet and I won," Shelby said.

"I know, but you have to be practical."

"I *am*. Now is everything set up for this afternoon?"

"I made the call."

"They've got to be there on time."

"They'll be there. Now, I tried to get back to you at your apartment, but you had already left for here."

"I'm supposed to be in East Hampton."

"Yes," Addison said, "I just thought that—"

"What?"

"Well…once here you'd come back home with me."

"That wouldn't solve our problem," Shelby said.

"If you stay home, it would."

"I want to live in this world. Not see it out from a kitchen window."

"And what if this sudden idea of yours doesn't work out? What if you should get into more trouble? What if my little girl should die?"

"The odds of my plan working are very good," Shelby said, "and don't forget that Colm Haydock is still searching for me, and the odds are that he'll find me—so why not let him?"

"Yes, but this whole idea of my little girl being bait—"

"That's the charm of it."

"Not if you're dead," Addison said.

"You *did* put that call in…?"

"I could put in another one, too."

"Then I'd be more vulnerable," Shelby said.

"What about Mr. Greer?"

"*Mr. Greer*….?"

"He's expecting you to ride in the winter events back home. I've even reserved a place for little Martha who'll be hunting for the first time in the children's pony class. She wants you with her and asks for you every day. She thinks you do not love her."

"*You* think I do not love her. I send her gifts and write her quick letters every day and call home at great expense."

"Yes," Addison said, "but all she does is ask for you. How can you hurt a little girl who loves you so much? Have you no heart?"

The second bell rang.

Shelby said, "You tell little Martha that I'll be home soon enough to steal her away and that we shall live happily ever after with more ponies than there are stars in the sky."

"What about your mother? Should anything happen to you, it would be the end of her."

"It would be the end of *me* if I came home and did what *she* wanted."

"But if anything should go wrong this afternoon—"

"You did put in that call?"

"I said that I did."

"Then don't worry," Shelby said.

"A father cannot but worry."

"Then you're missing the point," Shelby said.

"What?"

"That only a fool uses death as an excuse for never doing anything."

"That doesn't mean you throw caution to the wind," Addison said.

"That depends on the wind."

"…Well."

"Well, what?"

"…I've thought about it long hard," Addison said.

"Thought about what?"

"About you being a part of my business."

Shelby stared long and hard at her father.

"You heard me," he said.

"You're not just saying this to keep me on the train? Because I will not be fooled by easy sentiments."

"Child, you've proven to me your worth since last December. You've never lacked courage. Your ability to think quickly on your feet is priceless and, despite that you're a girl, you've proven to me your value… Now, did you send that letter?"

"To Haydock?"

"Yes."

"First thing after we hung up."

"This quick idea of yours better work," Addison said.

"You know as well as I that Colm Haydock needs to have the papers with all the corruption and dirt on him and the rest of them. How can he not take the bait?"

"Yes, but you've made so many enemies now," Addison said.

"That's why I'm now leaving town once Haydock is out of the way."

The last bell rang. The conductor shouted *All aboard* across the platform.

Addison approached her. "You're sure you won't come home with me?"

She kissed her father and said, "Fear not…Today we have the advantage, and it involves the heart."

"A cold one at that."

"No," Shelby said, "just a sadness that keeps it from getting warm." She left the Edendale.

69

Mott Haven Yard

The 20th Century Limited was in position to be sent south to Grand Central Terminal for the Chicago run. The Waldameer Observation car, the last one of the consist but the first going into the terminal, belonged to Beau and it was filled with porters who, for the moment, were enjoying the 1910 era big leather couches and deep slumbering chairs. Conductor Liston Truesdale entered by way of the observation deck with a new porter at his side. Everyone, including First Porter Beau LaHood, stood up to greet their boss.

Conductor Liston Truesdale said, "Y'all may sit down now."

The new porter was introduced to the crew and then was the first to be given the pre-trip quiz by the conductor.

"Porter Haley, how do you board a passenger?"

"Well, sir, when loadin' passengers, porter's got to put hisself at the entrance of his car and always be facin' the direction passengers comin' in. And don't make yourself look sloppy like leanin' on somethin' or puttin' hands in pockets. And never be smokin' and don't be chewin' gum. Always put on a smile and always say Welcome Aboard, but don't never tip your hat."

"What about pillows and blankets on a passenger's bed?"

"Well, sir, porter got to use the small step ladder for preparin' berths and he prohibited from standin' on seat cushions, mattresses and seat arms, 'cause it ain't sanitary and you' ruin 'em to boot anyway."

"What about breaking down berths?"

"Well, sir, when breakin' down berths, porter gotta be careful and fasten all mechanical attachments and safety devices for holdin' beds securely in position. Thems include upper berth safety support rods and bars, and safety guards, and safety curtain, and safety straps as well as hold-down latches, foldin' legs, and ladder attachments. In the event a bed is operated by a passenger, I got to explain him the operation of the bed and safety features so he don't kills hisself."

The porters all laughed. Conductor Liston Truesdale hushed them. "Now what about pillows? Because if you don't answer this right," the conductor said, "you're not riding with us to Chicago."

"Then ya should've asked me that first, sir."

"I ask how I want. Now give me the answer or you're leaving the train right now."

Porter Haley said, "Sir, all pillows got to be fluffed up by strikin' 'em smartly several times with open hands before placin' em on the passenger's bed, and when applyin' the slips don't never be holdin' 'em with your teeth nor chin on your chest or you'll get your ass fired."

The porters, again, broke out into laughter, and this time so did Conductor Liston Truesdale who said, "Okay, Haley, you're riding with us." Then he beckoned Beau to step off the train with him. He said to Beau, "The yard master was looking all day for you. Where were you?"

"I got in a little late, sir."

"How long we been riding together, Beau?"

"Since 1920."

"Then you know how things are when they get the way they are."

"I do most of the time, sir."

"That memorandum the yard master got from upstairs about the deal made with that lawyer who grilled you last December about that college boy who died of wood alcohol poisoning, some days ago, has been finalized."

"I didn't kill that boy," Beau said. "He came to our train drunk, and he kept on pesterin' me for somethin' more to drink, sayin': *Boy if you don't get me somethin', I'm gonna get you thrown off the train.* He was rude, disrespectful, and already half dead."

"I have no doubt, Beau, but the company made a deal."

"…What deal?"

"Beau—I went up myself to plead your case to keep you on the train and I tried everything I knew."

"*Keep* me on the train…?"

"Let me finish, Beau," resting his hand on Beau's shoulder. "President Cordley took a liking to you when you gave him that advice last December, because it done him a world 'a good since then. So, he sat me down and said this is the way things are gonna be. The company can't go to trial, because of all the bad publicity that would play out for months, so they settled outside of court and part of the deal is that you're fired."

Beau cried out, "I can't be fired."

"Beau—"

"That boy killed hisself. *I didn't.*"

"Beau, you're being rational. The parents don't want to believe their boy did it to himself. They have to believe that it was you. And on top of that, the railroad can't afford to have a public lawsuit. Everybody'll be thinking that porters are killing their children with coffin varnish and that would ruin business."

"So, I'm the one to pay for Prohibition and one stupid boy?"

"I don't know who's to pay, Beau, but they did say, upstairs, for you to come back in a year and they'll reconsider hiring you."

"And what am I to do in the meantime to earn a livin'? Join the Anti-Saloon League?"

Conductor Liston Truesdale reached into his coat pocket and pulled out an envelope. "The boys and I all chipped in 500 dollars for you, one month of their own pay. And if you're still in need of money, you wire me, and we'll help you out again."

"Ten years on the railroad," Beau said. "First Porter on the 20th Century Limited five years and now fired because of some stupid white kid and his self-pityin' parents."

"I couldn't have said it any better, Beau."

The last call rang for the consist to move south to Grand Central Terminal for the 2:45 departure. Beau got back on the train and said goodbye to all the porters he had worked with these past years. He even wished the new porter the best of luck. Then Beau stepped off the Waldameer with his grip in hand and for the first time in his life he had nowhere to go. He had seen other men who had shared the same fate, but now he understood it for himself. Conductor Liston Truesdale called to him from the observation deck as the midnight sleeper slowly rumbled south. "You can ride in with us, Beau, and save a nickel."

Beau couldn't ride. It would hurt too much. So, the 20th Century Limited moved on without him to the limestone halls of Grand Central Terminal. The whole train seemed to weep as the porters and the conductor stood by the windows and sadly waved to Beau, their old first porter. But it was he who wept.

70

Drawn to a Cause

Someone else was out of work and she was sitting right across from editor Emil Gauvreau of *The New York Evening Graphic*. He told her again. "Everyone's going to want to know your name and who you are, miss."

"I can't give you my name," she said.

"Why not?"

"Because I'll fear for my life."

"There'll only be more curiosity without your name."

"I don't care," she said. "There's isn't any stipulation in the contest that a winner has to reveal his or her name."

"Could you at least tell me how you got the negatives?"

"That would be like giving you my name."

"Open your pocketbook."

"Why?"

"*Open* it," the editor said, pointing to it.

She did. It was empty.

Emil Gauvreau reached into his desk. "When you wouldn't tell us your name, Miss Wirth, I had to make sure you weren't a plant for someone who had set this whole thing up to con us into giving away the contest prize of 10 grand."

She took her wallet back from the editor. "How can I trust you won't print my name after getting pickpocketed?"

"It has nothing to do with trust."

"It *doesn't?*"

"No, miss, see, our next contest will be to find the person who found the negatives and since I know your name, I'll know who's lying."

"So, you *will* print my name."

"Well, at least not for a while."

"You're a cheap low man, Mr. Gauvreau."

"Then you're not looking low enough," he said.

Ellen Wirth left his office. The anger in her face was livid as she quickly went down the hall where reporters noisily clanged away at their typewriters. A few stared at her as she made her way into the elevator with the valise full of cash.

Emile Gauvreau picked up one of the five candlestick telephones which were spread across his desk and put through a call. He waited and then said, "Good news, Zola. I just paid off the contest reward."

"Who won it?"

"I can't let you know at the moment, but she's a nice girl and I wouldn't want anything to happen to her—at least not yet. By the way, when do you want to pick up the negatives?"

Zola said, "I'll be right over."

"If you don't mind my asking, what do you plan on doing with them?"

"Darling, you're the last person I would tell," she said, hanging up. Zola then called Shelby, but she had to wait forever. When Shelby finally did pick up, Zola said, "Hey, what's this I hear about you sailing to Europe all of a sudden?"

"I'm busy packing and *can't* talk."

"Well, you're not the only one who has to leave town. Where are you heading?"

"Overseas."

"No kidding. Where?"

"*None* of your business," Shelby said.

"First-class I bet."

"The Kaiser suite."

"Well, you can't go alone. You're only nineteen years old and you know nothing of the world."

"Who said I'm going alone?"

"Good. We may fight but bottom line we're blood."

"I didn't mean *you*," Shelby said.

"Then who?"

"Sarah Remley."

"That old lady?"

"Better than with an old maid."

"You're an idiot."

Shelby hung up.

Zola quickly called the Biltmore Hotel concierge. "Which boat has the Kaiser suite?"

"It would have to be the Hamburg-Amerika Line, ma'am."

"Well, which one of its ships is sailing this afternoon?"

"The SS Albert Balin, and it's the only ship of that line in town today."

"Are you sure?"

"Yes, I'm sure," the concierge said. "We have hotel guests booked on it, and this time of year the line takes bookings up until departure. If you want passage, I'll call Hamburg-Amerika and you can settle up with the purser once aboard. They'll give you a temporary boarding pass at the gangway."

"I want a first-class ticket and nothing else." Zola said.

"Yes, ma'am."

Zola hung up the house phone. Then it rang. She picked it up. "*Shelby...?*"

"It's Beau, Miss Zola."

"What do you want?"

"Miss Shelby told me to call you."

"About what?"

"Say iffen she catch you on her boat she gonna throw you overboard and make you swim back to Mississippi for openin' your big mouth to Mrs. Buchanan about her and Miss Swain and where they all lived— her words, not mine, ma'am."

"Hey, aren't you supposed to be on that train to Chicago?"

"Well, ma'am, Miss Prevette got so used to Pullman service, I got me a new job soon as I walked in the door. Have a good day, Miss Zola."

Beau hung up and returned to Shelby's bedroom to help Caitlin with the packing. Shelby was running around barefoot in her slip-on giving orders as Caitlin and Beau kept coming in and out of the closets with shoes, gigolo hats, cloches, blouses, dresses, coats, and anything else the boss wanted. Beau didn't care. He was getting twice what the railroad paid and he didn't have to make one bed for it, plus he was going to Europe—might even learn to parlez-vous.

The phone rang. Beau picked it up.

"That you, Beau?"

"Yeah, Elgin, what happened?"

"That idea of yours worked. Bernarr MacFadden just paid me off so there'd be no demonstration about Carmela Knight and that cockeyed composograph they been runnin' in the *Graphic*."

"Good," Beau said, "next time he'll think twice about turnin' a colored girl into a white girl. You know where to send my half."

"It's already there……"

Beau then hurried out the building with Shelby's steamer trunks and squeezed them into her limousine. They headed crosstown to the West Side piers where the ocean liners were lined up and down the Hudson River. The SS Albert Balin's three smokestacks blocked out the sky. Beau handed off the trunks to the loading crew and then went up the gangway with her to the promenade deck. She told him, "You wait here and keep a lookout for you-know-who and, should I miss anything, I want a detailed account of what happened." Shelby was then taken to the ship's purser where she wrote out a check for their voyage. A personal steward, only for first class voyagers, escorted her to the upper deck Kaiser Suite for final approval. Next door was Sarah Remley's suite where cocktails were being served to friends who had crowded inside for the customary going-away party. She gave Shelby a hug and said, "I could never have done this on my own. He may be gone, but I still foolishly wait for his permission."

"Not anymore, Mrs. Remley. You're free of him, and in no time you'll be your own person. I'm sure of that… I see Gideon isn't here."

"He just called and said that he had something to do for school, which is odd because he's on winter vacation."

"Well, it doesn't matter, he promised to write me. Now, I've got some unfinished business that I must tend to first," Shelby said, "and then I'll be right back to join the party."

"I—I hope you're not leaving me," Sarah said, betraying a slight tremble in her voice.

"Mrs. Remley…" Shelby said, amused at how such a strong woman could also be so fragile, "I have a sense of humor, but it's not cruel."

Shelby hurried back to the gangway where Beau was still waiting. "Has he arrived?"

"No, not yet, miss. How's the suite?"

"Grand. Now, here's the key to your room. It's cabin class and private. You won't have to worry about sharing with white people as you would in third class. Take this pass. You'll be allowed in first class as my servant." Shelby then searched the crowded pier that was filled with excitement with the rush of people to and fro. Dock workers were busy loading steamer trunks and passenger cars into the ship's hull for those who were touring Europe. The second and third-class passengers boarded at the other end of the ship as if they were sailing on another vessel, but it was the size of the ship with its broad sweep of decks and black funnels which made onlookers dream of possibilities beyond the daily commute. An airship hovering over the city, with its cucumber contour, seemed to be looking on or just maybe into the future.

"…What if he doesn't come?"

"Miss, you set the trap, maybe late some," Beau said, "but then that note you sent invitin' him to your goin' away party just might do the trick."

"You *read* the note?"

"No, miss, it was sealed when you sent it out."

"So then how do you know what I wrote?"

"When I brought you coffee into your study, I heard you say it over and over while pennin' it, and it would've moved any man's heart."

"I see it moved yours," Shelby said.

"Yes, it did, miss," hearing her voice:

Dear Colm,

I write this letter in haste as time waits for no one. With great sorrow, I regret certain things done, but I have always been drawn to a cause, be it Ireland or someone I love. So, I will not waste your time with petty appeals. Please come to my going-away party this afternoon in the Kaiser suite, aboard the SS Albert Balin, Hamburg-Amerika Line. I shall then give you the documents pertaining to your mother and everything else, and they will be forever yours. If you choose not to come, then the documents shall remain with me, and should we encounter each other again in an unfitting spirit, I fear I may lose my mind and do something only to lose you forever.

With all my love,
Etta Jape

Beau said, "All you can do now is wait."

And they did, while they watched motorcars come and go as travelers with heavy steamship trunks moved their lives to the ocean liner and said goodbye to friends on shore. A man among them, attached to no one, left a taxi carrying white roses in one hand and a boxed bottle of champagne in the other. He wore his best suit, his best hat, and his best shoes. He had a goodness in his eye that always comes when love is imminent. His great height enabled him to see above the crowd, and as he searched the giant ship, he soon enough found Shelby standing by the gangway wearing a bold geometric patterned coat. His eyes met hers, but the pleasure went unreturned as her unnerving stare shifted to the black Packard sedan that stopped short of the district leader. Several men pushed him into the backseat of the car. Then the deep penetrating sound of the ocean liner's final horn drifted across the city and headed east along with Colm Haydock, now gagged and bound on the floorboard.

Shelby joined Robert Benchley on the first-class deck where they waved to the last of their friends still on the pier. Squat tugboats, way below, having just seen the white flag raised on the ship's bridge, pushed up against the gigantic ocean liner and nudged it out of its berth and brought it into New York Harbor. The inflexible ship made the maneuver seem treacherous, which it was. The captain, wearing a high winged collar and a bib of nautical whiskers, stood on the bridge with his crew and kept his eyes fixed on the shoulder wide wheel that was turned at his command. The first mate sent instructions down below to the engine boss who was busy keeping up the needed power to stay on course in reverse. It took three tugboats, one at the bow and two at the stern, to keep the ship from knocking out the pier. When the ship's bow finally inched past the edge of the pier, the tugs pushed the steamer out into the open harbor. The engine room then got the signal to reverse power. The SS Albert Balin sat still, for a moment, and then blew its booming horn and headed out to sea.

Shelby watched the city retreat into its staggered outline, a city that she had just gotten to know had now left her jilted blue. She turned to Mr. Benchley who was leaning against the first class railing and said, "…Then don't believe me, but that's why I'm sailing with you."

"Because you find me so *charming*?"

"What I find, and you can't, is of no matter to me."

"And what about this Sarah Remley?"

"What about her?"

"Someone with that surname died in the *Pair-a-Dice* explosion."

"A lot of people died that day," Shelby said.

"Yes, but that was Mrs. Remley's husband."

Shelby closed her coat against the wind. "Why don't you ask her?"

"I just might, but how did you get to meet her? She comes from one of the most prominent families in town, and you've only been here for a few days at most."

"Through someone I know," Shelby said.

"Who?"

"Someone."

"A cab driver…?"

"No," Shelby said, "and how's your German?"

"Like Milwaukee, dry."

"Zola told me you have many friends in Berlin."

"A few," he said.

"And that they're all journalists."

"Some. Why?"

"I have to meet them," Shelby said.

"…What for?"

"They know things you're not supposed to know."

Mr. Benchley, already used to her mischief, took in the long row of first-class passengers bundled up in lounge chairs drinking tea and coffee, and caring less about the weather than about the pleasure of chewing on a favorite biscuit as if nothing had any consequence. He said to her, "I'm going there as a political reporter, but why are you going?"

Shelby took him by the arm and said with half a smile, "To cause trouble…"

The SS Albert Balin sailed south through the Narrows, the Upper and Lower Bay, and then on out past the 12-mile limit where the armada silently waited. A deck steward came calling for Shelby and found her by the railing, He handed her a note written on the ship's stationary. She found no pleasure reading it: *Dear Young Lady, I'm two doors down from you and your new pal, and I got an earful from your going away* *party. I hope y'all're quieter the rest of the voyage. Z.N.*

Shelby handed the note to Benchley. "Guess who's here?"

He read the note. "You're going to need your cousin."

"I'm going to throw her overboard is what I'm going to do."

"You're making a big mistake," Mr. Benchley said.

"She's the one who made the mistake."

"Yes, but you'll be overseas all alone, and Zola knows Europe and also speaks German and French."

"So do I," Shelby said.

"Yeah, but she's seen war and knows what it's done to people over there."

"What's that supposed to mean?"

"It means, obstinacy doesn't make you right; it only distances you from the people you need." Mr. Benchley pulled up his coat collar and said, "I'm heading inside to the bar. It's too damn cold out here, despite how beautiful you are. Maybe the bartender knows what you're really up to."

"Then have him pour me a drink too, because I'll be right in." Shelby then saw Beau making his way down the open deck with her new field glasses. He handed them to her and then she searched the ocean far and wide."

Beau looked eastward out into the vast Atlantic Ocean. "We past the 12-mile limit yet?"

They then heard the familiar buzz of a powerboat like none other. Shelby handed Beau the binoculars and said, "Oh, yeah...."

He put them to his eyes and focused on the powerboat. "I thought you and that boy was in a feud, miss."

"We made up on the way back to the city. But I'm sore at him again."

"What happened now?"

"I brought him upstairs for breakfast and then for no reason he bugged me about a sock."

"A sock?"

"Yes," Shelby said.

"Why would he be angry about a sock?"

"He thinks he knows whose foot was in it."

"Well," Beau said, "this is between you and me, but your father did ask me iffen you was in love with that boy?"

"…And what did you tell him?"

"Well, I done told him love is like learnin'. It can take a while to get it, and some never do." Beau then stared into the ocean where nothing above it could hide. "I heard 12 minutes is all it takes to drown this time of year."

"You heard right," Shelby said, thinking of the man who had come to the pier with flowers, champagne, and the turbulence of love in his veins.

But then she was off to Berlin, and it had a turbulence of its own.

www.RaederLomax.com

Contact the author if you have any questions about the making of the Midnight Sleeper Series

http://eepurl.com/b2F_E5

More books by the author

Midnight Sleeper 3:

Voodoo Child

Has your worst nightmare ever come true?

Voodoo Child takes place in long gone Berlin of the 1920s amidst the sexual and social chaos that is politicized and then savagely battled over.

KIRKUS Reviews: VOODOO CHILD

"Skulduggery abounds in the third novel in Lomax's Midnight Sleeper series, which brings more intrigue and crazy adventures, set in Berlin in 1926…The intrigue among people and groups builds…this book delivers."

www.ingramcontent.com/pod-product-compliance
Lightning Source LLC
Chambersburg PA
CBHW020349120726
47904CB00002B/518